# IT'S NOT JUST AN ENCHANTED FOREST—IT'S HOME

Azzie selected four more stones from the chamois bag of jewels and gave them to Merioneth. "Will that do?"

"That takes care of the forest and the basic landscaping. But you also want it enchanted. Right?"

"That's what I told you. What good would it be if it weren't enchanted?"

"Don't get huffy with *me*," Merioneth said. "This forest is nothing to me. I'm just trying to understand the order. What sort of enchantments did you have in mind?"

"The usual stuff," Azzie said. "Animated flame trees will do nicely. There are always plenty of them in stock."

"You're a horticulturist that you know that?" Merioneth said caustically. "Fact is there are damn few flame trees available at this time of year. And I suppose you want them to have magic thorns?"

"Of course."

"Magic thorns aren't standard."

A few more gems changed hands.

"Now, let's see," Merioneth said. "What exactly should these magical thorns do?"

"The usual thing," Azzie said. "When a traveler passes who is not pure in heart, or not in possession of the proper magical counterspells, they impale him."

"I thought you'd want that! Impaling's extra!"

"Consistently amusing and occasionally hilarious . . . filled with reversals, plots twists, and wonderful absurdities."

—*Science Fiction Chronicle*

Bantam Books by Roger Zelazny and Robert Sheckley:

BRING ME THE HEAD OF PRINCE CHARMING
IF AT FAUST YOU DON'T SUCCEED

Mr. Sheckley wishes to thank Honor P. Vallor for her help with plotting and editing his portion of this collaboration.

BRING ME THE HEAD OF PRINCE CHARMING
*A Bantam Spectra Book*

*PUBLISHING HISTORY*
*Bantam hardcover edition published December 1991*
*Bantam paperback edition / December 1992*

ISBN 0-553-29935-2
*Published simultaneously in the United States and Canada*

PRINTED IN THE UNITED STATES OF AMERICA

*OPM*   0 9 8 7 6 5

# BRING ME THE HEAD OF PRINCE CHARMING

## Roger Zelazny and Robert Sheckley

BANTAM BOOKS

NEW YORK · TORONTO · LONDON · SYDNEY · AUCKLAND

# BRING
# ME THE
# HEAD OF
# PRINCE
# CHARMING

# MATINS

HERO SANDWICH

# Chapter 1

The bastards were shirking again. And Azzie had just gotten comfortable. He had found a place just the right distance between the fiery hole in the middle of the Pit and the hoarfrost-covered iron walls which encircled it.

The walls were kept close to absolute zero by the devil's own air-conditioning system. The central Pit was hot enough to strip atoms of their electrons, and there were occasional gusts that could melt a proton.

Not that that much heat or cold was needed. It was overkill; overharass, actually. Humans, even when dead and cast into the Pit, have very narrow ranges (speaking on a cosmic scale) of tolerance. Once past the comfort zone in either direction, humans soon lost the ability to discriminate bad from worse. What good was it subjecting a poor wretch to a million degrees Celsius if it felt the same as a mere five hundred degrees? The extremes only tormented the demons and other supernatural creatures who tended the damned. Supernatural creatures have a far wider range of sensation than humans; mostly to their discomfort, but sometimes to their exceeding pleasure. But it is not seemly to talk about pleasure in the Pit.

Hell has more than one Pit, of course. Millions upon millions of people are dead. More are dying every day. Most of them spend at least some time in the Pit. Obviously, there have to be arrangements to accommodate them all.

The Pit Azzie served in was called North Discomfort 405. It was one of the oldest, having been put into service in Babylonian times, when people really knew how to sin. It still bore rusty bas-reliefs of winged lions on the walls and was listed in the Hell Register of Places of Historical Distinction. But Azzie cared nothing for serving in a well-known Pit. All he wanted was to get out.

Like all Pits, North Discomfort 405 consisted of a circle of iron walls enclosing an enormous garbage pit, in the center of which was a hole from which poured exceeding hot fire. Hot coals and burning lava spat from the hole. The glare was unremitting. Only full-fledged demons like Azzie were permitted to wear sunglasses.

And the torments of the damned were accompanied and amplified by music of a sort. Menial imps had scraped clear a semicircle in the midst of the dense, matted, moldy, and rotten debris. The orchestra was seated in this semicircle on orange crates. It was composed of inept musicians who had died in the act of performing. Here in Hell they were forced to play the works of the worst composers ever known. Their names are not remembered on Earth, but in Hell, where their compositions are played without stop, and even broadcast on the Kazum circuit, they are famous.

The imps worked away, turning and adjusting the damned on their griddles. The imps, like the ghouls, liked their people well rotted, and served up marinated in an admixture of vinegar, garlic, anchovy, and maggoty sausage.

What had pulled Azzie from his repose was that in the

sector directly ahead of him, the dead were stacked only about eight or ten high. Azzie gave up his comfortable (relatively) berth and scrambled down through rotting eggshells and squashy entrails and chicken heads to the level ground where he could trample comfortably over the bodies.

"When I said stack 'em high," he told the imps, "I meant a whole lot higher than that."

"But they topple over when we try to stack them any higher!" said the head imp.

"Then get some bracing material to hold them in! I want those piles at least twenty bodies high!"

"Difficult, sir."

Azzie stared. Dared an imp talk back to him? "Do it or join them," he said.

"Yes, sir! Bracing material going right up, sir!" The imp ran off, shouting orders to his work crew.

It had started out as another typical day in one of the Pits of Hell. But it was to change dramatically, unexpectedly, in another moment. So it is with change! We go about our accustomed ways with lowered head and hangdog eye, tired of our accustomed round, sure it will go on forever. Why should it change when there is no change in sight, no letter, no Federal Express, not even a telephone call presaging a great event? So you despair, never realizing that your messenger has already been dispatched, and that hopes are sometimes realized, even in Hell. Indeed, some would say, hopes are *especially* realized in Hell, since hope itself is counted by some as one of the diabolic torments. But this may be an exaggeration of the churchmen who scribble about such things.

Azzie saw that the imps were beginning to perform satisfactorily. He only had another two hundred hours to work on his shift (days in the Pit are long) until he could get his three hours' sleep before beginning again. He was just about to return to that comfortable—relatively comfortable—spot he had just abandoned when a messenger came running up.

"Are you the demon in charge of this Pit?"

The questioner was a violet-winged Efreet, one of the old Baghdad crowd, now mainly working courier service since the Evil Powers of the Upper Council liked their gaily colored turbans.

"I am Azzie Elbub," our demon said. "And yes, I am in charge of this particular subpit."

"Then you're the one I'm looking for." The Efreet handed Azzie an asbestos document inscribed in letters of fire. Azzie drew on his gloves before handling it. Such documents were used only by the High Council of Infernal Justice.

He read, "Know all demons by these presentiments that an Injustice has been done; namely, a human has been brought to the Pit before his time. The forces of Light have already made remonstrations on his behalf, since, if he were to live out his allotted days, he would still have time to repent. The betting against this taking place is on the order of two thousand to one, but the chance exists, albeit but mathematically. You are therefore requested and ordered to take this man out of the Pit, sponge him off, and restore him to his wife and family on Earth, and there remain with him until he has adjusted sufficiently to get his own living, since otherwise we are responsible for his upkeep. After that, you will be released to normal demonic duties on Earth. Sincerely, Asmodeus, Head of North Pit Section of Hell. P.S. The man answers to the name of Thomas Scrivener."

Azzie was so elated that he embraced the Efreet, who stepped hastily back, adjusting his turban and saying, "Take it easy, buddy."

"I was just excited," Azzie said. "I'm going to get out of this place at last! I'm going back to Earth!"

"A disappointing place," the Efreet said. "But to each his, her, or its own."

Azzie hurried off to find Thomas Scrivener.

·   ·   ·

He located the man at last in row 1002WW. The Pits of Hell are laid out like amphitheaters. Every location can be traced. A master plan exists. In practice, however, what with the imps carelessly throwing people onto piles and the piles falling over onto other piles, people's locations in the Pits are known only approximately.

"Is there a Thomas Scrivener here?" Azzie asked.

The mound of sinners at location 1002WW turned away from their discussion and looked at him, those whose heads were faced in the right direction. Instead of repenting their sins, they considered Pit time a social occasion, a chance to get to know neighbors, exchange opinions, have a few laughs. Thus do the dead continue to deceive themselves, just as in life.

"Scrivener, Scrivener," an old man in a middle position said. He turned his head toward his armpit with difficulty. "Sure, he's here. Any of you fellows know where Scrivener is?"

The request was carried up and down the great mound. Men turned from their preoccupation with sports (there are plenty of sports in Hell, but the home team always loses—until you bet against them) to say, "Scrivener, Scrivener, sort of a tall skinny loony fellow with a cast in one eye?"

"I don't know what he looks like," Azzie said. "I assumed he answered to his name."

The mound of people mumbled and coughed and discussed it among them, as humans, living or dead, are wont to do about anything. And if Azzie had not had a demon's preternatural hearing, he would not have heard the faint squeak that came from somewhere deep in the pile.

"Hi there! Scrivener here! Was somebody asking for me?"

Azzie directed his imps to pull Scrivener out of the pile, but gently, without tearing off any of his appendages. They could be replaced, of course, but the procedure was painful and apt to leave a psychic scar. Azzie knew he was supposed to bring the man back to Earth intact so that Scrivener wouldn't create trouble for the Dark Forces for reaping him prematurely.

Soon enough Scrivener scrambled out of the pile, brushing himself off. He was a small, balding, jaunty little man.

"I'm Scrivener!" he cried. "You found out it was a mistake, eh? I told them I wasn't dead when they first brought me here. That Grim Reaper of yours doesn't do much listening, does he? Just keeps grinning that great big idiotic grin. Plucked me away just like that. I've a good mind to complain to someone in authority."

"Listen to me," Azzie said. "You're lucky the mistake was found at all. If you begin litigation, they'll put you in a holding tank until your case can be heard. That could take a century or two. Do you know what our holding tanks are like?"

Scrivener shook his head, wide-eyed.

"They're so bad," Azzie said, "that they even contravene infernal law."

Scrivener seemed impressed. "I guess I'm lucky to be getting out at all. Thanks for the tip. Are you a lawyer?"

"Not by training," Azzie said. "But all of us down here have a little lawyer in us. Come on, let's get you back home."

"I've a feeling I have a few problems at home," Scrivener said hesitantly.

"That's what life is," Azzie continued. "Problems. Be glad you have problems to worry about. When you come down here to stay, you'll have nothing to worry about. Whatever's happening to you just goes on and on."

"I won't be back," Scrivener said.

Azzie wanted to ask him if he wanted to bet on it, but decided that it wouldn't be appropriate under the circumstances.

"We'll have to wipe your memory of this experience," he told Scrivener. "You understand we can't have you fellows going back to Earth and telling a lot of stories."

"Fine with me," Scrivener said. "Nothing here I want to remember, anyhow. Although earlier, in Purgatory, I met this blond succubus—"

"Save it," Azzie growled, grabbing Scrivener by the arm and steering him to the gate in the wall that leads to other parts of Hell and, eventually, to everywhere else and vice versa.

# Chapter 2

Azzie and Scrivener proceeded through the iron gate in the iron wall and up the spiraling road that leads through the outer suburbs of Purgatory, a region composed of great crosshatched depths and startling heights exactly as Fuseli drew it. They trudged along, demon and man, and the way was easy, for easy are the roads of Hell, but it was also boring, because Hell is the state of not being amused.

And after a while Scrivener said, "Is it much farther?"

"I'm not sure," Azzie confessed. "I'm new in this sector. In fact, I shouldn't be here at all."

"Just like me," Scrivener said. "Just because I fall into a corpselike coma from time to time is no reason for your Grim Reaper fellow to grab me up without making proper tests. It was slipshod, I tell you. Why shouldn't you be here?"

"I was intended for better things," Azzie said. "I got good grades in Thaumaturgy College. Finished in the top three in my class."

He failed to tell Scrivener that all of his class except three had wiped out when a sudden infestation of good blew in from the south, freak metaphysical weather that killed all but Azzie and two others, who seemed to have a natural immunity against good halations. And then there had been the poker game.

"So why are you here?" Scrivener asked.

"I'm working off a gambling debt," Azzie said. "I couldn't pay up, so I had to serve time." He hesitated, then said, "I like to gamble."

"Me too," Scrivener said, with what sounded like an air of regret.

They walked for a while in silence. Then Scrivener said, "What's going to happen to me now?"

"We're going to insert you back into your body."

"Will I be all right? Some people wake up from the dead and are all funny, so I've heard."

"I'll be around to look out for you. I'll stay until I'm sure you're all right."

"That's good to hear," Scrivener said. He walked for a while in silence, then said, "But of course, when I wake up I won't know you're there, will I?"

"Of course not."

"Then I won't be reassured."

Azzie said testily, "When you're alive, nothing can reassure you. I'm just telling you this now. It's only when you're dead you can appreciate it."

They walked on. After a ways more, Scrivener said, "You know, I can't remember a thing about my life back on Earth."

"Don't worry, it'll all come back to you."

"I think I was married, though."

"Fine."

"But I'm not sure."

"It'll all come back to you as soon as you are back in your body."

"What if it doesn't? What if I've got amnesia?"

"You'll be fine," Azzie said.

"Do you swear that on your honor as a demon?"

"Certainly," Azzie said, lying with ease. He had taken a special course in forswearing and had proven adept at it.

"You wouldn't lie to me, would you?"

"Hey, trust me," Azzie said, using the master mantra that makes docile even the most suspicious and bellicose.

"You can understand why I'd be a little nervous," Scrivener said. "Being born again, I mean."

"Nothing to be ashamed of," Azzie said. "Here we are.

"Thank Satan," he added under his breath. Talking long with humans made him nervous. They went *around* subjects so! The Demon Fathers had offered a survey course in Human Tergiversation at Demon U, but it was an elective and he hadn't bothered to take it. False Dialectic had seemed more interesting at the time.

Up ahead he saw the familiar scarlet and chartreuse stripes of the North Pit ambulance. The ambulance stopped a few yards away and a medical demon got out. He was an obelisk-eyed pig-snouted fellow and very different from Azzie, who was a fox-faced demon with red hair, pointed ears, and startling blue eyes, accounted quite handsome by those who have a taste for demons.

"Is this the fellow?"

"This is him," Azzie said.

"Before you do anything," Scrivener said, "I just want to know—"

The pig-snouted medical demon reached out and touched a spot on Scrivener's forehead. Scrivener stopped talking and his eyes went unfocused.

"What did you do?" Azzie asked.

"Put him on idle," the medical demon said. "Now it's time to ship him."

Azzie hoped Scrivener would be all right: it's never good news when a demon messes with your head.

"How do you know where to send him?" Azzie asked. The medical demon opened Scrivener's shirt and showed Azzie the name and address tattooed on his chest in purple ink.

"It's the devil's identification mark," the medical demon said.

"You'll take that off before you send him back?"

"Don't worry, he can't see it. That's for *us* to read. You going along with him?"

"I'll get there on my own," Azzie said. "Let me just see that address again. Okay, I got it.

"See you later, Tom," he said to the blank-eyed man.

# Chapter
## 3

A nd so Thomas Scrivener was returned to his home. Luckily the medical demon had been able to get him back before irreparable damage had been done to his body. The doctor who had bought it had been about to start an incision in the neck to trace out the arterial system for his students. Before he could begin, Scrivener opened his eyes. "Good morning, Dr. Moreau," he said, and then fainted.

Moreau proclaimed him alive and demanded a refund from his widow.

She paid it grudgingly. Her marriage to Scrivener hadn't been particularly successful.

Azzie had traveled to Earth by his own means, not wanting to go with Scrivener in the Vehicle of the Undead, whose rotting smells were a trial even for supernatural beings. He arrived just after Scrivener's resuscitation. No one could see him since he wore the Amulet of Invisibility.

Invisibly, except to those with the second sight, Azzie

followed the procession that carried Scrivener back to his home. The good people of the village, rustics all, proclaimed it a miracle. But Scrivener's wife, Milaud, kept on muttering, "I knew he was faking it, the wretch!"

Shielded by his invisibility, Azzie drifted around Scrivener's house, where he would live until Scrivener was past the claims period. Probably a matter of a few days. It was a fair-sized house, several rooms on each floor, and a nice dank basement.

Azzie took up his abode in the basement. It was just the sort of a place for a demon. He had brought along several scrolls to read and a sack of rotted cats' heads for snacks. He was looking forward to a quiet time. But no sooner had he settled in than the interruptions began.

First it was Scrivener's wife, a tall wench with coarse brown hair, wide shoulders, and a big bottom, coming down to the cellar for provisions. Then it was the oldest son, Hans, a weedy lout who looked just like his father, searching for the honey pot. Then Lotte the maidservant, down to pick out some potatoes from last year's harvest.

What with one thing and another, Azzie got little rest. In the morning he looked in on Scrivener. The resuscitated man seemed to be on the mend. He was sitting up and taking herb tea, arguing with his wife and scolding the children. One more day, Azzie decided, and he'd be all right and it would be time to move on to more interesting matters.

The two dogs of the household knew he was there, and slunk away whenever he came by. That was to be expected. But what happened next was not in his plans.

That night he went to sleep in the moldy part of the cellar where some turnips had rotted and he'd made a noisome little nest for himself. But he awoke abruptly when he sensed the presence of light. It was a candle's glow. Someone was standing there looking at him. A child. How insufferable! Azzie tried to bound to his feet and fell back. Someone had tied a piece of string around his ankle!

Sheer reaction made him rear up. A child. A little fat-faced flaxen-haired girl of seven or so. Somehow she must be able to see him: in fact, she had trapped him.

Azzie swelled himself up to his full height, deciding he'd better impress this child at once. He tried to loom menacingly over her, but the strangely glowing string, one end of which she had tied to a beam, pulled him up short and he fell again. The little girl laughed and Azzie shuddered: nothing sets a demon's teeth on edge quite so much as innocent young laughter.

"Hi, little girl," he said. "Can you see me?"

"Yes, I can," she said. "You look like a nasty old fox!"

Azzie looked at the tiny dial set in his Amulet of Invisibility. As he had feared, it showed that the power was down close to zero. Those fools at Supply! But of course he should have checked it himself.

He seemed in a bit of a fix. But nothing he couldn't talk his way out of.

"A *nice* fox, though, eh, snubkin?" Azzie said, using a term of endearment common among demon parents. "How nice to see you! Please undo this bit of string and I'll give you a whole bag of sweets."

"I don't like you," the child said. "You're bad. I'm going to keep you tied up and call the priest."

She stared at him accusingly. Azzie could see he was going to have to employ some cunning to get out of this one.

"Tell me, little girl," he said, "where did you come by this bit of string?"

"I found it in one of the storerooms of the church," she told him. "It was on a table with a lot of bits of bone."

Relics of the holy saints! That meant that the string had to be a spirit-catcher! The best spirit-catchers were made from the rope that girdled the robes of saints. It was going to be difficult getting out of it.

"Little girl, I'm just here to look after your father. He

hasn't been well, you know, what with dying and coming back to life and all. Now be a dear and undo the cord, that's a sweet good girl."

"No," the little girl said, in that adamantine way little girls have, and some big ones, too.

"Well, curse and blast," Azzie said. He struggled but couldn't get his foot out of the spirit-catcher, which had the annoying property of tightening each time he tried to loosen it. "Come on, little girl, fun's fun but now it's time to let me go."

"Don't call me 'little girl,' " the little girl said. "My name is Brigitte, and I know all about you and your kind. The priest told us. You are an evil spirit, aren't you?"

"Not at all," said Azzie. "I am actually a *good* spirit, or at least a *neutral* spirit. I was sent here to make sure your father gets well. I must look after him now, then go away and help others."

"Oh, I see," said Brigitte. She thought for a while. "You look awfully like a demon."

"Looks can be deceiving," Azzie said. "Let me go! I must see to your father!"

"What'll you give me?" Brigitte asked.

"Toys," Azzie said. "More than you've ever seen before."

"Good," the little girl said. "I need new clothes, too."

"I'll give you a new wardrobe. Now let me go!"

Brigitte came close and picked at the knot with a grubby forefinger. Then she stopped. "If I let you go, will you come back and play with me whenever I call for you?"

"No, that's going too far. I have other things to do. I can't be at the beck and call of a little village girl with a dirty face."

"Well then, promise you'll grant me three wishes whenever I ask for them."

Azzie hesitated. Granting wishes could get you into trouble. A demon's promise in this regard had to be kept.

But granting human wishes could take you into some difficulties. Humans were so extravagant!

"I'll grant one wish," he said. "As long as it's reasonable."

"Well, all right," Brigitte said. "But not too reasonable, all right?"

"All right! Untie me!"

Brigitte did so. Azzie rubbed his ankle, then searching through his pouch, found a spare charge for his Amulet of Invisibility. He plugged it in and vanished.

"Don't forget, you promised!" she cried.

Azzie knew he couldn't forget even if he wanted to. Promises made by supernatural creatures to humans are registered with the Office of Equilibrium, operating under the rule of Ananke. If a demon tried to forget a promise, the forces of Necessity quickly and painfully reminded him.

Scrivener was all right, eating a bowl of cereal, giving orders to his hired hands and to his wife. Azzie exited. It was time to get on with his life.

# Chapter
# 4

It was a pleasure for Azzie to be free and able to roam the green earth once again. He had really hated his stay in the Pit, for its simpleminded repetitiousness as much as anything else—you can get very tired of the dreary daily round of roasting sinners. Azzie was an energetic demon, enterprising, forward-looking. He was an agent of evil, and despite a certain air of frivolousness, he took his hellish duties seriously.

After leaving Scrivener's village, the first thing he wanted to do was orient himself. This region was not familiar to him. Azzie had visited Earth last during Imperial Roman times and had even been present at one of Caligula's notable feasts. Now, flying low over the land that had been called Gaul, he was guarded from mishap by his Amulet of Invisibility. The Amulet also conferred a degree of impalpability upon its wearer, which was just as well when he passed through a large flock of trumpeter swans. As he flew Azzie noted the forest stretching out on all sides. The village had been but a patch in that great

forest that covered most of Europe and stretched from
Scythia to Spain. Azzie found a muddy track running
through it and followed it at an altitude of about five
hundred feet. The track stretched on and on, at last opening out into a proper paved Roman road. He accompanied a group of horsemen down the road and into a city of
fair size. Later, he learned this was Troyes, a part of the
kingdom of the Franks, who were large barbarians with
iron swords who had taken over all of Gaul and much
more since the decline of Roman power.

Azzie flew low and slow over the city, noting the
many small houses and, among them, the palaces of lords
and high churchmen. On the outskirts of the town a fair
was being held. He flew above its tents and pennants,
attracted to its cheerful bustle. He decided to pay it a
visit.

He came to Earth and changed into one of his standard disguises: a kindly, portly man, balding, and with a
twinkling eye. His toga, which came with the disguise,
looked out of place, so he purchased a cloak of homespun
at a booth and looked more or less like everyone else.

He strolled along, looking around, still slightly disori-
ented. There were several permanent structures and a
field scattered with tents. All sorts of things were sold
here—weapons, clothing, foodstuffs, livestock, tools,
spices.

"Hi there! You, sir!"

Azzie turned. Yes, the old crone was beckoning to
him. She sat in front of a small black tent, cabalistic figures painted on its sides in gold. She was dark-skinned,
and appeared to be an Arab or a Gypsy.

"You called me?"

"I did, sir," she said, in a villainous North African
accent. "Come inside."

A human might have been more cautious, because you
can never tell what might happen inside a black tent with
cabalistic figures. But for Azzie that tent was the first
familiar thing he had seen in a long time. There are whole

tribes of demons who live in black tents and wander up
and down the waste places of Limbo, and Azzie, although
Canaanite on his father's side, was related to some of the
wandering Bedouin demons.

Inside, the tent was lined with richly figured rugs.
There were oil lamps of finely wrought pewter on the
wall, and embroidered cushions lay all over. At the far
end was a low altar with a table for offerings. Behind it,
looming high, was a heroic statue in the Grecian manner,
of a handsome young man with a wreath of laurel in his
hair. Azzie recognized the features.

"So Hermes is here," Azzie said.

"I am his priestess," said the crone.

"I was under the impression," Azzie said, "that we
were in a Christian country and that worship of the old
gods is strictly forbidden."

"What you say is true," the crone said. "The old gods
are dead, but not really dead because they have returned
to life in new forms. Hermes, for example, has changed
into Hermes Trismegistus, patron saint of alchemists. His
worship is not approved, but neither is it forbidden."

"I'm happy to see that," Azzie said. "But why have
you called me here?"

"You are a demon, sir?" the crone inquired.

"Yes. How did you know?"

"There is something lordly and sinister in your mien,"
the crone said, "an air of brooding, implacable evil that
would set you apart from others no matter how large the
crowd."

Azzie knew that Gypsies were capable of subtle per-
ceptions which they then phrased to flatter their clients.
Nevertheless, he reached into his pouch, found a gold
denier, and gave it to her.

"Take that for your cunning tongue. Now, what do
you want of me?"

"My master wants to have a word with you."

"Well, good," Azzie said. It had been a long time since

he had had a chat with one of the old gods. "Where is he?"

The crone knelt down at the altar and began mumbling. In a moment the white marble was suffused with a rosy glow. The statue came to life, stretched, stepped down from its pedestal, and sat beside Azzie. To the old woman Hermes said, "Go find us something to drink."

When she had left, he said, "So, Azzie, it's been a long time."

"Quite long," Azzie said. "It's good to see you again, Hermes. I wasn't on Earth when Christianity defeated paganism—other commitments, you know—but I do want to offer my condolences."

"Thank you," Hermes said, "but actually we lost nothing. We're all at work, all the gods. We move with the times, and we sometimes hold honored positions in both camps—saint or demon. Does wonders for one's perspective. There's much to be said for a kind of intermediate status."

"I'm glad to hear it," Azzie said. "There's something sad about the thought of an out-of-work god."

"Never worry about us. I had my servant Aissa call you, Azzie, because she said *you* looked lost. I thought I could help."

"That is good of you," Azzie said. "Perhaps you could just fill me in on what's been going on since Caligula."

"Well, in brief, the Roman thing collapsed under barbarian invasions and lead poisoning. The barbarians are all about now. They call themselves Franks and Saxons and Visigoths. They have formed an empire which they call the Holy Roman Empire."

"Holy?" Azzie asked.

"That's what they call it. I don't know why."

"But how did the real Roman empire fall?"

"You can look it up in any history," Hermes said. "Just take my word; it fell, and that was the end of the Classical Age. The period we are now in is called—or will be, shortly after it's over—the Middle Ages. You just

missed the Dark Ages. We had some fun then, I promise you! But this time is good, too."

"What year is it?" Azzie asked.

"The year one thousand," Hermes said.

"The Millennium!"

"Yes."

"Then it's almost time for the contest."

"That is correct, Azzie. It is the time when the forces of Light and the forces of Darkness hold their great contest to see who shall dictate the essence of human destiny for the next thousand years, and whether it shall be for good or for evil. What are you going to do about it?"

"Me?" Azzie said. "What can *I* do?"

"You can enter the contest."

Azzie shook his head. "The representative of Evil is chosen at the Grand Council by the High Evil Powers. They always play favorites, giving the making of the contest to one of their friends. I wouldn't stand a chance."

"That is how it was in the old days," Hermes said. "But I've heard that Hell is reforming itself. They are being sorely pressed by the Powers of Light. Nepotism, excellent though it is, is no longer sufficient to carry their point of view. Now, as I understand it, the selecting of the contestant must be awarded on merit."

"Merit! What a novel concept! But there's still nothing I can do."

"Don't be a defeatist like so many other young demons," Hermes said sternly. "So many of them are lazy, content just to lie around, take drugs, swap tales, and take the easy way through eternity. You are not like that, Azzie. You're clever, and you have principles, initiative. Do something. You may actually have a chance."

"But I don't know what to do," Azzie said. "And even if I did, I have no money to carry it out with."

"You paid the old woman," Hermes pointed out.

"That was fairy gold. It vanishes after a day or two. If I want to make an entry in the contest, it calls for real money."

"I know where some is," Hermes said.

"Where? How many dragons do I have to slay to get it?"

"No dragons at all. You merely have to best the other players in the Founder's Day Poker Game."

"Poker!" Azzie breathed. "My passion! Where's the game?"

"It is taking place three days hence in a graveyard in Rome. But you must play better this time than last, else you'll be returned to the Pit for a few hundred more years.

"In fact," Hermes said, "you need what gamblers of a later day will call an edge."

"An edge? What is that?"

"Any device that helps you win."

"There are watchers at these games to prevent cheating."

"True enough. But there's no law, heavenly or infernal, against a good-luck charm."

"But they're rare indeed! If only I had one!"

"I can tell you where to get one. But you will have to inconvenience yourself to get it."

"Tell me, then, Hermes!"

"In my nocturnal wanderings around the city of Troyes and its environs," Hermes said, "I have noticed a place at the edge of the woods to the west where a small orange flower grows. The people hereabouts know it not, but it is Speculum, which grows only in the presence of felixite."

"There's felixite around here?" Azzie said, marveling greatly.

"You must find that out for yourself," Hermes said. "But the indications are good."

# Chapter
# 5

Azzie thanked Hermes and took his leave. He walked
through a low field, toward the woods that surrounded the city. He found the rare flower, which was
low and inconspicuous. Azzie sniffed it (the odor of the
Speculum is delicious) and then bent low and put his ear
to the ground. His preternaturally alert sense of hearing
brought to his senses the presence of something below-
ground, something that moved and thumped, moved and
thumped. It was, of course, the characteristic sound a
dwarf makes as he cuts a tunnel with his pick and shovel.
The dwarves are well aware that the sound of their digging gives them away, but what can they do; a dwarf
needs to dig to feel alive.

Azzie stamped his foot and sank into the earth. This is
a talent that most European and Arabian demons have.
Living in the earth is as natural for them as living on the
earth is for men. The demons experience earth as something much like water, through which they can swim,
though they much prefer to walk in tunnels.

It was cool underground. The lack of light did not prevent Azzie from seeing around him very nicely, in a dim infrared sort of way. And it is rather pleasant underground. There are moles and shrews near the surface, and other creatures glide along the differing densities of the soil.

At last Azzie came out in a large underground cavern. Phosphorescent rocks gave off a dim glow, and he could see, at the far end of the cavern, a solitary dwarf of the north European variety, dressed in a well-made green and red moleskin suit, with tiny jackboots of gecko hide and a little mouseskin cap on his head.

"Greetings, dwarf," Azzie said, adjusting his height upward as far as the rocky ceiling allowed so that he could loom over the dwarf impressively.

"Hail, demon," the dwarf said, sounding not too pleased at stumbling over one. "Out for a stroll, are you?"

"You could say so," Azzie said. "And what about you?"

"Just passing through these parts," the dwarf said. "On my way to a reunion in Antibes."

"Is that a fact?" Azzie asked.

"Yes, it is."

"Then why were you standing here digging?"

"Me? Digging? Not really."

"Then what were you doing with that pick in your hand?"

The dwarf looked down and seemed surprised to find the pick there. "I was just tidying up." He tried to rake a few rocks together with the pick, but of course, since it was never intended for that purpose, it didn't do a good job.

"Tidying up the earth?" Azzie said. "What'dye take me for, a moron? Who are you, anyhow?"

"I am Rognir, a member of the Rolfing Dwarveria from Uppsala. Tidying up the earth may seem absurd to you, but it comes naturally to dwarves, who like everything to remain the same."

"Frankly," Azzie said, "what you are saying makes no sense to me at all."

"That's because I'm nervous," Rognir said. "As a rule I talk quite sensibly."

"Then do so now," Azzie said. "Relax, I mean you no mischief."

The dwarf nodded but looked unconvinced. He didn't trust demons, and you couldn't really blame him. There are many rivalries in the spirit kingdom which are unknown to man, since a Homer or a Virgil wasn't around when something was going on. The dwarves and the demons had been having quite a tense time of it recently, due to territorial disputes. Demons have always had a claim on the underground, despite their distant birth as fallen creatures of the Light. They love the underground ways of Earth, the deep caverns, bogs, and sinkholes, caves and declivities, the passageways that present vistas of beautiful strangeness to their poetic but gloomy imaginations. The dwarves had their own claim on the underworld, considered themselves children of it, born spontaneously out of the chaotic fiery writhings of the deepermost regions of primal flame. They were romanticizing, of course; the true origin of the dwarves is interesting, but there is no time to go into it here. What is important is the power of imagination, to take an idea and cling to it stubbornly. Thus the dwarves, and their insistence on being free to wander the underground ways as they pleased, without stint or restraint. This wasn't to the demons' way of thinking, however. They preferred territories. Demons like to stomp along alone, and other creatures tend to get out of their way. Not so the dwarves, who trooped along in their bands, white whiskers flowing, pickax and spade always ready, pounding and chanting (for they are great chanters), often passing directly through a demon convocation: for demons are always holding meetings on crucial points of doctrine, though their discussions are rarely noted by those who really dispose the power. Be this as it may, they hate being disturbed, and the dwarves had an uncanny power of choosing just the wrong place and time to dig to disturb a demon sitting deep in thought, motionless on a block of basalt, hands to his ears, as we see in some of the family portraits done in stone on the turrets of Notre Dame. The demons feel the dwarves are crowding them. Wars have been started on lesser issues.

"I believe," Azzie said, "our tribes are currently at a state of peace. In any event, I have come only for something which will not even interest you, since it is not a precious gem."

"What exactly are you looking for?" Rognir asked.

"Felixite," Azzie said.

In those days, charms and talismans still had great power in the world. And there were many of them about, though the dwarves hid them in secret places, to keep them from the dragons, without much luck, since dragons knew that where you find dwarves, you find gold. Dwarves and dragons go together like lox and bagels, herring and sour cream, good and bad, memory and regret. The dwarves worked hard to extract felixite luck stones from the depths of the earth. Felixite is found only in small quantities, in beds of Neptunic basalt, the very oldest and hardest kind.

This stone of good omen, felixite, was much in use back when everything was happier, better, dearer, truer, the Golden Age, which ended just before true humans came on the scene. Some say that the deposits were laid down by the ancient gods who ruled the earth in the distant long-ago time before things had names. Even then felixite was the rarest mineral in the world. A tiny amount of it could transmit its own inherent joyous and buoyant karma to the holder thereof, thus predisposing a favorable outcome to whatever enterprise he was engaged in. That was why men killed for it.

One thing is sure. If you want a magic good-luck charm, you must either steal one (which is difficult, since a real good-luck charm preserves itself for its owner, and thus tends to be more than a little theft-resistant), or you must find a lode of felixite in the bowels of the earth and fashion one for yourself. You might think that all the natural felixite would be gone by now, since dwarves have been looking for it (among other things) under the earth for as long as mankind has been on the face of it; but you would be wrong; felixite is so lucky that even the earth feels blessed by it and tends to produce more of the stuff from time to time, ecstatically, as it were, but always in small amounts.

"Felixite!" Rognir gave a small, unconvincing laugh. "What makes you think there's any around here?"

"A little mouse told me," Azzie said, making a clever allusion to Hermes' former occupation as Mouse god, before he was abolished or transformed along with the rest of the Olympians. This was completely lost on Rognir.

"There's no felixite around here," Rognir said. "The place was mined out long ago."

"That hardly explains what you are doing here."

"Me? I was just taking a shortcut," Rognir said. "This place happens to be on the underground great circle route from Baghdad to London."

"If that's the way it is," Azzie said, "you won't mind if I look around?"

"Why should I mind? Dirt's free for everybody."

"Well put," Azzie said, and started nosing around. His keen fox's nose soon picked up the faintest strand of a smell that once, not long ago, might have been associated with something else, itself associated, perhaps only fleetingly, with felixite. (Demons have great powers of smell in order to render their time of service in the Pit all the more onerous.)

Sniffing like a fox, Azzie followed this elusive scent around the cavern and directly to the lemur-skin bag that rested at Rognir's feet.

"You don't mind if I take a look in this, do you?" Azzie asked.

Rognir minded very much, but since dwarves are no

match for demons in equal contest, he decided to let discretion reign and to hell with valor.

"Help yourself."

Azzie emptied out the bag. He kicked aside the rubies which Rognir had garnered in Burma, ignored the Colombian emeralds, pushed aside the southern African diamonds with their sinister future connotations, and picked up a small piece of pink-colored stone, shaped in a cylinder.

"Looks like felixite to me," he said. "Would you mind if I borrowed this for a while?"

Rognir shrugged since there was nothing he could do about it. "Just be sure to give it back."

"Don't worry," Azzie said, and turned to leave. Then he looked again at the precious stones scattered underfoot. He said, "Look here, Rognir, you seem a good sort for a dwarf. How about if you and I strike a bargain?"

"What did you have in mind?"

"I have a certain enterprise afoot. I can't say much about it now, but it has to do with the upcoming Millennial celebrations. I need the felixite and your jewels, because without money a demon can do nothing. If I get the backing I expect from the High Evil Powers, I will be able to repay you tenfold."

"But I was planning to take these home and add them to my heap," Rognir said. He stooped down and began to pick up his jewels.

"You probably have a pretty big heap already, haven't you?"

"Oh, it's nothing to be ashamed of," Rognir said, with the complacency of a dwarf whose heap could bear comparison with the best.

"Then why not leave these stones with me? Your heap at home is plenty big already."

"That doesn't stop me from wanting it to be bigger!"

"Of course not. But if you add them to your heap, your money won't be working for you. Whereas if you invest this with me, it will."

"Money working for me? What a curious concept! I hadn't known money was supposed to work."

"It is a concept from the future, and it makes very good sense. Why shouldn't money work? Everything else has to."

"That's a good point," Rognir said. "But what assurance do I have that you will keep your word? All I'll have is your word that your word's good if I take this offer, whereas if I don't take the offer, I'll still have all my gems."

"I can make this offer irresistibly attractive to you," Azzie said. "Instead of following normal banking procedure, I am going to pay you your profit in advance."

"My profit? But I haven't even invested with you."

"I realize that. Therefore, as an inducement, I am going to give you the interest you will make in a year's time investing with me."

"And what do I have to do?"

"Just open your hands."

"Well, all right," said Rognir, who, like most dwarves, couldn't resist a profit.

"Here you are," Azzie said. He gave Rognir two of the smaller diamonds, one ruby with the tiniest flaw, and three perfect emeralds.

Rognir accepted them and looked at them uncertainly. "But aren't these mine?"

"Of course! They are your profit!"

"But they were mine to begin with!"

"I know. But you loaned them to me."

"I did? I don't remember."

"You remember accepting the profit, don't you, when I offered it?"

"Of course. Who turns down a profit?"

"You did quite right. But your profit was based on loaning me the stones so I could make your profit from them. Now you have several of them back. But I still owe you those that I returned as well as the rest. They are principal. In a year you will get them all back. And you have already gotten the profit."

"I'm not so sure of this," Rognir mused.

"Trust me," Azzie said. "You've made a wise investment. It has been a pleasure to do business with you."

"Wait a minute!"

Azzie scooped up the rest of the stones and, not forgetting the piece of felixite, vanished into the upper world. Demons are able to vanish, of course, and this generally gives them a working sense of theater.

# Chapter
# 6

I t was long since Azzie had visited Rome. This city was
an especial favorite of demons, and they had long been
accustomed to travel there for sight-seeing, sometimes in-
dividually, often in groups of hundreds, complete with
women and children demons, and accompanied by guide
demons who lectured on what had gone on in this place
or that. There was no lack of good things to see. Above
all, the cemeteries were high on the list of attractions.
Reading the tombstone inscriptions afforded much
amusement and cemeteries were good melancholy places
for reflection, what with their tall dark cypresses and ancient moss-covered monuments. And, too, Rome was an
exciting place to be in those days, what with the continual
electing of this Pope and excommunicating of that Pope,
as well as the opportunity to help things go a little worse.

And it was especially exciting because this was the
Millennium, the year A.D. 1000. Otto III was Holy Roman Emperor, and there was much contesting between
his German followers and the Italians who supported the

local candidates. The Roman nobles were regularly up in arms against Otto, and there was continual attack and rout. It wasn't safe for a human to walk the streets after dark, and there were perils even by day. Bands of lawless mercenaries roamed the streets, and woe to man or maid who fell into their hands.

Azzie flew in just at dusk, when the sun was setting over the Adriatic, illuminating the domes and towers of Rome with brightness while the terra-cotta rooftops were already darkened with evening gloom. He flew low over the twisted streets, dipping down to take an appreciative look at the Forum and the Colosseum. Then he gained altitude again and soared to the Palatine. Here there was a very special cemetery, the Narbozzi, and this was the place where the demons, since time out of mind, had been holding their annual poker games. With luck, the game would be held here again this year.

The Narbozzi cemetery, stretching for many hectares along the undulating northern limit of the Palatine, was covered with marble sarcophagi, stone crosses, and family tombs. Azzie wandered among the Narbozzi's overgrown grassy ways, which became clearer to him as the sun went down, for demons see better at night, it being their natural medium. The cemetery was large and he feared he might miss the location of the game altogether. He hoped not. He had his good-luck amulet, Rognir's felixite, securely wrapped in parchment with a sign of King Solomon on it. Also in his pouch were the gemstones of Rognir's heap, his stake for the coming game.

He hurried along, and soon the twilight had given way to full night. A horned moon appeared overhead, and Sirius the Dog Star glowed red in the heavens, a fine omen for evil. There was a sound of locusts and a throbbing of frogs from the nearby swamps. Azzie began to wonder if he had come to the wrong cemetery—Rome at this time held the world record for cemeteries of high antiquarian interest. It would take him too long to check them all out, and he didn't even have a complete list.

He was just starting to curse himself for his lack of
preparedness—he should have gotten in touch with the
Supernatural Convention Committee to find the exact location of the game—when he heard a sound, reassuringly
unhuman. He moved toward it, and it distinguished itself
as laughter. It was coming from the east side of the
Narbozzi, the side known in antiquity as "the Accursed."
As he came closer he heard oaths being sworn, and then
he made out the tremendous kettledrum laughter of
Newzejoth, one of the great lords among demons, the
sound of whose voice was unforgettable. Swiftly he flew
to the source of the sound.

The demons were camped in a little hollow between
the great marble sarcophagus of Romulus and the more
recent tomb of Pompey. They were in a small grove surrounded by a circle of ilex trees. Although they had been
there no more than a few hours, the area already showed
the signs of chaos and squalor which characterize demon
gatherings. Huge vats of ichor had been brought in for
refreshment. There were fires here and there, and kitchen
familiars roasted people-parts of many different nations
over hot charcoal.

Azzie was soon made welcome by the other demons.
"Light meat or dark?" a succubus asked him. But Azzie
had no time to eat, delicious though the young humans
appeared to be, all golden brown from the spit.

"Where's the game?" he asked.

"Right over there," the succubus told him. She was an
Indian demon, as Azzie could tell by the ring in her nose
and the fact that her feet were turned backward. She
smiled at him seductively. She was indeed beautiful, but
Azzie had no time for dalliance right now, nor the appetite, because gambling fever was raging in his veins, and
he hastened toward the circle.

The card-playing demons were gathered in a circle lit
by balefires and tallow candles made of unsavory waxy
substances. There was also an outer circle of demons,
gathered to watch and comment on the action. As Azzie

came to the circle a big hand was in progress. In the pot were a scattering of gold coins, some silver denarii, and a human torso, worth plenty since blood was still dripping from the stumps of its arms and legs. The final bet was made, and a small, potbellied demon with skinny arms and legs and a great long nose (a Laplander, to judge from his reindeer sweater) won it and raked it all in.

"New player!" someone called out, and they slid over and made room for Azzie.

Azzie sat down, laid out his jewels in front of him, and was given cards. He was cautious at first. It had been quite a while since he had sat in on a game. This time, even with the lucky amulet of felixite, he was determined to be cautious, bet only good hands, fold when he was in doubt, and do all the other things that poker players, human or demonic, are forever telling themselves to do. He converted some of his gems into body parts and began to play. There in the darkness, lit by the uncanny green-tinged flames of the balefires, the game went on, with demons laughing and swearing as fortune shifted from one to the other.

Demons playing poker are jolly companions as long as things are going well for them. They start out a game in fine high fettle, betting entire human heads and raising limbs with gay abandon. All this is accompanied by the sorts of jokes demons consider hilarious but other beings consider in poor taste. "Anyone for a hero sandwich?" one of the serving demons asked as a tray of human parts was passed around.

Azzie's caution soon left him. He began to plunge, betting more and more wildly. He was thinking of the Millennial Evil Deeds banquet and how much he would like to participate. If only he could be a winner! He really wanted to represent evil in the great Millennial contest between Light and Dark.

But unfortunately, his pile of parts kept dwindling. He knew he was betting wildly, stupidly, demoniacally, but there was nothing he could do about it. Caught up in the pace of the game, he scarcely noticed how the bigger demons seemed to be getting all the big pots. What was going wrong with his felixite? Why wasn't he winning any big hands?

Then it occurred to him that all demons carry good-luck charms, and the more important the demon, the better the charm he could afford. It stood to reason that the charms of the others were nullifying his own charm. He was being wiped out again! It was unthinkable, and very unfair.

The night passed rapidly, and it wasn't long before Azzie noticed a faint lightening in the eastern sky. Soon it would be dawn, when the game would have to break up, unless someone had the keys to a private tomb. At this point Azzie had lost most of what he had started with.

Feelings of rage and chagrin flooded his foxy head. The hand he was holding was another bust, a pair of deuces and three middle cards. He was about to fold it and give up when a feeling came over him. No, not exactly a feeling, more a sensation. It was a warm glow that came from the vicinity of his pouch. Was his good-luck amulet trying to tell him something? Yes, it had to be! And it occurred to him that if the felixite really wanted to help him, it would wait for a single hand, then put all its capacity into winning that one for him.

So certain was he that this was the true state of affairs that he wagered recklessly on his bad hand, raising again and again.

He was given his final cards. He didn't look at them, but continued betting.

There came the showdown. Spreading his cards, Azzie saw his deuces, and saw that he had picked up another pair of deuces. He was about to declare two pairs, when it dawned on him that he had four of a kind. No one else was even close. The others grumbled and threw in their cards. The pot, biggest of the night, was raked over to Azzie.

In it, aside from the pile of golden coins and gems and

miscellaneous body parts, was the hilt of a sword, its blade broken off, and tied around it, a red silk lady's favor. There was also a pair of human legs, in very good condition, scarcely gnawed at all. And a fair amount of lesser stuff, knucklebones, septums, a set of kneecaps, which he turned in for gold.

Azzie, being a true demon, would have gone on gambling as long as he had a penny or a body part to his name. But the sun had just peeped cautiously above the eastern horizon and it was time for everyone to leave the graveyard. Azzie stuffed his winnings into a stout canvas bag which he had been carrying around for just such a purpose. The beginnings of an idea were starting to form in his mind. It was still vague, but there was something there.

# LAUDS

FRIKE

# Chapter
# 1

After leaving the poker game, Azzie flew north. He had decided to look in on the great convention of demons being held at Aachen, Charlemagne's old capital, as part of the opening ceremonies for the Millennial contest. But strong head winds held him up, since being invisible and slightly tenuous does not reduce all air pressure and drag. By evening, he had gotten no farther than Ravenna. He decided to pass up the convention and found a nice graveyard to rest in outside the city walls.

It was a pleasant place, with plenty of big old trees, oaks and willows, a pretty combination, and, of course, cypress, the stately death tree of the Mediterranean. There were nicely decaying tombs and mausoleums. In the distance, he could see the sagging graystone outline of the city wall.

He made himself comfortable near a weathered headstone. What he needed now was a cozy fire. He raided a nearby mausoleum and found several exceedingly dry cadavers. These, together with some dead cats, who had been poisoned by some busybody from the town, fed the flames.

As night wore on, Azzie found that he was getting hungry. He'd had a fine feed last night at the poker game, and demons can go a long time between meals, but flying into head winds all day had given him an appetite. He emptied his sack to see what provisions he had left.

Ah, there were a couple of candied jackal's heads he had taken from the party, wrapped in a bit of moldy winding-sheet. They were delicious morsels, but they left him unfilled. He looked to see what else was in the sack and discovered the pair of legs he'd won.

They looked delicious but he didn't really want to eat them. He remembered some stirring of an idea when he'd first seen them, though now it was forgotten. He was sure there was something he could do with them other than eat them, so he propped them against a tombstone. They brought on an almost irresistible desire to soliloquize. Demons at this time thought nothing of traveling hundreds of miles to find a really good object to soliloquize over. It was an especially pleasant exercise on a desolate Italian upland with a thrusting wind and the distant bark of jackals.

"O legs," Azzie said, "I warrant you trooped nicely to your lady's favor, and bowed well, too, since you are a pair of muscular and nimble legs, of the sort the ladies look upon with favor. O legs, I imagine you now, widespread in antic mirth, and then coiled tight together in that final paroxysm of love. When you were young, O legs, you climbed many a stately oak, and ran near running streams, and across the green friendly fields of your homeland. I daresay you dove over thicket and hedge as you careened your way. No path was too long for you, and you were never tired."

"Think you so?" a voice said from above and behind him. Azzie turned and beheld the mournful cloaked figure of Hermes Trismegistus. He was not surprised that the mage had followed him here. Hermes and the other old gods seemed to follow a different destiny from demons or ghosts, a destiny unaffected by questions of good and evil.

"Good to see you again, Hermes," Azzie said. "I was just philosophizing over this pair of legs."

"I'm not going to stop you," Hermes said.

He had been floating in the air about five feet above Azzie's head. Now he drifted gracefully to the ground, bent, and examined the legs.

"What sort of man do you suppose these belonged to?" Hermes asked.

Azzie turned and considered the legs. "A merry sort, obviously, for look you, they are still wrapped around with gaily colored woolen strips, of the sort that dandies and fellows who think well of themselves affect."

"A dandy, do you think?"

"Most certainly, for look how exquisitely the calves are turned. And notice how perfectly formed and finely muscled the thighs are. You might also notice the small foot, with high, aristocratic arch, well-shaped toes, and evenly clipped nails. Nor is there much in the way of callusing on the heel and along the sides. This fellow did not have to do much to get his living, certainly not with his feet! How do you suppose he met his fate?"

"I know not," Hermes said. "But we can soon find out."

"Have you some trick?" Azzie asked. "Some feat of conjuration unknown to the common lot of demons?"

"Not for nothing," Hermes said, "am I the patron saint of the alchemists, who invoke me when they concoct their mixtures. They seek to turn base metal into gold, but I can turn dead flesh into living memory."

"That seems a useful trick," Azzie said. "Can you show me?"

"With pleasure," Hermes said. "Let's see how these legs spent their last day."

As is customary in conjurations, there was a puff of smoke and a sound as of a brazen gong. As Azzie watched, the smoke parted and he saw . . .

• • •

A young prince marching off in defense of his father's
castle. A fair young man he was, and well set up for the
warrior trade. He marched at the head of his troop of
men, and they were a brave sight, their banners of scarlet
and yellow fluttering finely in the summer breeze. Then,
ahead, they saw another body of men, and the prince
pulled his mount to a halt and called up his seneschal.

"There they are," the prince said. "We have them
fairly now, between a rock and a hard lump of ice, as they
say in Lapland."

This much Azzie saw. And then the vision faded.

"Can you read what fate befell him?" Azzie asked.

Hermes sighed, closed his eyes, lifted his head.

"Ah," he said, "I have tuned in on the battle, and what
a fine engagement of armed men it is! See how furiously
they come together, and hear the well-tempered swords
singing! Yes, they clash, they are all brave, all deft. But
what is this . . . One of the men has left the circle. Not
even wounded, but giving retreat already! It is the former
owner of these legs."

"Poltroon!" cried Azzie, for it was as though he could
see the engagement.

"Ah, but he gets not off unscathed. A man is following, his eyes red with the blood fury, a huge man, a berserker, one of those whom the Franks have been fighting
for hundreds of years, whom they call the madmen from
the north!"

"I don't like the northern demons much, either," Azzie
said.

"The berserker is running down the cowardly prince.
His sword flashes—a sidewise blow struck with an uncanny combination of skill and fury."

"Difficult to strike such a blow," Azzie commented.

"The blow is well struck—the poltroon prince is clo-
ven in twain. His upper half rolls in the dust. But his
cowardly legs are still running, they are running now

from death. Relieved of the weight of his upper body, they find it easy to run, though it is true they are running out of energy. But how much energy does it take for a pair of legs to drive themselves, when no one else is attached? Demons are pursuing these running legs, because they have already passed the boundaries of the normal, already they run in the limitless land of possibilities that is the preternatural. And now, at last, they totter a last few steps, turn, sway, and then crash lifeless to the ground."

"In short, we have here the legs of a coward," Azzie said.

"A coward, to be sure. But a sort of divine coward who would run from death even in death, so afraid was he that what had in fact happened would happen."

# Chapter 2

After Hermes left him to preside over a meeting of maguses in what would someday be Zurich, Azzie sat and brooded. Moodily he poked the legs. They were much too valuable to waste on snacking. That's what Hermes had implied in his usual roundabout fashion.

What should he do with them? He thought again about the great event, the Millennial contest. What he needed was an idea, a concept. . . . He stared at the legs, rearranged them this way and that. There must be something. . . .

Suddenly he sat up straight. Yes, the legs! He had it! A wonderful idea, one that was sure to make his name in circles of evil. He had an idea for the contest! It had come in a burst of demoniac inspiration. He must lose no time, must hurry and get it on record, get cooperation from the Evil Powers. What day was this? He calculated swiftly, then moaned. This was the last day in which entries could be made. He must go to the High Demon Council, and quickly.

Taking a deep breath, he propelled himself away from Earth to the region of Limbo where the high council was meeting. It is not generally realized, but demons have as much trouble getting in to see someone in the top level of command as mortals do. If you're not high up in the hierarchy, if you're not related to someone important, if you are not a gifted athlete, then forget anything immediate; you have to go through channels, and that can take time.

Azzie didn't have time, however. Next morning, the High Committee would pick a winner, and the game would be set.

"I gotta see the Game Committee," Azzie said to the demon guard at the gate of the Ministry, the great group of buildings, some baroque and ornamental with onion-shaped domes, others severely modern and rectilinear, where the affairs of demons, imps, and other evil supernatural creatures were regulated. Many demons worked here as clerks: a lot of paper was required in the never-ending attempt to codify the behavior of supernatural creatures. The government of Supernatural Creatures of Evil was more extensive than any on Earth and employed most of the demons of Hell in one capacity or another. And this was despite the fact that the governing of demons had never been sanctioned by a higher power. The only recognized power above Good and Evil was the strange and misty thing called Ananke, Necessity. It was not certain whether the chain of command stopped at Ananke or went on to even higher levels. Ananke was as far as demoniac theorists had reached. The theorists had difficulty communicating with Ananke because it was so mysterious, so difficult to pin down, so unbodied, and so uncommunicative that it was impossible to be sure of anything about it except that it seemed to exist. Ananke judged the contests between Good and Evil which were held every thousand years. Its decisions were reached mysteriously. Ananke was a law unto itself, but it was a law that showed only glimpses of itself, and never stood still for explication.

· · ·

But why should demons have to be ruled? In theory, demons were autonomous creatures who followed their impulses, i.e., to do evil. But there seemed to be a built-in perversity in the makeup of intelligent creatures, whether natural or supernatural, that made them go against the grain, against what was best for them, against all the things they should believe. Thus the demons needed the first necessity of government, a bureau of Conformity, and this cheered them no end because their top theorists believed that the enforcing of the standards of evil was worse, evilwise, than the doing of evil itself. It was difficult to be sure of this, but it seemed reasonable.

Azzie was acting in a nonconformist manner as he burst past the guards, who stared at him slack-jawed, taken aback because this was definitely undemonic behavior. Demons are usually toadies to those above them. But they hesitated to chase after and stop him because the fox-headed young demon had seemed more than a little crazed, and if that were so, he might be divinely inspired, that is, inspired by Satan himself, in whose invisible service all of the powers of evil toiled as an act of faith.

Azzie ran through the corridors of the Ministry, well aware why the guardian demons had not tried to stop him. That was all very well, but *he* knew he was not inspired, and he also knew that the high council would not be amused by any of this. It occurred to him that he had made a very big mistake, had taken more upon himself than he could deal with. But he thrust that thought from his mind, his determination stiffening. Now that he had begun, he would have to continue.

He raced up one side of an impressive double stairway, turned to his left, almost overturning an urn filled with freshly picked spring weeds, and continued down the corridor, making left turns whenever the choice presented itself, racing past subordinate demons with their hands full of papers, until he came to a high bronze door.

He knew this had to be the place. He pushed open the door and entered.

When Azzie burst in, the meeting of the Powers of Evil was in full session. It was not a happy meeting. Discontent was manifest on the bestial faces of the major demons. Mouths were turned down, eyes red and swollen.

"What is this?" Belial said, standing up on his goat feet to better peer at Azzie, who was now bowing low.

Azzie, tongue-tied, could only stammer and stare.

"It's obvious, isn't it?" Azazel said, hunching his mighty shoulders and ruffling his dark wings. "It's a demon of the common sort who has presumed to break in upon us. I don't know what the young are coming to these days. It wasn't like this in my time. Young demons were respectful then, and desirous of pleasing their elders. Now they barge around in gangs, sewer gangs I have heard them called, and they don't care whom they offend with their noisy behavior. Not satisfied with this, they even elect one of their number to break into our inner sanctorum and taunt us."

Belial, an old rival of Azazel's, pounded with his hoof on the table and said, in mincing words, "The right honorable member is sufficiently talented to expand a single demonic intrusion into an onslaught by a sewer warfare gang. I see no gang: only a single rather foolish-looking demon. I would also point out that *sanctum* is more correct than *sanctorum* in this case, which the honorable member would know if he had ever mastered the dear old mother tongue, Latin."

Azazel's eyes smoldered, little wisps of blue smoke came out of his snout, corrosive acid dripped from his nose and ate holes in the ironwood table. "I'll not be mocked," he said, "by a jumped-up nature spirit who has been *made* a demon rather than born one and who, because of his ambiguous ancestry, cannot be relied upon to understand the true nature of evil."

Other members clamored to be heard, because demons loved to argue about who really understood evil,
who was most evil, and by extension, who was insuffi-
ciently bad. Azzie, however, had now regained his poise.
He realized that the attention of the Lord Demons would
soon be turned to him. So he made haste to speak in his
own defense.

"Gentlemen," he said, "I am sorry to be the cause of
this dispute. I would not have broken in on you if I had
not something urgent to say."

"Yes," Belial said. "Why *have* you come? And I notice
that you haven't brought any presents, as is customary.
What have you to say for yourself?"

"I come without presents," Azzie said, "that is true. It
was my haste, and I beg apology. But I do bear something
more important."

He paused. It was that dramatic demon sense working
in him that made him stop at that moment rather than
blurt on.

The Demon Lords also knew a thing or two about
drama. They stared at him in accusing silence. After what
seemed like forever, Belphegor, who was anxious to ad-
journ this committee and get a little sleep, said, "All right,
damn you, what do you bear that is more important than
presents?"

In a low, husky voice, Azzie said, "What I bear, gentlemen, is that most precious of things: an idea."

# Chapter
# 3

Azzie's words hit upon a common concern among the Lord Demons, namely, their need for an idea for the coming Light versus Dark festivities, a drama that would be their entry into the contest of Good versus Evil, and whose outcome would demonstrate, homiletically, as it were, the superiority of Evil, thus giving them the right to dominate man's destiny for the next thousand years.

"What is this idea?" Belial asked.

Azzie bowed low and began to tell them the story of Prince Charming.

Fairy tales have great weight and resonance for demons as well as for humans. All of the Demon Lords knew the Prince Charming story—of how a youth came forth to save a princess who had been enchanted by a spell and cast into a perpetual sleep. This prince was Prince Charming, who, aided by his pure heart and loyal spirit, fought his way through the various dangers that beset the Princess, conquered them all, won through the wall of thorns to her castle, climbed to the top of the mountain of glass upon which her palace had been set, and kissed her. Whereupon she awoke, and they married and lived happily ever after.

Azzie proposed to stage this pretty story, but with characters of his own devising.

"Gentlemen, give me a grant so that I can draw freely upon Supply, and I will create a Prince and a Princess who will act out the Prince Charming–Sleeping Beauty story and turn this insipid tale on its ear. My couple will demonstrate a different ending. Their conclusion to the tale, arrived at by their own free will, with only a minimum of behind-the-scenes tampering on my part, will show conclusively, to the enjoyment of our friends and the confusion of our enemies, that given a free hand, evil must inevitably win in the contests of the human spirit."

"Not a bad idea," Azazel said. "But what makes you think that your actors, given free will, will act the way you want them to?"

"That can be ensured," Azzie said, "by careful selection of the body parts, and appropriate education once they are selected and animated into persons."

"Careful selection?" Phlegethon asked. "What do you mean by that?"

"Here is the very first item," Azzie said, "around which I intend to build my Prince Charming."

He removed from his canvas bag the pair of legs he had won at the demons' poker game. The Lord Demons leaned forward to regard them. By the combined weight of their gaze a cloud of body memory issued forth, and each demon could see for himself the history of this pair of legs, and how their owner had come to lose them.

"A devilish cowardly pair of legs indeed," Belial said.

"True, my lord," Azzie said. "A prince with these legs would never stay the course of a difficult trial. The legs themselves would almost haul him back to shameful safety!"

"Is that the destined outcome of your planned charade?" Belial asked.

"No, it is not, lord," Azzie said. "I crave your indulgence not to force me to reveal the conclusion of my scheme too soon, for much of the pleasure in its making lies in following a creative intuition without knowing too firmly in advance its outcome."

There may have been difficulties about Azzie's plan, but the time to select an entry was at hand, and nothing better had come along. The assembled Lord Demons nodded. "I think we have something here," Belial said. "What do you think, my colleagues?"

The others humphed and griffed but finally gave their assent.

"Go forth, then," Belial said to Azzie, "and do what you have promised. You are our entry, our chosen one. Go, and produce horror and evil in our name."

"Thank you," Azzie said, genuinely moved. "But I'll need money to do this. Body parts such as I want don't come cheap. And there is the matter of the other things I'll need—two castles, one for each protagonist, and a mansion for myself from which to operate. Also the wages of a servant, and quite a few other things."

The lords issued him a black credit card with his name embossed in fiery letters above an inverted pentagram, insertable anyplace dark and sinister. "With this," Belial said, "you will have instant and unlimited credit with Supply. You can call them up anytime and anywhere, so long as you find someplace foul in which to insert the card. But that should be no difficulty, the world being what it is. It is also good for control of meteorological phenomena."

"But you must supply your own hero and heroine," Azazel told him. "And, of course, the directing of the action is all your responsibility."

"Accepted," Azzie said. "I wouldn't have it any other way."

# Chapter 4

If someone had been watching, from a high window in the steeply pitched narrow old house above the main square in the village of Hagenbeck, he might have seen a man arriving in the public coach from Troyes. This man was tall and attractive. He was neither young nor old. His face was not displeasing, and had about it a sternness that marked its owner as a person of some consequence. He wore clothing of good English cloth, and his shoes had fine brass buckles. He got off at Hagenbeck, went directly into the inn, and asked for rooms. When the owner, Herr Gluck, wondered about the new arrival's ability to pay, Azzie (for such it was) produced a purse in which rested innumerable pieces of Spanish gold cast in doubloons.

"Very fine, indeed, sir," the innkeeper said, cringing to show his appreciation. "We have our finest apartment open. Usually it is occupied, but everyone is gone to the great fair in Champagne."

"Then it is mine," said Azzie.

It was very fine, the main room having a large bower window. There was even a little bathroom in which to clean up, not that demons make much use of such things.

At first Azzie lay down on the big bed with its feather down coverlet and its fine plump pillows. It seemed to him that his career was finally beginning. He was amazed at how quickly he had moved, from a lowly servitor in North Discomfort 405 to the impresario of a fine new game for the Millennial celebrations. He lay on the bed and pondered his good fortune for a time, then bestirred himself, anxious to get his scheme started.

The first thing he needed was a servitor. He decided to consult the landlord about this requirement.

"Of course you must have a servitor," the fat landlord said. "I was amazed that such a fine gentleman as yourself didn't come equipped with servants and a considerable traveling chest. Since you have money, that shouldn't be hard to put to rights."

"I need a special sort of servant," Azzie said. "One who may be called upon to do deeds of a most unusual nature."

"Might I inquire," the landlord asked, "just what nature your excellency is speaking about?"

Azzie looked keenly at the landlord. He was fat and complacent looking, but there was a sinister cast to his features. This man was no stranger to evil deeds. He was a man who would stop at nothing, and who knew a sort of glee at the thought of evil deeds, finding in them the excitement his normal life lacked.

"Landlord," Azzie said, "the deeds I will require may not be entirely within the ken of the king's law."

"Yes, sir," the landlord said.

"I have prepared here," Azzie said, "a little list of the requirements I need in a servitor. I wish you could tack this up somewhere. . . ."

He handed a sheet of parchment to the landlord. The landlord took it, moved it back and forth to get into reading range.

It read: "Servitor needed, a man not squeamish, accustomed to blood and gore, honest and reliable, up for anything."

He read it several times, then said, "A man like this might be found, if not in our village of Hagenbeck, then in nearby Augsburg. But I shall be pleased to nail this on our front wall, along with the listings for hay and oats, and we shall see what comes of it."

"Do that," Azzie said. "And send me up a flagon of your best wine, in case the wait becomes onerous."

The landlord louted low and took his departure. Within minutes he sent up the servant girl, a poor creature with deformed face and halting gait, carrying not only the flagon of wine, but also some small cakes which the cook had baked just that day. Azzie rewarded her with a silver penny, for which she was pathetically grateful. He then sat himself down and feasted. Demons do not really require food, of course, but when they take human form they also take on human desires. This appetite for food was one of them. Azzie dined well, and afterward sent for the blackbird pie he could smell baking in the inn's well-founded kitchen.

It was not long before the first applicant knocked at his door. He was a tall young man, thin as a weed, and with wild light blond hair that floated around his head in a sort of nimbus. His clothing was presentable, although much patched. He held himself well, and bowed low when Azzie opened the chamber door.

"Sire," the stranger said, "I read your notice belowstairs, and I have come quickly to present myself to you. I am Augustus Hye, and I am a poet by trade."

"Indeed?" said Azzie. "This is a somewhat unusual post for a poet."

"Not at all, sire," Hye said. "Poets must perforce deal with the most extreme of human emotions. Blood and gore would suit me fine, since they would prove good subjects for my poems, in which I will consider the vanity of life and the inevitability of death."

Azzie was not entirely satisfied with what he heard. The poet didn't seem really suited for the task. But Azzie decided to give him a trial.

"Do you know the local graveyards?" Azzie asked.

"Of course, my lord. Graveyards are a favorite place for poets who crave contemplation to bring to their minds great and dolorous deeds."

"Then hie you to such a place this evening, when the moon is down, and bring me a nicely aged human skull, with or without hair, it makes no difference. And if you can bring me some ladies' fingers, all the better."

"Ladies' fingers, sire? You are referring to the confection of that name?"

"Not at all," said Azzie. "I am referring to the actual and literal objects."

Hye looked uncomfortable. "Such items are hard to come by."

"I know that," Azzie said. "If they were easy, I would go forth and get them myself. Now go and see what you can do."

Hye left, not happily. Already his hopes were fading. Like all poets he was more used to talking about blood and gore than actually getting his hands into it. But still, he decided to attempt the task because Lord Azzie, as he called himself, was evidently a wealthy man and might be counted upon to give out much largess.

Azzie's next caller was an old woman. She was tall and lean, dressed entirely in black. She had small eyes and a long nose; her lips were thin and bloodless.

"I know you advertised for a man," she said, after dropping a deep curtsy, "but I hoped that you might not be adamant in that choice. I will make a wonderful servitor for you, Lord Azzie, and you can enjoy my favors into the bargain."

Azzie shuddered. This old beldame really fancied herself if she thought that any lord, or any demon masquerading as a lord, would fancy her for anything more than pulling off his boots after a hard day's riding. Nevertheless, he decided he would be fair about it.

He repeated the instructions he had given the poet Hye. The aged beldame, whose name was Agatha, also seemed taken aback. She was one of those who believed that appearance was the better part of evil. For many years she had gotten by in Hagenbeck solely by her appearance, and the reputation it had given her for evil deeds. She had thought this job would be just the right thing for her, since she already looked the part of one who would stop at no evil deed and would take delight in blood and gore. But, despite her appearance, she was one who had difficulty even in cutting off a chicken's head. Nevertheless, she said she would do her best and promised to return at midnight with her spoils.

That was the end of the applicants for that day. Azzie was not well satisfied. The people in these parts seemed to have little appetite for his sort of work. But he would see. Having a servant was absolutely necessary.

# Chapter
# 5

That afternoon, Azzie went to nearby Augsburg and spent the rest of the day strolling about observing its ancient churches. Demons are very interested in churches, which, though Powers of Good reside in them, can as often as not be twisted to serve evil. In the early evening he returned to the Inn of the Hanged Man in Hagenbeck, but learned from the landlord that no other persons had applied for the post he had offered.

He took out the black credit card and looked it over carefully. It was a beautiful thing, and he had the desire to call up something that would amuse him, like dancing girls. But he decided against it. First things first. He needed a good human servitor. After that, both the work and the fun would begin.

In the evening he decided to take his dinner downstairs with the tradespeople. He had a special table for himself, curtained off from the crowd. But he kept a bit of the curtain drawn back so he could watch their antics.

The people ate and drank and caroused, and Azzie

wondered how they could be so light of heart. Did they not know that the Millennium was approaching? Elsewhere in Europe men knew about this, and were taking whatever precautions they could. There were Dances of the Dead being held on blasted heaths, and all manner of signs and portents. Many people were sure the end of the world was coming. Some turned to prayer. Others, deciding they were doomed, passed their time in eating and sexual activity. The Angel of Death had been sighted in a dozen places around Europe, surveying the territory and making a preliminary census of all who would be taken. In churches and cathedrals anathemas were intoned against promiscuity and license. But all this was to little or no avail. People's spirits had been roused and frightened by the approach of the grim year when it was said the dead would rise in the streets, the figure of the Antichrist would be seen in the land, and all things would gather themselves for Apocalypse, the last great battle between the forces of Good and Evil.

Azzie himself had no need for such vulgar superstitions. He knew that mankind's game was a long way from being played out. There would be contests like this for many thousands of years into the future, as there had been for thousands of years into the past, though the memory of mankind retained only the most confused memories of this.

At last Azzie grew tired and went up to the bedroom. It still lacked a half hour or so of midnight. Azzie didn't believe either Hye or Agatha would return. They seemed not to be made of stern enough stuff. But he decided to show them the courtesy of staying up for them anyhow.

The minutes dragged by, and a hush fell over the village. This was the time Azzie loved best, the minutes approaching midnight, when the complexion of the world changed, when the dusky sanctities of evening had been forgotten, and the saving grace of dawn was still far away. It was in these hours, between midnight and dawn, that evil always felt most at peace with itself, most experimental, most in need of strangeness and sin, most in need of producing the ever-pervading perversions which needed constant renewal, and the doing of which was a delight to the evil soul.


Midnight came and passed and no one knocked at his door. Azzie was growing bored, and the big four-poster bed with its fluffy eiderdown looked exceedingly comfortable. It was a temptation, and since demons are not supposed to resist temptation, he gave in, got up on the bed, and closed his eyes. He fell into a deep sleep, and in that sleep a dream came to him. In his dream three maidens clad all in white came to him carrying holy articles in their hands. They beckoned to him, saying, "Come, Azzie, join us in our frolic." And Azzie, looking at them, was greatly desirous of joining them, for they smiled and winked at him most enticingly. But there was something about them he didn't like, something which said to his trained eye that they really didn't care for evil, were merely feigning it in order to lure him into their clutches. Nevertheless, he was drawn toward them, almost against his will, even though he repeated to himself lines from the Credo of Evil: that the good is capable of assuming a pleasing form and that a demon must take care not to be seduced by that which only seems evil. The Credo didn't help. They reached out to him. . . .

He never learned the outcome because he was awakened by a tapping at the door. He sat up and pulled himself together. How ridiculous it was to be afraid of being tainted by good! It was a standard fear among demons, and it gave him a turn, dreaming of it.

The tap came again.

Azzie checked his appearance in the cracked mirror. He smoothed his eyebrows, brushed back his red hair, and gave an experimental leer. Yes, he was decidedly horrific tonight, ready for any applicant who came through the door.

"Come in," he said.

When the door opened and he beheld his visitor, he was more than a little surprised.

The person who entered was not familiar. He was a very small man with a large hump upon his back. He had on a large black cloak which was wrapped completely around him, its hood raised. His long, bony face was dead white, sepulchral. As he advanced Azzie noticed that he walked with the help of a cane.

"And who," Azzie asked, "are you, to come calling upon me at this hour?"

"I am Frike," the lame hunchback replied. "I have come in answer to your ad. You wanted a servant, it seems, one who would be up for anything. I put myself forth as just such a person."

"You are not afraid to recommend yourself," Azzie said. "But there are two applicants ahead of you. I set them a simple task and now I await their return."

"Ah, yes," Frike said. "I happened to meet them, the poet and the beldame. They were at the gates of the cemetery, trying to get up the courage to do what you required of them."

"They should not have delayed so long," Azzie said. "The time set for their appearance is already past."

"Why, master," Frike said, "they met with certain unfortunate accidents. And so I have come in their stead."

"What accidents?" Azzie asked.

"My lord," Frike said, "I brought the items you requested of them."

Frike reached inside his cloak and took out a leather satchel of tanned cowhide. Opening it, he removed two packets wrapped in sackcloth. Opening one, he removed eight fingers and one thumb, neatly severed, perhaps with a razor.

"Behold," Frike said. "The lady's fingers."

"These are somewhat gummy," Azzie said, examining the fingers and nibbling one of them.

"They are the best I could provide on short notice," Frike said.

"And why is there not a full set? A thumb is missing!"

"Your lordship might not have noticed," Frike said, "since to notice such a thing would be beneath your dignity. But I would point out, sire, that Agatha, who aspired to the post of your servant, had a thumb missing. I do not know the story of its loss, and I'm afraid now I can't find it out for you."

"It is of little importance," Azzie said. "But I also asked for a head."

"Ah, yes," Frike said. "The quest you set for the poet. Now you would think, sir, that his would be an easy task, since our local cemetery is full of the sort of specimens you asked for. But he walked around outside the graveyard, then finally went in and put his spade here and then changed his mind and put it there, until at last I got sick of waiting for him to complete the task. So I took the liberty, my lord, of procuring the object and eliminating my opposition in a single stroke."

So saying, he opened the satchel and displayed the head of Hye, the poet.

"Not cleanly severed, I notice," Azzie said, but it was just for form's sake, for he was well pleased with the work of this applicant for the position of his helper.

"I regret there was no time to wait for the perfect stroke," Frike said. "But since he is well known hereabouts as a bad poet, I daresay he's missed many a clean stroke himself."

"Frike, you have done very well. You shall enter my employ at once. I think that you are a paragon among mortals. And since you have done so well at this, I'm sure you will have no problem getting me the things I need, once I have explained them and scouted out the territory."

"I expect to serve you well, master," Frike said.

Azzie went to his chest, opened it, and from a small

deerskin bag, extracted four golden thalers. He gave these to Frike, who louted low in gratitude.

"And now," Azzie said, "we must go to work. Midnight is past; the time of evil is at hand. Are you up for what may come, Frike?"

"Indeed I am."

"And what do you expect as your reward?"

"Only to continue serving you, lord," Frike said, "after death as before."

Thus Azzie knew that Frike knew who, or rather, what he was. He was pleased to find so intelligent a servant. He bade Frike pack the things. They would set to work at once.

# Chapter 6

Before anything else could be done, Azzie needed a place from which to operate. The Inn of the Hanged Man possessed many fine features, but the space was too limited and the other customers too apt to be curious. And as Azzie and Frike gathered their specimens there was the problem of the smell. Azzie knew several master spells to keep human meat relatively fresh, but not even a magic spell could take away the odor of death and decay that hung over his work. Even hiring men to bring down ice from the Alps was insufficient, for keeping constant relays going would be a monumental enterprise. And the Powers of Darkness had vetoed his scheme in this regard, saying it didn't warrant the expense, and it would call too much attention to him and his work.

The question, then, was where to locate the home and alchemical laboratory that would be needed. He needed to stay close to the heart of Europe because that was where the action was. He settled finally upon the town of Augsburg, in the Alps near Zurich. It was a fine small city, located on a trade route. This meant that he could purchase from passing vendors the spices and simples he needed for the work. Augsburg was also good because it was a well-known center for witchcraft. Since everyone there suspected everyone else of sorcery, no undue suspicion was likely to fall upon him.

He met with the burgomeister and arranged the long-term rental of the high-steepled Château des Artes on the northern edge of town. This noble old building, built over the ruins of a Roman villa which had been lived in by a praetor in the old days of the Roman empire, suited him admirably. Since the cellar was extensive there was no problem over where to keep his growing collection of body parts. And finally, he was near enough to Zurich and Basle to ensure a good supply of additional material from the medical schools in those areas.

But it was summer, and even his preserving spells were pushed to their limits. Finally, he had to resort to an additional remedy. It was known of old that when anything organic was put into a vat containing ichor, it kept for a long time. Indeed, ichor was the universal solution, good to drink, capable of miracles when used for other purposes.

Obtaining a sufficient quantity of ichor proved a problem, however. Supply tried to keep every drop of it for themselves. It was only after asking Hermes Trismegistus to intercede for him that Azzie received a quantity adequate for his purposes. And even then he had to counsel Frike, on pain of great torture and possible death, not to touch the precious supplies.

The breasts, haunches, kneecaps, and elbows were easy enough. Ribs and shoulders were in good supply. But Azzie wanted to know the antecedents of every piece of meat he bought, and this knowledge was often beyond the ken of the men he dealt with. Bit by bit, as the warm days wore on with a deepening of greens and the spread of summer flowers, he collected a goodly mess of pieces. But these were the least important parts. The heads, the faces, the hands—these were crucial, and hard to come by.

More days passed, summer storms rattled and rolled, and it seemed he was getting no closer to his goal. He assembled a sample human which stumbled about gibbering until he put it back in the rendering vat, a poor dottering idiot. The creature's brain had evidently decayed before it could be preserved. Azzie began to wonder whether he hadn't bitten off more than he could chew.

But the bright days of summer made the year's-end deadline seem an eternity away, and he called in laborers to repair the château. He hired husbandmen from nearby villages to put in quick-growing crops. He found these chores an oddly satisfying way of passing the time while the head-hunt went on.

The Château des Artes was conveniently situated for journeys south to Italy, west to France, east toward Bohemia and Hungary. So while he filled his time with householder's tasks, he sent Frike far and wide on a big gray horse, two pack animals trailing behind. While Frike turned up many curious and useful items, it seemed a slack season for heads. Heads . . .

He told the mayor of the town, Estel Castelbracht, that he was engaged in various researches to find cures for the plague, the ague, and the tertian fever, which had been sweeping these parts since Roman times. He explained that it was necessary to conduct his researches on human flesh, with methods learned from the great alchemists of the period. The mayor, and then the people, took him at his word, for he seemed a jolly sort, never reluctant to treat local sick, very often with good results.

While doing this, Azzie was also considering the props he would need for his Prince Charming game. He sent to Supply for lists of goods, but their replies were always vague, filled with stipulations such as "if still in stock" or "out of stock, more expected soon." What was especially annoying was their response to his request for two castles, one for Prince Charming, the other for Princess Scarlet. The powers at Supply, speaking to him through an oracular owl, told him that they were clean out of castles at the moment. Azzie argued with them, explaining that this was a priority job which had the imprimatur of the High Demon Council. "Yes," they said, "they are all priority jobs, and we can only do what we can. . . ."

He decided he'd better go to Supply, look over their stores himself, and set aside what he would need when his Prince and Princess were ready to be assembled. Yes, it was time to go to Limbo, that ill-defined region where are shaped the supernatural events that push and pull at the mixed destiny of mankind.

And keep an eye out for the proper head . . .

# Chapter
# 7

Azzie departed with a feeling of regret. He knew that he should not allow himself to get sentimental over land he would occupy for only a short time, and which he lived on only in order to serve a special purpose. Still, all that work on the mansion and fields . . . He had never put that much of himself into a place before, watching it change in accord with his wishes. It was beginning to feel kind of . . . homey.

And the journey to Limbo was not without its dangers. There was always difficulty passing from one realm to another. The laws of a realm, like those of Earth itself, are not to be understood completely. How less completely, then, were understood the strange laws which governed the movement between realms.

Luckily, nothing went wrong this time. He made the necessary preparations and spoke the Greek words, the Hebrew exclamation. The fire flared and he suddenly occupied a spot on a long plain, bleak black mountains on either side. The sky was white and hot and there were occasional green swirls in it, as of djinns flying fast in formation.

Just to get around in Limbo was a considerable chore, since its extent was limitless. Luckily, some of its more important places existed reasonably close together and they exerted something of a pull which drew visitors to them. And there was the Roc service, of which Azzie was able to avail himself. The huge birds had been extinct on Earth for a long time, because of difficulties in making a living after the Pleistocene. But with their broad backs, they were admirably suited for taxi service in this place.

Supply looked like a huge series of warehouses set in the middle of the plain. Supply had wanted plenty of room. Here, Supply's space was sufficient to store all of the living rooms on Earth, with plenty of room left for kitchens and stables. In actual fact, they had never tried to fill all their warehouses. The number of things they would need was limited only by human imagination, which at one time or another sought all things. The number of things that could be of use in the invisible powers' continual attempt either to enlighten or subvert humanity was never-ending and called upon everything under the suns. You could never tell when some demon would need a Thracian spear from A.D. 55 or something equally esoteric. Supply simulated most of what was asked for, and Supply possessed some of the most imaginative scene designers ever known.

Supply was built on a bank of the Styx, that stupendous river that runs through Earth and all the heavens and hells, and upon whose dusky surface the ancient boatman, Charon, plied his way between the centuries and the worlds. The supernatural powers he sometimes served considered Earth the greatest game ever conceived and had no wish to be disconnected from any aspect of it, no matter how far in the future or the past.

Azzie dismounted from the Roc. He walked rapidly, occasionally gliding when walking grew onerous, and made his way down the long streets, both sides of which were flanked with warehouses. All of the warehouses had the sign, UNAUTHORIZED PERSONNEL STAY OUT. Armed Salis, the neutral spirits of Limbo, stood guard. They were armed with energy dissipators. These weapons, which resembled spears with gun sights and triggers, let forth rays of pattern-disrupting particles (though some said waves) which would disrupt the personality pattern of even the greatest of the demons, "whipping his brains to tapioca" in the phrase popular that year. Azzie gave them a wide berth. Limbo had become a dangerous place of late, and this was due more to the guards than the guarded.

At length he came to a warehouse which had an unguarded door. Over it was the sign, INQUIRIES MAY BE MADE HERE. It was a surprisingly blunt statement for so vague and conceptual a place, but Azzie lost no time going to it.

Inside he found about twenty demons of all sorts and degrees waiting their turn to lodge complaints with a bored young demon clerk who wore a plaid golfing cap in defiance of temporal clothing regulations (demons can go into the past or future, but they are not supposed to bring back souvenirs).

Azzie flashed his black credit card and pushed his way to the head of the line. "This is top priority," he told the clerk. "I've got full clearance from the High Demon Council."

"Is that a fact?" the young demon asked, unimpressed.

Azzie showed his black credit card.

"Is what he says true?" the clerk asked the card.

"BELIEVE IT!" the card flashed back.

"All right," the demon said. "What can we do for you, Mister Big Shot?"

Azzie resented the young demon's attitude but decided now was not the time to make an issue of it.

"The first thing I need," Azzie said, "is two castles. I know that's a lot to ask, but I really need them."

"Two castles, huh?" The young demon eyed him unsympathetically. "I suppose your whole plan will fail if you don't have them."

"That's exactly right."

"Then resign yourself to failure, buddy, because we have only one castle, and even that isn't a proper castle; it's mostly an outline with a real wall and barbicon, but all the rest is mental construct held together by old magic spells."

"That's ridiculous," Azzie said. "I thought Supply had an unlimited number of castles."

"That was true quite some time ago. But recently the premise has been changed. The possibilities have been narrowed. It means a lot more trouble for everyone, but it keeps things interesting. That, at least, is the theory of the Supply-side deviltry."

"I never heard of it," Azzie said. "Do you know what you're talking about?"

"If I did," the clerk said, "would I be in this menial job, telling guys like you they can only have one castle?"

"All right," Azzie said, "I'll take the castle you've got."

The clerk scribbled something on a sheet of parchment. "You'll have to take it as is. We haven't got time to patch it up any further."

"What's the matter with it?"

"I told you about the magic spells that hold the place together. There're not enough of them, so parts of the castle disappear every now and then."

"Which parts?" Azzie asked.

"That depends on the weather," the clerk said. "Since the castle is bound together by dry-weather spells, long periods of rain play hell with its provisional existence."

"Isn't there a plan of some sort showing which parts vanish when?"

"Of course there's a plan," the clerk said. "But it needs updating. You'd be crazy to trust it."

"I want it anyway," Azzie said. He had a lot of respect for scratchings on parchment.

"Where do you want me to put this castle?" the clerk asked.

"Just a minute, this won't work. I really do need two castles. I have two different beings. One of them has to get from his castle to the castle of the woman he loves, or thinks he loves. I really need two castles."

"How about one castle and one very large house?"

"No, it's entirely out of the spirit of the game."

"Make do with one," the clerk suggested. "You can shuttle them around. It's easy enough to change the appearance of a castle. Especially when rooms keep on disappearing."

"I suppose I'll have to," Azzie said. "Or I could use my château for one of them. How soon can you send it?"

"Hey, for you I'll get on it right away," the clerk demon said, in a voice that implied Azzie wouldn't see that castle before Hell froze over. Azzie caught the tone and tapped the black credit card. It flashed: "DO WHAT HE SAYS! NO HORSING AROUND!"

"All right," said the clerk. "I was only kidding. Where do you want this castle delivered?"

"Do you know a region of Earth called Transylvania?"

"Don't worry. I'll find it," the clerk said.

"Uh, wouldn't know where I could turn up a good head, would you? Human? Male?"

The clerk just laughed.


And so it was that Azzie left Supply and returned to Earth, where nearly a week had passed. He went to the Château des Artes and was irritated to discover that Frike was nowhere to be found. He went outside and mounted his horse. He was going to ride into Augsburg and seek him out.

Storming into the office of Estel Castelbracht, he asked directly whether he had seen the man. There seemed no need for great subtlety.

"Indeed I did," Castelbracht said. "He was hurrying down the street, and he went into the house of Dr. Albertus over yon. I heard him muttering something about a head—"

"Thank you," Azzie said, passing him money, as was his wont on dealing with anyone in an official capacity, when he could afford it.

# Chapter
# 8

The doctor's house was at the end of the little lane that led to the town wall. The house stood all by itself, a tall, narrow old building with ground floor of stone and upper levels of dressed timber. Azzie marched up the steps and swung the great bronze knocker.

"Who knocks?" came forth a voice from inside.

"One who requests knowledge," Azzie said.

The door was opened. Standing in the doorway was an elderly, white-haired gentleman who wore a fine Roman tunic in spite of this garment having been out of fashion for some hundreds of years. He was tall and stooped, and he walked with the aid of a long cane.

The old gentleman said, "I believe it is Lord Azzie, is it not?"

"That is correct," Azzie said. "I've been told that my servant, Frike, might be found here."

"Ah, of course, Frike," the old gentleman said. "Won't you come this way, sir? By the way, I am Master Albertus."

He led the way into a gloomy interior, past a cluttered parlor, past an unkempt kitchen and scullery, to a cheerful little drawing room in the back.

Frike was standing by the fireplace at the far end of the room. He smiled when Azzie came in.

"Frike!" cried Azzie. "I thought you had deserted me."

"Nay, master," Frike said, "I would not dream of it. What happened was that during your absence, I took myself to the village tavern in search of companionship, and there to quaff the strong red wine that gives this region its ferocious valor. There I met this gentleman, Messer Albertus, who is my old master from the days when I was an apprentice in Salerno."

"Yes," Messer Albertus said, his eyes twinkling, "I know this rogue Frike well enough, Lord Azzie. I was overjoyed to hear of his good luck in getting into your employ. I brought him to my house to give him assistance in the matter he is helping you with."

"What help exactly are you speaking of?" Azzie asked.

"Why, lord, it seems that you require a few first-rate body parts. And I happen to have a particularly choice item in my laboratory."

"Are you a doctor?" Azzie inquired.

Albertus shook his white-tressed head. "I am an alchemist, my lord, and body parts are often useful in my occupation. If you will come this way . . ."

Azzie followed the aged gentleman, and was followed in turn by Frike. They went down the hall to a barred door. Albertus unlocked it with a key carried on a thong around his neck, and they followed him down winding flagstone stairs to a well-made alchemist's laboratory in the cellar. There Albertus lit an ancient oil lamp. By its glow, Azzie could see tables covered with alembics and cysters, and on one wall, a chart of chakra locations from India. On the bookcases that lined one side of the room there were mummified bits and pieces of persons.

"A pretty place," Azzie commented. "My compliments, doctor! But these specimens are very old. They may have an antiquarian value, but they are of no interest to me."

"These are simply surplus items," Albertus said. "Now, look here and see what I have."

He went to a small vat resting on a side table. From it Albertus lifted a human head severed at the neck. The face was that of a young man, deathly pale, but quite handsome, and this despite the fact that where eyes had been there were now only reddened holes.

"How did he meet his fate?" Azzie asked. "And what happened to his eyes?"

"He had the bad fortune to lose them, my lord."

"Before or after his death?"

"Before, but only moments before."

"Tell me about it."

"With pleasure," Albertus said. "This fellow's name was Phillipe, and he lived in a village not far from here. Handsome indeed he was, far handsomer than a young fellow had any right to be. Everything came easy for him, and the more he got, the more he wanted, and the less satisfied he became. One day he beheld Miranda, daughter of a wealthy man hereabouts. She was just fifteen at this time, and beautiful as dawn upon the mountain. Delicate and pure she was, and she had planned to live her life in utmost purity, aspiring only to do good.

"Having seen her, Phillipe became inflamed of her, and though it is said he was a coward, he aspired still to winning her. One day Phillipe climbed the wall around her father's house and went into the churning room and spoke to her. Miranda had been raised in isolation, and had never seen a man like this. Everyone in her father's household was old except for her three brothers, and they were away fighting in one war or another.

"Phillipe seduced her with sweet words and impassioned tales of his own trials. Miranda was softhearted, and she was greatly moved to learn that he was sickly and apt to live but a little while longer. A lie, so he thought, but a prophecy as it turned out! He feigned a fainting spell, and she let him put his arm around her to support himself. They touched. And so one thing led to another.

"It is a tale often told, alas. In brief, he seduced her, and she ran away with him, for he swore that he would take care of her. But when they came to the first large city, Civalle in Provence, Phillipe abandoned her and went his own way.

"Alone, Miranda had a desperate time of it until she became the model for the painter Chodlos. She lived with him for some months as his mistress and they seemed happy enough. Chodlos was a big bear of a man, but not strong despite his size. He was always jolly, though too much given to drink. He painted his famous Magdalene with Miranda as his model. He could have been truly great. But before the year was out, he was dead, his head broken in a tavern brawl.

"Miranda was heartbroken, because she had loved the painter. Chodlos' creditors took away all the furniture and his paintings, and turned Miranda out of the apartment. She had no money and no place to go. Finally, as the only alternative to starvation, she went to work in a brothel. But bad luck was not through with her yet. One night a madman came to the brothel. No one knows what transpired between him and Miranda; but before anyone could stop him, he had put out her eyes, and then cut her throat.

"Hearing of this, her brothers, Ansel, Chor, and Hald, came to the city for revenge. The madman was already dead, torn to pieces by a mob. The brothers found Phillipe drinking in a tavern with a new light o' love. They bent him back over a table, told him he would die as Miranda had died. Then they tore his eyes out and cut his throat. That is the history of the head that you here behold."

"It's actually a very nice head," Azzie said, lifting the head and looking into its ruined eye sockets. "Now what I need is a matching female head. This Miranda. A madman killed her, eh? Master Albertus, do you know what happened to her body? And most especially, her head?"

"Alas, I know not," said Albertus.

"You have helped me greatly," Azzie said. "Name your price for this head."

# PRIME

HL
D 666-999-0214
42
ETRN 702112
X7
AZZIE ELBUB

DON'T LEAVE HELL
WITHOUT IT

# Chapter 1

"Master, look at this."

It was the fourth head Frike had brought in that week. This one was a dark-tressed lady who still looked pretty good, especially if you could repair her nose, which the worms had gotten at.

"No, Frike, it won't do." Azzie sighed and turned away.

"But why, lord? She's perfect!"

"There's only one who could be considered perfect."

"Who is that, lord?"

"Frike, the perfect accompaniment to our Prince Charming will be Miranda, the girl Phillipe seduced."

"But we do not know where she is!"

"Not yet." Azzie got up, prowled around restlessly for a moment. "But we will find her."

"The head has probably gone moldy by now."

"You can never tell. If by some good fortune her face is not obliterated, she will be my Princess Scarlet in the little charade I am preparing."

"But, lord, we have no clues as to its whereabouts."

"We'll start in Civalle, where she died. She's probably buried there."

"Master, it's a waste of time. You have little time left anyhow before the contest, and there is much to do."

"Pack our horses, Frike. I am an artist in these matters. I must have Miranda's head for my Princess."

"She had a gaudy history, master, but why this particular wench?"

"Don't you see, Frike? It makes my plan more elegant. We will bring these lovers together again after death. Their conscious memories will be gone, of course. But something will remain. Something that will help bring a fine conclusion to my tale of Prince Charming and Princess Scarlet. We must find her body and hope that the face is still all right. Go, ready the horses."


Frike packed the horses and they set out to Civalle in southern Provence. It was late June and travel was easy and pleasant. Frike had hoped that Azzie would transport them by supernatural means. Azzie said the distance was too close to go to all the bother of setting up a travel spell and activating it.

They arrived in Civalle, a pleasant southern city near Nice. From Albertus' description it was easy to find the brothel where Miranda had been killed. Azzie made inquiries of the madam and learned that her brothers had taken her remains away, no one knew where. Azzie rewarded her well for the information and asked if a garment of Miranda's remained. The madam found an old shift and sold it to him for two gold soldi. Whether it was indeed the genuine article, he could not be certain—yet.

When they left the brothel, Frike said, "What now, master?"

"You'll see in due course," Azzie replied.

He and Frike departed the town and passed into the forest. After a long while they camped, making a dinner of cold meat pie and boiled leeks. Afterward, at Azzie's instructions, Frike built a fire. When its flames finally leaped high, Azzie removed a small vial from the chest in which he carried his magical paraphernalia. He removed from it a single drop of dark liquid and let it fall into the fire.

The flames flared even higher. Frike cringed back.

"Pay attention," Azzie ordered, "for this is educational. Perhaps you have heard of the fabulous hunting dogs of the old gods? We have something better nowadays."

As the flames subsided three large birds flew into the camp and landed near Azzie. They were ravens, with small, sinister eyes.

"I hope all is well with you," Azzie said to them.

"We are well, Lord Demon," one of them replied.

"Meet my servant, Frike. Frike, meet the Morrigan. They are supernatural Irish birds, and their names are Babd, Macha, and Nemain."

"Pleased to meet you," Frike said, remaining well back, for they looked upon him with fierce appraisal.

"What can we do for your lordship?" Macha asked.

Azzie brought out Miranda's gown. "Find this woman," he said. "The one who last wore this. She is dead, by the way."

Babd sniffed at the cloth. "You didn't have to tell us that," he said.

"I forgot the extent of your powers. Go, peerless ones. Find this woman for me!"

When the ravens had flown away, Azzie said to Frike, "Let's make ourselves comfortable. This may take a while, but they will find her."

"I never doubted it," Frike replied.

Azzie and Frike ate more cold meat pie and leeks. They discussed the weather and the possible nature of the heavenly entry in the Millennial contest. The day wore on. The brassy blue sky of Provence was a huge dome radiating sunlight and heat. They ate more leeks.

After a long while a raven returned, announcing itself as Nemain. It circled twice, then settled upon Azzie's outthrust wrist.

"What did you find?" Azzie asked.

Nemain cocked his head, then, in a small voice, replied, "I believe we've located the one you want."

"Where is she?"

The other two ravens fluttered down. One perched on Azzie's head, the other on Frike's shoulder.

Macha, the eldest, said, "Yes, it's definitely the woman you want. The scent is unmistakable."

"I suppose she *is* dead?" Azzie asked.

"Of course she's dead," Macha said. "That's the way you wanted her, isn't it? If not, you could always have her killed."

Azzie didn't bother explaining that there were rules against that sort of thing. "Where will I find her?"

"Go a couple of leagues down this road and you'll come to a town. She'll be in the second building on your left."

"Thanks, baleful bird," Azzie replied.

Macha nodded, then rose into the air. The others followed. In a moment they were gone.

Azzie and Frike mounted and headed downroad, south. It was an old Roman road that crossed southern Europe, headed toward the great fortress city of Carcassonne, in better condition than many roads they had taken. They passed along it in silence, and after a time they came to a fair-sized village. Azzie sent Frike on ahead to locate accommodations while he tended to the matter of Miranda's head.

He walked to the house the ravens had indicated. It was the largest in the lane, and dark, with an unpleasant look to its little slit windows and ill-thatched roof.

He knocked at the door. No answer. He tried the latch. It was not secured. He walked into the main room. It was dark inside, with only a little light showing through cracks in the ceiling. There was a strong smell of wine.

His sense of danger kicked in, a moment too late. He plunged through a hole in the floor and fell into the room below, landing heavily. When he sat up, he found himself inside a bottle.

# Chapter 2

It was a glass bottle with a wide neck, of a type not seen much in these days, large enough to hold a medium-sized demon like Azzie. The fall had made him dizzy for a moment, and he heard a noise above his head but didn't know what it was until he looked up. Then he saw that the bottle had been stoppered with a wooden plug. Azzie recovered his senses quickly. What was he doing in a bottle, anyhow?

Peering through the green-tinged sides, Azzie saw that he was in a room illuminated by many candles. There were three rough-looking men standing around a little table, arguing.

Azzie tapped on the glass to get their attention.

They turned. One of them, the one with the ugliest features, came forward and spoke to him. Since the bottle was stoppered, no sound came through. Azzie indicated this by pointing to his own ear and shaking his head.

When the loutish fellow understood, he told the others. Once again their argument raged, this time more furiously. Finally, they came to a decision. The first man climbed up a ladder set alongside the bottle and loosened the wooden plug slightly.

"You can hear now," he said, "but if you try anything, we'll push the plug in tight and go away and leave you here forever."

Azzie made no move. He figured he had a decent chance of driving it out before they could hammer it in securely. But he was interested in hearing what they had to say.

"You came for the witch, didn't you?" the man said.

"It might be easier if I knew your names," Azzie said.

"This is Ansel, here is Chor, and I am Hald. We are brothers, and the dead witch Miranda is our sister."

"Indeed," Azzie said. "Where is she?"

"We have her close by. We've preserved her with ice."

"Bought at great expense," his brother Ansel reminded him. "We must get back the cost of the ice. And that's only the beginning."

"You're going too fast," Azzie said. "What makes you think this sister of yours, whom you call a witch, is worth anything at all?"

"The doctor told us."

"What doctor is that?" Azzie asked.

"Old Dr. Parvenu. He is also our local alchemist. After that crazy fellow killed Miranda and we brought her back, our first thought was to consult Dr. Parvenu, who is an expert on these matters. This was after we had killed Phillipe, of course."

"Yes, I know about her seducer, Phillipe," Azzie said. "What did Dr. Parvenu tell you to do with your sister's body after she'd been murdered?"

"He advised on the entire affair—and he told us to keep her head."

"Why?"

"He said that beauty like hers would surely tempt a demon!"

Azzie saw no need to enlighten these fellows as to

what he intended to do with Miranda's head. He felt quite at ease. Demons learn early how to cope with the bottle trick, and these fellows didn't seem too clever. . . .

"This crazy fellow who killed Miranda—who was he?"

"We heard only that his name was Armand. None of us ever saw him, because he was dead by the time we reached the brothel. After the people found out what he had done to Miranda, they were so incensed that they beat him to death and tore his body into rags."

"And now you would sell your own sister's head?"

"Of course! She was a whore! What difference does it make what we do with her head?"

"I guess I could give you a few pieces of gold for her," Azzie said. "Unless her features are all battered and distorted."

"Not in the slightest!" Ansel said. "She looks as good now as she did while she was alive. Better, perhaps, if you like the languid type."

"Before I buy," Azzie said, "I must see her."

"You shall. But from the bottle, of course!"

"Of course," Azzie said. "Trot her out."

Ansel called to his brothers to bring out Miranda's head. Chor and Hald scuttled to the back of the cellar. Soon they returned, bearing an object. Before presenting it, Ansel wiped it with his shirt, to get off the ice crystals.

Azzie saw that she was quite lovely, even in death. The long, sad lips were slightly parted. Her ash-blond hair clung to her forehead. A drop of water glistened on her cheek. . . .

Azzie knew at once that his instinct had been correct; she was indeed the one he needed.

"So what do you think?" Ansel asked.

"She'll do," Azzie said. "Now let me out of here and we'll discuss the fee."

"How about granting us three wishes first?" Ansel asked.

"No," Azzie said.

"Just that? No?"

"That's right."

"No counteroffer?"

"Not while you have me in this bottle."

"But if we let you out, we won't have anything to threaten you with."

"That's right," Azzie said.

Ansel and his brothers held a whispered conference. Ansel came back. "They told me to tell you that we know an incantation that can make life very difficult for you."

"Do you really?" Azzie said.

"Yes, we do. Really."

"Then incant away."

The three brothers began to chant.

"Excuse me, fellows," Azzie said, "but I think you have some of the words a little wrong. You should say fan*ta*go, not fan*dra*go. Subtle, but there it is. Pronunciation is everything in the matter of magic spells."

"Come on," Ansel said. "Grant us a couple of wishes, what's it to you?"

"I know you think demons have all sorts of special powers," Azzie said. "But that doesn't mean we have to use them."

"What if we don't release you? How would you like to spend years in a bottle?"

Azzie smiled. "Have you ever wondered what happens when the demon and the people who have captured him can't reach an agreement on his ransom? The old stories don't tell about that, do they? Be sensible now. Don't you think I have any friends? Sooner or later they'll see I'm missing and come looking for me. When they find me here, your prisoner—well, perhaps you can imagine what they might do."

Ansel thought about it and didn't like what he came up with. "But why should they do anything to us? By the rules of magic, we are allowed to trap demons. We caught you fair and square."

Azzie laughed. It was a horrible sound he had practiced for occasions such as this.

"What do you poor fools know of the rules of magic, or for that matter, of the laws that govern the conduct of creatures supernatural? You'd do better to confine your dealings to human things. Once you get into the supernatural area, you can never tell what might happen."

Ansel was trembling now, and his two brothers looked ready to flee. "Great demon," he said, "I didn't mean to intrude. It's just that Dr. Parvenu said it would be so simple. What do you want us to do now?"

"Unstop the bottle," Azzie said.

Ansel and his brothers tugged out the stopper. Azzie stepped out. He adjusted his height so that he was about one and a half feet taller than Ansel, the tallest of the three.

"Now then, my children," Azzie said. "The first thing to learn about dealing with supernatural creatures is this —despite the folklore to the contrary, they will get the better of you every time. So don't try to trick them or cheat them. Note how you opened the bottle for me when actually I was helpless."

The brothers exchanged looks.

After a moment, Ansel asked, "You mean we actually had you at our mercy?"

"Indeed you did," Azzie replied.

"That you were a helpless prisoner?"

"That is correct."

"Sure fooled us," one of the others observed, nodding slowly.

Another round of glances was exchanged.

Ansel cleared his throat then. "You know," he said, "at your present size, great demon, I don't see any way you could be gotten into that bottle. I daresay your excellency couldn't even put yourself into it now if you wanted to."

"But you'd like to see me try, is that it?"

"Not at all," Ansel said. "We are entirely at your orders. I just wish you would show me that you can do it again."

"If I did," Azzie said, "would you play fair with me and not close the stopper?"

"Yes, sir, that I would."

"Would you swear it?"

"On my immortal soul," Ansel said.

"And the other brothers?"

"We also swear," they said.

"Okay, then," Azzie said. "Watch this." He stepped into the bottle and maneuvered so that he fit entirely inside. As soon as he was all the way in the brothers put in the stopper.

Azzie looked out at them. "Okay, quit horsing around and unplug this bottle!"

The brothers chuckled; Ansel motioned to them. Chor and Hald took up a flagstone from the floor, revealing a stone-lined well. From far below came the sound of water.

"Take note, demon," Ansel said. "We'll push you, bottle and all, into the well, and cover it up, and paint a skull and crossbones on it so people will think it's poisoned. Fat chance your friends will have of finding you then."

"You broke your word," Azzie said.

"Well, what of it? Nothing much you can do about it, is there?"

"All I can do," Azzie said, "is tell you a story."

"Come on, let's get away from here," the two other brothers said. But Ansel said, "No, let's hear him out. Then we can laugh and go away."

Azzie said, "Bottles to contain demons have been in constant use for several thousand years. Indeed, the first man to ever make a bottle—a Chinaman, by the way—did so in order to trap one of us. The ancient Assyrians and Hittites kept their demons in clay pots. Certain African tribes keep us in tightly woven baskets. We are aware of this, and of how the customs for trapping us vary from one part of the world to another. In Europe, demons always wear these."

He held up his hand. On his forefinger, or foreclaw, there glistened a brilliant diamond.

"And with it we do this." Azzie swung his arm in an arc, the point of the diamond in contact with the greenish glass. Azzie swung a circle, then pushed against the glass. The circle he had cut fell out. He stepped through.

Ansel, his face frozen with fear, said, "We were only kidding, boss. Isn't that right, boys?"

"That's right," said Chor and Hald, both of them grinning from ear to ear, sweat dripping from their rudimentary brows.

"Then you'll like this," Azzie said. He waved his fingers and muttered under his breath. There was a flash of light and a puff of smoke. When it cleared, a very small demon with horn-rim glasses became visible, sitting nearby, writing something with a quill pen, on a parchment.

"Silenus," Azzie said. "Record these three to my account and take them away. They are self-damned."

Silenus nodded, waved his hand, and the three brothers vanished. A moment later, Silenus vanished.

As Azzie remarked later to Frike, it was the easiest three souls he had ever helped damn themselves, and with practically no urging on his part.

# Chapter
# 3

O h, master, it's so good to be home!" Frike said,
throwing back the bolt of the front door of the big
mansion in Augsburg.

"It *is* nice," Azzie said. "Brr." He rubbed his claws
together. "It's chilly in here! You must build a fire as soon
as you put away the body parts."

Demons, despite or because of their long association
with hellfire, enjoy a roaring hearth.

"Yes, master. Where do they go?"

"In the cellar laboratory, of course."

Frike hurried out and unloaded the cart. On it,
wrapped in various ichor-soaked cloths, were a number
of body parts; enough, if Azzie's calculations proved correct, to make up two entire bodies, one male, the other
female, to be known thereafter as Prince Charming and
Princess Scarlet.

They began working on the bodies the next day. Frike
proved to have a useful hand with needle and thread. He
put Charming together as neatly as a tailor makes a suit.

There were seams and stitch marks, of course, but Azzie told him not to worry about them. Once the bodies were reanimated, they would lose these stigmata of their rebirth.

Those were pleasant domestic evenings. Azzie would settle into a corner of the lab with his copy of *King Solomon's Secrets*, which he had always meant to read but never found the time for. Now it was very pleasant to sit in the lab with its smells of fusel oil, kerosene, sulfur, ammonia, and permeating it all, the rich, complex odors of scorched and putrid flesh; to sit there with his book open on his knee glancing up every now and again to watch old Frike, his hunchbacked shadow thrown monstrously against a wall by a low-set light, bent over his work with a tiny steel needle.

The needle had been hammered out for him by the Ruud, smallest and most cunning of the dwarves of central Europe. The thread was the finest silk from Taprobane, so gossamer and transparent that it seemed as if the lips of the gaping wound separating an arm from shoulder were adhering to each other by some sort of physical magnetism, or by magic. But the only magic in this case was Frike's tiny needle, making its neat little holes and forming, bit by bit, a whole man from the pile of body parts stacked neatly at his left side on a bed of glacial ice.

Frike was a careful workman, but he did bear watching. More than once he put feet where arms should be, either because of dim-sightedness or some perverted sense of humor. But when he joined the Princess' midsection to Charming's head, Azzie decided that this was too much. "Stop that nonsense," he told Frike, "or I'll put you in a Pit where you can fuse gravel into rock for a few centuries to teach you seriousness."

"Sorry, master," Frike said, and worked with exactitude and propriety thereafter.

And so the bodies took shape. Apart from the pending matter of appropriate eyes, the only real problem was Princess Scarlet's mismatched hands. It was not so important that they were of different sizes. But one was yellow and the other white, and this could not be permitted. Azzie discarded the yellow one and made a quick expedition to the Schnachtsburg Doctoring Center. There, in a shop dedicated to necrophilious memorabilia, he was fortunate enough to find a pickpocket's hand for Princess Scarlet.

Soon after his return, Azzie received word from Supply that his castle was ready for delivery to his coordinates in Transylvania. Azzie departed immediately, flying across the Alps to the plain of Hungary. The land stretched ahead of him, lushly green, tree-scattered. He found the exact spot he had picked, which he remembered from the grove of tall purple trees that bloomed there, the only ones of their kind in the world, trees whose existence ended before modern science could declare them anomalous. Merioneth was there waiting for him, a thin, ill-favored demon from Supply who wore pince-nez and carried a scroll attached by brass studs to a well-smoothed piece of wood—the progenitor of the clipboard.

"You Azzie Elbub?" Merioneth asked.

"Of course I am," Azzie said. "Why else would I be here?"

"You could have your reasons. Got some ID?"

Azzie showed the black credit card with his name engraved on it.

"It doesn't have a picture," Merioneth noted, "but I'll accept it all the same. Okay, where do you want it?"

Azzie looked around. The site he had chosen was rolling countryside. He looked it over critically.

"I want the castle right there," he said.

"Over there on that flat piece?"

"That's it. But first you must put down a glass mountain."

"I beg your pardon?" Merioneth said.

"I want a glass mountain. The enchanted castle must sit on top of it."

"You want the castle on top of a glass mountain?"

"Of course. That's where enchanted castles always stand."

"Usually, maybe even often, but not always. I can cite several traditional tales—"

"This castle is going to stand on a glass mountain," Azzie said.

Merioneth took off his pince-nez, polished them on his gray fur, put them back on. He opened his briefcase. It was made of well-tanned human skin, and its clasps were yellowed teeth. Azzie admired it and decided to get one like it when he had the time. Merioneth opened the case and shuffled through papers. At last he selected a sheet and read it with pursed lips.

"This is your original work order," he said. "It says nothing here about a mountain."

Azzie came over and read the work order. "It says here you will supply standard landscaping."

"Standard landscaping does not include a mountain of glass. Why not have us move in an existing mountain?"

"It has to be of glass," Azzie said. "As far as I know, there are no existing mountains of glass."

"So why not take a dead volcano instead?" Merioneth said. "With lots of obsidian?"

"It won't do," Azzie said. "Glass mountains have been a feature of folklore since people began telling tales. Surely you have one somewhere in Supply?"

Merioneth pursed his lips and looked doubtful. "Maybe we do and maybe we don't. The point is, it isn't on the work order."

"Can't we put it there now?"

"No, it's too late."

"Can't we get around that somehow?" Azzie asked.

"What do you mean?"

"I'll pay the extra myself. Can I put it on the card?"

Merioneth shrugged again. "It's not a matter of that. The work order has already been filled out and signed."

Azzie looked at it. He pointed. "You could write it in

right there, just above the signature. 'One glass mountain, and one enchanted forest.' "

"If my supervisor ever found out . . ."

"And I'll make it worth your while," Azzie said. He reached into a pocket inside his cloak and took out a small satchel. It was here that he kept his valuables. Here, in a chamois bag, he had the gemstones Rognir had invested with him. He took out a handful and showed them to Merioneth.

"So?" Merioneth said.

"Yours," Azzie said, "if you write me in a glass mountain."

Merioneth looked at the jewels. "I could get into a lot of trouble over this."

Azzie added a few more gems.

"I guess I can do it," Merioneth said, taking the stones. He bent over the work order and scribbled, then looked up. "But an enchanted forest—that's another matter."

"Enchanted forests are no big deal," Azzie pointed out. "They're not rare, like glass mountains. Everywhere you go you find enchanted forests."

"Until you need one in a hurry," Merioneth said, his gaze on Azzie's chamois bag. "I suppose you want a road through it, too, huh?"

"Nothing fancy. A dirt track would be fine."

"And who's to survey it, eh? I'd need a surveyor. And a surveyor's services—"

"I know, it isn't on the original work order." Azzie selected four more stones and gave them to Merioneth. "Will that do?"

"That takes care of the forest and the basic landscaping. But you also want it enchanted. Right?"

"That's what I told you. What good would it be if it weren't enchanted?"

"Don't get huffy with *me*," Merioneth said. "This forest is nothing to me. I'm just trying to understand the order. What sort of enchantments did you have in mind?"

"The usual stuff," Azzie said. "Animated flame trees will do nicely. There are always plenty of them in stock."

"You're a horticulturist that you know that?" Merioneth said caustically. "Fact is there are damn few flame trees available at this time of year. And I suppose you want them to have magic thorns?"

"Of course."

"Magic thorns aren't standard."

A few more gems changed hands.

"Now, let's see," Merioneth said. "What exactly should these magical thorns do?"

"The usual thing," Azzie said. "When a traveler passes who is not pure in heart, or not in possession of the proper magical counterspells, they impale him."

"I thought you'd want that! Impaling's extra!"

"Extra! What in hell are you talking about?"

"I got more to do than hang around here jawing with you," Merioneth said, and unfolded his wings.

Azzie paid over a few more gems. The chamois bag was empty. He had gone through Rognir's treasure in a surprisingly short time.

"I guess we're in agreement on basics now," Merioneth said. "There are a few more refinements I can think of, stuff you might like, but it'd cost more."

"Never mind the refinements," Azzie said. "Just do what we've agreed upon. And quickly, please! I have other matters to attend to."

Merioneth called up a work crew and the demons started building the forest. They worked rapidly, thorough professionals once they got moving. Some of the younger demons were obviously unaccustomed to manual labor. But the supervisors kept them up to the mark and things proceeded nicely.

As soon as the basic forest was in place, with the spells set up but not yet activated, the head work-crew demon left an underling to put in the shrubs and wildflowers and turned his attention to setting up the castle. Crews up in Limbo threw down the building blocks with gusto, and the demons below cursed and dodged and caught up the pieces and put them together. Piece by piece a high structure of crenellated walls and pointed turrets rose into the air. It was historically inaccurate but definitely of fairy-tale design. At this stage there were a few small mix-ups. When it came time to dig the moat around it, they found they lacked earth-moving equipment. A team of dragons was summoned and bribed with an offering of maidens. After they had dined, the dragons scooped out a fine moat, twenty feet wide, thirty feet deep. But of course there was no water in it, and no one seemed to know who was in charge of getting the water. Azzie finally solved the problem by ordering a weather spell from Supply and calling up a brief but very heavy rain. This, plus the water from the runoffs, did the trick nicely. A pair of swans added a touch of class.

Soon the castle stood, tall and stately, a lofty collection of stone towers in the midst of domed shapes. From the topmost towers bright banners floated in the breeze. The place was unfurnished, of course, and extremely drafty, because no one thinks of closing up the chinks and gaps in magical castles. Azzie ordered furniture from Supply. There was a problem on how to light the place. He decided upon magical lighting, since it was difficult to see anything with oil lamps.

At last it was all together. Azzie stood back a few hundred yards and admired. It was a castle that Mad King Ludwig would have loved. It would do.


Azzie returned to the mansion to finish work on the principals. The bodies looked fine now in their vats, all seams faded. The ichor and spells had done their work to perfection. But the bodies had no intelligence as yet, since that comes last, and they did some strange things as one part of the body or another came to life. Azzie worked to stabilize them and, at last, had them set up properly.

Then Frike pointed out that both creatures were still blind.

"You're right," Azzie said. "I was saving that for last."

He sat and remembered Ylith. Yes, he'd saved that for last.

# Chapter
## 4

Azzie liked witches. He considered them a sort of permanent dating pool where a demon could always find a companion for a Saturday night. Back in those days, Witches' Sabbaths were the primeval form of nightclub.

"Frike! Bring me chalk! Candles!"

Frike hurried to the pantry where the magic supplies were stored. There, in a stout chest, he found the things Azzie needed. The candles were as thick as a man's wrist, and they stood almost as high as Frike himself. He bundled five of them under his arm, one for each point of the pentagram. The candles were as hard as petrified flesh and slightly greasy to the touch. Frike brought them and the chalk to the front room. Azzie moved the trestle table out of the way. He had taken off his cloak and doublet. Long muscles gleamed under his shirt as he tugged an extra suit of armor into a corner.

"I don't know why I keep all this junk around," Azzie

said. "Give me the chalk, Frike. I'll inscribe the figure myself."

Azzie bent low and, lump of chalk in his right hand, inscribed a large five-sided figure on the stone floor. A ruddy glow from the fireplace outlined his figure, tingeing it red, accentuating his foxlike look. Frike almost expected to see Azzie's legs change into the furry red legs of a fox. But despite his excitement, Azzie retained his human shape. He had worked on it for a long time, since demons of experience take great pains to shape their human forms to suit their self-ideals.

Frike watched as Azzie inscribed the Hebrew letters of power, then lighted the candles.

"Ylith!" Azzie intoned, crossing his claws and genuflecting in a manner that hurt Frike's eyes. "Come to me, Ylith!"

Frike could see the beginning of movement in the center of the pentagram. The candles gave off coiled streamers of colored smoke. These danced up and down, coalesced, gave off bright sparks, then settled into a solid shape.

"Ylith!" he cried. But it was not. The being in the pentagram was a woman, but there all resemblance to the Ylith he remembered ceased. This was a short, stout female with orange hair and a hooked nose. This female crossed her arms and glared at Azzie.

"What do you want?" she asked severely. "I was just leaving for my coven meeting when you conjured me. If I hadn't been caught by surprise, I would have canceled your spell, which was wrongly cast anyhow."

"You're not Ylith, are you?" Azzie asked.

"I'm Mylith," the witch replied.

"From Athens?"

"Copenhagen."

"I'm dreadfully sorry," Azzie said. "I was trying to conjure up Ylith from Athens. The Spirit Exchange must have gotten things mixed up."

Mylith sniffed, rubbed out one of Azzie's Hebrew

characters, and scribbled in another. "You had the wrong exchange. Now, if there is nothing more . . . ?"

"I'll be happy to conjure you back to your home," Azzie said.

"I'll do it myself," Mylith said. "No telling where your charm would land me!"

She made a gesture with both hands and vanished.

"That was embarrassing," Azzie remarked.

"I think it amazing," Frike said, "that you can conjure anything. My last master, the demon Throdeus, was quite unable to conjure at all on Saturdays."

"Why, do you suppose?" Azzie said.

"He had been an Orthodox rabbi before becoming a demon," Frike said.

Again he conjured. Again colored smokes coiled in the center of the pentagram. But this time, when they coalesced, instead of a short, ugly orange-haired witch standing in the pentagram, there was a tall, good-looking black-haired witch in a silk shorty nightgown.

"Ylith!" Azzie cried.

"Who is it?" the witch asked, rubbing her eyes. "Azzie? Is it really you? My dear, you should have sent a messenger first. I was sleeping."

"Is that a sleeping garment?" Azzie asked, for through and around the peach-colored diaphanous garment he could see her plump and well-shaped breasts and, by walking around her, get a look at her rosy bottom, too.

"Shorty nightgowns are the newest sensation in Byzantium," Ylith said. "I don't suppose they will catch on in Europe. Not soon, anyhow." She stepped out of the pentagram. "It is wonderful seeing you, Azzie, but I really need some clothes."

"I've seen you in less than that," Azzie said.

"I know, but this is not one of those times. And your loutish servant is staring at me! I must have a wardrobe, Azzie!"

"And so you shall!" Azzie cried. "Frike!"

"Yes, master?"

"Get into the pentagram."

"Master, I really don't think—"

"Don't think. Just do it."

Grumbling, Frike hunched his way into the center of the pentagram.

"I'm sending you to Athens. Pick up all the lady's garments you can. I'll bring you back in a few minutes."

Ylith said, "There's a fur-collared deep blue dress in the anteroom. It's the one with three-quarter-length sleeves. Please be sure to bring that! And in the little closet near the kitchen you'll find—"

"Ylith!" Azzie said. "We can bring more clothing later, if there proves to be a need. Right now I'm in just the slightest hurry."

Raising his hands, Azzie recited a spell. Frike vanished in mid-grumble.

"Well now," Ylith said. "We are alone. Azzie, why didn't you call me sooner? It's been centuries!"

"I was in the Pit. Lost track of time," he explained.

He escorted Ylith to the big couch that was pulled up to the fire. He brought her wine and a plate of little cakes he knew she liked. They settled down onto the couch, and Azzie employed one of his minor music spells to call forth a chorus of popular airs of the day. He sat down beside her and looked deep into her eyes.

"Ylith," he said, "I have a problem."

"Tell me about it," Ylith said.

Azzie did, forgetting Frike for several hours, so earnest was his explanation. When he finally conjured Frike back, it was dawn, and the servant arrived yawning, draped in ladies' clothing.

# Chapter
# 5

Azzie took Ylith to the lab where Charming and Scarlet, now entirely assembled, lay side by side on marble slabs, veiled with two linen tablecloths, since Azzie had often observed that people look better slightly clad than not clad at all.

"They make a cute couple, don't they?" Azzie said.

Ylith sighed. Her long, mobile face was beautiful one moment, sinister the next. Azzie tried to adjust his perception so that he would see only her beautiful side, but it was difficult; witches have obscure feature cyclings. Azzie had felt ambivalent about Ylith for a long time. Sometimes he thought he loved her; sometimes he hated her. Sometimes he tried to solve the problem by attacking it head-on; sometimes he preferred to forget it in favor of simpler problems, such as how best to spread evil and further the general bad. Sometimes—a lot of the time—he didn't know what to do. He loved her but he didn't always like her. But she was also his best friend, and when he had a problem he turned to her.

"They're real cute," Ylith agreed, "except for the lack of eyes. But you know that."

"It's why I'm showing them to you," Azzie said. "I've already told you that I'm going to enter them in the Millennial contest. They are going to act out the Prince Charming tale, entirely on their own, no urging from me, utilizing the famous free will that all intelligent creatures are said to possess. And they are going to come to the wrong conclusion and condemn themselves forever. But I need eyes for them, not just any eyes: special eyes. I need enchanted eyes. I need them in order to give the story that special air, that flavor, that fairy-tale savor—if you know what I mean."

"I understand perfectly, my dear," Ylith said. "And you want me to help? Oh, Azzie, you are such a child! What gave you the idea that I would find eyes for you?"

Azzie hadn't considered that. He scratched his scalp —scaly—that's what the Pit did to you every time—and considered. He said, "I thought you'd do it because it's the right thing to do. I mean, you want evil to win as much as I do, don't you? Consider if good rules human destiny for the next thousand years: it could put you out of business."

"You have a point," Ylith said. "But it is not entirely persuasive. Why should I help you? I do have a life of my own, and other business in progress. I'm into administrative work for the coven, and I've been doing some teaching. . . ."

Azzie took a mental breath, the kind he always took before embarking on one of his really big lies. As he drew in that mental breath his genius and all his faculties took heed and helped him into the role he knew was needed.

"Ylith," he said, "it's very simple. I love you."

"Oh, really!" she said, scornfully, but not closing off the conversation. "That's rich! Tell me more!"

"I have always loved you," Azzie said.

"You sure acted like it, didn't you?" Ylith said.

"I can explain why I never called," Azzie said.

"I'll just bet!" Ylith said, waiting.

"There were two reasons," Azzie said, not knowing at the moment what they were but saying there were two in case one wasn't enough.

"Yes? Let's hear them!"

"I've already told you I was in the Pit."

"And you couldn't even send a postcard? I've heard that 'I was in the Pit' excuse before!"

"Ylith, you must simply believe me. There are some things a man can't speak about. But take my word for it, things came up. I could explain if there were time, but the important thing is, I love you; the bad enchantment has ended at last, and we can be together again, just as you have always wanted and as I secretly have wanted, too, though I said otherwise."

"What enchantment?" Ylith said.

"Did I mention an enchantment?"

"You said, 'Now the bad enchantment has ended.' "

"I said that? You're sure?"

"Of course I'm sure!"

"Well, I shouldn't have," Azzie said. "One condition for ending the bad enchantment was that I never speak about it. I just hope we haven't set it off again."

"What bad enchantment?"

"I don't know what you're talking about."

Ylith drew herself up to her full height and glared at him. He was really the most impossible demon. Demons are expected to lie, of course, but even the worst would occasionally tell the truth. It's almost impossible not to tell the truth sometimes, by accident. Except for Azzie. But that was not because he had a lying heart. No, it was because he was trying so hard to be really bad. She couldn't help but feel for him. He still appealed to her. And it was not the amusing season in Athens.

"Promise you'll never leave me again," she said.

"I promise," Azzie said. Then, realizing that he had capitulated too soon, added, "Under normal conditions, that is."

"What do you mean, normal conditions?"

"Conditions that are not abnormal."

"Such as what?"

"How would I know?"

"Oh, Azzie!"

"You must take me as I am, Ylith," Azzie said. "It really is nice to see you. Have you any ideas about those eyes?"

"Yes, as a matter of fact, I do have an idea or two."

"Be a doll and rush off and get them," Azzie said. "I'm running out of ichor and I don't dare resurrect these creatures before I have eyes for them. It might change their development."

"They'll have to wait," Ylith said. "Two special pairs of eyes aren't come by quite as fast as all that."

"We will all await you, my queen!" Azzie said.

Ylith gave a raucous laugh, but he could tell she liked to hear that stuff. Azzie waved, Ylith twirled, turned into a rotating column of violet smoke, and then disappeared entirely.

# Chapter
# 6

She had been content for many years to hang around in Athens, enjoying parties and good times, having many lovers, and redecorating her house. Witches grow lazy with the passing of time, and tend to rest upon their laurels. The sins that witches try to make people commit turn up later to haunt them. They lose their knowledge bit by bit, forgetting what they studied in the great witch schools. Ylith had been vegetating for a long while, before she was called up by Azzie.

Her reaction now was surprise at herself for volunteering to find eyes for the young couple. Was this really what she wanted to do? Did she love Azzie so much? Or was it more a matter of trying to find a duty to perform, to serve something greater than herself? Either way, she felt the need for advice when it came to the second pair of eyes.

And when it came to wise advice, the sagest counsel she knew was that of Skander. . . .

Dragons live a long time, and smart dragons not only

live a very long time, but also change their names from time to time so that people don't get wise to just how long they're living and get jealous. There's nothing a hero likes to kill more than a really old dragon. The years on a dragon are like the rack on a buck.

Skander and other dragons became aware of how many heroes were hunting for them, and they grew more and more cautious. Gone were the old days, when they hung around and guarded treasure and took on anyone who came along. The dragons were doing very well at that game, too, although all you hear about are hero victories. There were plenty of dragon victories, but there were only a few dragons and an endless supply of heroes. The heroes kept coming, until the dragons got wise to the whole game.

There was a big conference held, at which many views were heard. The Chinese dragons were the most numerous at that time, but they were so jealous of their wisdom and so determined that no other dragon would get it, that all they said, when their advice was asked, were things such as, "It furthers one to see the great man." "You will cross the water." "The superior man is like sand." And the Chinese philosophers, who had a taste for obscurity, collected these into books, which they sold to Westerners in search of wisdom.

The final decision at the conference was to bow to necessity, give up some of the more aggressive tactics, which had given dragons bad repute, and maintain a low profile. Dragons voted universally to give up their time-old pursuits of Hoarding and Guarding in favor of the new disciplines of Ducking and Dodging. Don't just stand around guarding treasure, they announced to each other. Fade into the landscape, live at the bottoms of rivers—for many dragons were able to live underwater—gilled dragons, they were called, that fed on sharks and killer whales and mahimahi. The land dragons had to adopt a different strategy. Land-based dragons learned to conceal themselves as small mountains, hills, even as clumps of trees. They gave up their old habits of ferocity, contenting themselves with an occasional hunter who strayed into their territory. Once in a while a dragon went back to the old practices, and eventually got hunted down and killed. That dragon's name would go down in the Dragon Hall of Heroes, and the rest would be advised not to act like him.

Skander was old even by dragon standards. He was therefore super wily and stayed out of trouble. He lived in central Asia, somewhere near Samarkand, but he had been around since before the city was founded. You could have searched for ages and not found Skander if he didn't want to be found. But if you did find him he was often a helpful dragon, and he had a vast store of lore. He was also quirky, however, and given to mood swings.

Ylith knew this, but she had to make the attempt. She picked up a bundle of powerbrooms, the sort you can fly on. These were the witches' greatest accomplishment. They ran on spells, which the Witches' Sisterhood put together at their headquarters in Byzantium. The power of spells ran in cycles, some years good, others not so good. Spells were subject to natural forces, but these were not clearly understood, and there were occasional recalls.

The logical starting place, it seemed to her, was the place she had met Skander last time: Dragon Rock. Dragons are clever enough to know that men will never search for a dragon at a place called Dragon Rock.

Many heroes had ridden through the area, most of them bearing only the light curved sword of the region, which would do no good against a dragon anyway. Not that Skander cared to try issues even with these lightweights. Skander's hide with its overlapping scales was able to withstand the blow of an avalanche, and he thought nothing of swords unless they were backed up with really powerful spells. But humans were sneaky;

they'd seem to be aiming at a shoulder, and then, *pow*, you'd get an arrow in the eye. Somehow dragons, despite their extreme intelligence and centuries of experience, were prone to getting arrows in the eye. They never fully caught on to the trick that men used, of pretending to shoot in one direction and then actually shooting in another. It wasn't according to dragon practice, and went against their idea of a warrior's ethics.

For whatever reason, Ylith had met Skander at Dragon Rock, where she had been visiting relatives who had recently moved to the area from Scythia. Skander at that time had been taking advantage of a rare shape-changing spell that had come his way. Dragons are always in search of shape-changing spells because, being intelligent, they aspire to appear in human society. Although humans don't know it, dragons in altered shapes have been present in many of the courts of the world, where they love to argue with philosophers. More often, though, dragons simply get tired of all the years alone, all the more alone since dragons of either sex are suspicious of dragons of the opposite sex. It is for this reason, not for lack of opportunity or lustiness, that dragons rarely mate, and it is even more rare that they have young. Among the dragons who do have young, there's no agreed-upon rule as to which parent is to bring up the children. There's not even consensus on who bears them. The dragons did away with most of that instinctual stuff ages ago. Creatures of reason now, they fought over these matters among themselves. It is said that in the settling of these arguments, much of the race of dragons was wiped out.

And heroes had a field day against dragons in their confusion. It amazed dragons to think that knights—beefy guys in metal suits—could kill them, since the humans were so obviously unintelligent and had only their court rituals going for them. But the humans were winning because they were single-minded about killing, while the dragons were single-minded about nothing at all.

Ylith flew to the Samarkand region and made inquiry

in the town of Yar Digi, the nearest village to Dragon Rock. It was a low, miserable place, and there was nothing on its one street but souvenir shops. These were filled with dragon lore, but there were no customers. When Ylith asked about this, a bookstore owner named Achmed told her, "It is because the long-awaited boom in dragon lore has not yet come to pass. Other places are getting all the attention. In Britain, for example, where no dragons have stirred for centuries, they run guided tours of where they used to be, and outsell us a hundred to one. Where is the dragon? Somewhere up the trail over in his cave at Dragon Rock. But no one ever seems able to find it unless the dragon wants visitors. And you never know about that. He's quirky."

Ylith went in the direction indicated and, after paying her entrance fee, was allowed onto the path. Moving along it, she rounded a number of turns, passed a small refreshment stand, passed Dragon Rock itself. Nothing resembling a cave was apparent at either hand.

It was not until she heard a deep, resonant chuckle that she halted.

"Skander?" she called.

The sound came again.

"It's me, Ylith."

Suddenly she became aware of a shadowy place between two boulders which might be more than shadow. Moving to it, she saw that it continued back into a greater darkness. She entered there.

At what point she passed within the greater darkness of the hillside she could not be certain. Yet, after a time, the echoing of her footfalls convinced her that she was entirely indoors.

"Skander?" she repeated.

There was still no reply, but she became aware of a faint illumination ahead and to the right. Following it around a bend, she entered an area where the stone itself seemed to glow—overhead and at either hand. With this visibility, she increased her pace. The passage branched several times, and in each instance she followed the path of greater brightness.

At length, she came to a chamber where the dark, scaled form she sought reclined, staring at her. Save for the eyes, she might have missed him in the stillness. She halted upon the threshold, uneasy.

"Skander. It's me. Ylith," she said.

He cocked his head and lowered his eyelids slightly.

"Yes. It is, isn't it?" he observed. "How long has it been?"

"Long. What are you doing?"

"I was dreaming of the Renaissance."

"What is a Renaissance?"

"I'm sorry, I'm getting my centuries mixed up," he replied. "The Renaissance comes later. That's the trouble with being prescient. You can never tell then from now."

"Skander," Ylith said, "I need help."

"Just as I thought," the dragon said. "What else would bring you out to this remote place? What is it you want, my dear? The old flames are still plenty hot. Want me to burn someone up for you?"

"I need eyes," Ylith said, and explained about Azzie and Prince Charming and Princess Scarlet.

"Eyes," Skander murmured, and his hide, normally a reddish brown, turned pasty white. There was a prophecy she had suddenly brought to mind.

"Why do you stay in this place?" Ylith asked.

"It's the quest for fame, you see," Skander said. "The people here are going to publicize me. I promised to put this place on the map. It hasn't happened yet but it's bound to come."

"Where can I get some really good eyes?" Ylith asked.

"Eyes," Skander mused. "Why, there are eyes everywhere. Why do you bother asking me?"

"You know where the best ones are. All dragons do."

"Yes, of course," Skander said. "But I'd really rather not discuss eyes, if you don't mind."

"You don't want to discuss eyes?"

"Just superstitious, I guess. Sorry."

"Care to tell me about it?"

"All right," he said. "Long ago, in China, I saw that whenever the court artist painted dragons he always put in the eyes last. When I asked him of this, he told me that this act gave the painting a special sort of life, and it wouldn't do to summon this life until everything else was done. A wise man had told him that the eyes of my kind are the focus of the spirit. They hold the life, they are the last things to go. I looked up that wise man then—an old Taoist monk—and he assured me that this was true. He also prophesied that a witch asking after eyes in my presence represented a total reversal of Yin and Yang."

"What does that mean?"

"Rosebud . . ." he answered, and closed his eyes.

She waited, but he did not continue. After a time, she cleared her throat.

"Uh, Skander? What then?"

There was no reply.

"You asleep, Skander?"

Silence.

Finally, she moved forward and held her hand before his nostrils. She could feel no breath. Moving even nearer, she placed her hand between the scales of his breast. There was no heartbeat.

"Oh dear!" she said. "What now?"

But she already knew.

When she had done, she stroked the dead dragon's nose, a thing it had loved feeling in life. Poor old dragon! she thought. So old and wise, yet reduced to this, a mound of cooling flesh in a mountain cave.

She knew that it would be evening soon, and that was not a good time to be about in a foreign country. Local demons were apt to be abroad, and they could cause some rare mischief if they were of a mind to. There was no love lost between European and Asiatic demons in those days, and the wars between the two still awaits their chronicler.

The eyes she wrapped in a small silk handkerchief,

then placed in a casket of rosewood which she kept on hand for the transport of delicate and precious objects. Then she turned and departed the cave.

Ylith stood tall as the light of the falling sun bounced off the ice peaks of the highest mountains. She shook out her glorious black flag of hair, mounted her powerbroom, and soared away into the west, the land of the dragon dwindling beneath her.

# Chapter
# 7

It was still daylight when Ylith arrived in Augsburg, for, with a favorable tail wind, she had managed to outrace the sun itself. She came down near the front door of Azzie's mansion and banged hard with the big brass knocker. "Azzie! I'm back! I've got them!"

A cavernous silence followed. Although it was a summer afternoon, there was a chill in the air. Ylith felt faintly uneasy. Her witch's sense warned her that something was amiss. She touched the protective amulet of amber she wore around her neck. She knocked again.

At last the door was opened. Frike stood there, meager face screwed into an expression of grief.

"Frike! What is the matter!"

"Alas, mistress! Things have gone very wrong indeed!"

"Where is Azzie?"

"That, milady, is what has gone most wrong. He is not here."

"Not here? But where could he be?"

"I do not know," Frike said, "but it wasn't my fault!"

"Tell me what happened."

"A few hours ago," Frike said, "the master was preparing a solution to wash the hair of Princess Scarlet, since it had become dirty and tangled. He had finished it, and I was drying the lady's hair. I recollect it was somewhat past the noon hour, for the sun was full and high when I went out to gather firewood—"

"Get on with it," Ylith said. "What happened?"

"I came in with the firewood and Master Azzie was humming a merry tune as he clipped Prince Charming's fingernails—he always takes great care with details, you know. All of a sudden he stopped humming and looked about. I looked, too, though I had heard no sound. Master Azzie looked entirely around him, and when his gaze rested on me again, I could swear he was a changed demon. Some of the fire had gone out of his hair, and he had grown pale. I said to him, 'Did you hear something, master?' and he said, 'Yes, a keening sound, and it will bring me no good. Quick, fetch me my Master Spell Book.' And so saying, he slumped to his knees. I rushed to do his bidding. He had not the strength to open the book—it is that very large brass-bound one you see on the floor near your feet. He said to me, 'Frike, help me turn the pages. Some cunning trick of weakness is undemoning me.' I assisted him, and he said, 'Faster, Frike, faster, before the heart goes out of me entirely.' And so I turned the pages faster, doing it all myself now since the master's hand had fallen away and it was all he could do to keep his eye, which had lost its usual luster, focused upon the page. And then he said, 'Right, stop there. Now let me see. . . .' And that was all."

"All?" said Ylith. "What do you mean, all?"

"All that he said, mistress."

"I understand that well enough. But what happened?"

"He vanished, Mistress Ylith."

"Vanished?" Ylith said.

"Before my very eyes, he vanished entirely out of

sight. I was beside myself, knowing not what to do. He had left no instructions. So I went into hysterics for a time, then decided it best simply to await your arrival."

"Describe to me the manner of his vanishing," Ylith said.

"The manner?" Frike asked.

"Yes. Was it a smoke vanishment, in which he dwindled quickly to nothing? Or was it a flash vanishment, in which he disappeared with perhaps a small clap of thunder? Or did he shrink down to the size of a point first?"

"I know not, mistress. I shut my eyes."

"Shut your eyes! You are a fool, Frike!"

"Ah, mistress, but I peeked."

"And what did your peek tell you?"

"I saw the master become very thin and slide off sidewise."

"Which side?"

"The right side, mistress."

"Did he slide away smoothly or with a sort of up-and-down motion?"

"With motion."

"This is very important, Frike. Did he at any time change color before vanishing completely?"

"You've got it, Mistress Ylith! He changed color indeed, just before he slid away into nothingness!"

"What color did he change into?"

"Blue, milady."

"It is as I thought," Ylith said. "Now let us look at his conjuring book."

Frike lifted the heavy volume to a lectern where Ylith could read it more easily. It was still turned to the page Azzie had regarded just before his disappearance. Ylith bent over it and quickly translated the runes.

"What is it?" Frike asked.

"It is a General Unbinding, Frike," she told him. "This is the spell that demons use when something or someone is trying to conjure them. It is called the Grand Counterveillance."

"Was he too late?"

"Obviously."

"Conjured!" said Frike. "But the master is a conjurer himself!"

"Of course he is," Ylith said, "and a very good one. But all who conjure, Frike, are subject themselves to conjuration. It is one of the great laws of the Unseen Realm."

"So I have heard," Frike said. "But who could conjure the master away like that?"

"There are many possibilities," Ylith said. "But given the sequence of events, it is most likely that it was some mortal—a witch perhaps—or an alchemist, or some other demon—who had a hold of some sort over Azzie, and thus was able to call him away without his consent."

"But when will we see him again?" Frike asked.

"I have no idea," Ylith said. "It depends on who did the conjuration, the spell used, and the nature of the obligation that Azzie had incurred."

"But will he be back soon?"

Ylith shrugged. "He could be back in an instant. Or he could be gone for days, months, years, even forever. It is difficult to unravel the truth of these matters a posteriori."

"I'd be glad to sacrifice my posterior if it would bring him back!" cried Frike. He wrung his hands in grief and uncertainty, and then a thought crossed the shadowy places of his mind and he called out afresh, "Oh, no!"

"What is it?" Ylith asked.

"The bodies!"

"What about them?"

"They run peril of decaying, lady! For only this morning we used up our last bit of ice, and we're very low on ichor. I reminded the master of this as soon as he arose, and he said, 'Never fear, Frike, I'll call Supply and get some more as soon as I've had my nap.'"

"Nap? But you said he had just arisen."

"He liked a nap soon upon awakening, mistress."

"Now that you mention it, I remember it well," Ylith said.

She went to the part of the laboratory where the bodies slept in their coffin-shaped open boxes, side by side, awaiting resuscitation. The ice of the high Alps was gone. In the bottom of each box was no more than a little pool of ichor.

"Your master has been very slack," Ylith said.

"He had not expected to be conjured, mistress," Frike said.

"I suppose not. Well, first things first. We must refrigerate these bodies, Frike."

"Beg pardon, mistress?"

"We must find a means of lowering their temperature."

"Can you call up glacial ice, mistress?"

"Not I," said Ylith. "Witches' conjurations do not lean to that sort of thing. Fetching things is demons' work. But our demon has been taken from us. This is a tricky situation." She crossed to the couch and sat down. "Stop whimpering, Frike, and let me think."

She returned to the boxes, bent over, and touched the bodies. They were still perceptibly cold, but Ylith could tell that they were warmer than they ought to be. Another hour or two and Azzie's prize specimens would be rotten meat, probably filled with blowflies. And then it wouldn't matter if he came back or not. The contest would be over.

"I'm going to do something about those bodies, Frike," she said. "I'm going to talk to some people. You had better not watch me depart. This is women's magic, not for men's eyes."

"I'll be in the den when you need me," Frike said, slinking away. Ylith turned to her work.

# Chapter 8

Ylith selected a freshly charged broomstick and, first making sure her protective amulets were in place, flew out of the mansion window and up, straight up, into the empyrean blue of the highest atmosphere. As she went she murmured a protective spell to herself, for she was unhappy over what she was about to do. Still, to keep those bodies cold, her first thought had been to ask assistance of the Harpies.

Harpies and witches were friendly toward one another. The Harpies were female demons inducted into the Powers of Darkness after the collapse of classical mythology. Not only did they do evil, but their very presence was disturbing. Their breath was foul, and their table manners disgusting. But it was to the Harpies that Ylith had decided to go, because, although they were foul, they were quick-witted. There were many other demonic deities she could have called upon, but only the Harpies and their sisters, the Sirens, could be counted upon to understand at once what was desired, and sufficiently honorable to follow through on what they promised.

She flew hard and fast, soon passing through the crack that separates the realms of the human from that of the inhuman and superhuman.

Immediately she found herself in a vast cloudland of snowy hills and mountains. And there were rivers, too, and little temples along the riverbanks, all made of clouds. She flew on and, dipping low over this land, saw the manticore and the chimaera and, in a little valley of its own, Behemoth snorted and reached for her with a great talon. She eluded the beast easily and flew on, to a region where the clouds were colored blue, and everything below was stained with blue and gold, like the borders of a dimly remembered dream. Descending, she saw, very tiny at first, the figures of beautiful women on the banks of a sleepy river, and close to them, a waterfall where they could sport and slide.

Then Ylith directed her flight downward and came to one of the regions where the Harpies and the Sirens lived together. She slowed and came to a stop on the left bank of the river. This was the Styx, the great river that traveled from deepest past to furthest future. There were trees along it of no known variety, for they still awaited their birth on the earth. Beneath these trees were maidens, lolling at their ease on the grassy banks. There were eight of them, Sirens, and several Harpies. The Sirens were famed for luring people, especially sailors, to their doom with their sweet songs. The Harpies were the more advanced stage of Siren, beautiful and golden-haired, with firm, well-shaped breasts, but with table manners that would make a hyena blush. They were in charge of tormenting damned souls of a classical sort, by snatching food from their mouths and splattering them all over with fiery excrement.

Although Ylith put on a bold front, she was more than a little afraid, as these ancient demons were given to odd perversions and strange thoughts, and their mood was always uncertain.

But she put on a bold face and said, "Sisters, I bring you greetings from the world of humans."

One of the Sirens stirred herself. She was large, ash blond, and had a sweet little rosebud of a mouth. It was difficult to believe that this was Poldarge, one of the most ominous of the Chthonian women deities.

"What do we care for the world of humans?" Poldarge said. "The banks of this fine river are our home. Here we entertain each other by singing of fine exploits of the past. And, from time to time, a man falls into our hands, having escaped over the side of Charon's boat. Then we get him from the river deities, and we play with him until he goes mad, and then we eat him, each of us tearing off her share."

"I thought," Ylith said, "that you might care for some diversion, as long as it is in good cause. Because, excellent though this riverbank is, you must sometimes miss the world of humans, where fine deeds can be done."

"What do we care about human deeds?" Poldarge asked. "But go on, sister. Tell us what you want."

And Ylith told them about the great Millennial contest, and about Azzie, and about how he was going to enter the lists against the Powers of Good by utilizing two human creatures, resuscitated and set into an inverted fairy tale of ominous import. The Sirens and Harpies applauded. The very thought of the next thousand years being consecrated to evil gave them goose bumps of pleasure.

"I am glad you approve," Ylith said. "But there is a problem. Azzie has disappeared, conjured up by someone."

"Now, sister," Poldarge said, "you know we can do nothing about that. We are forbidden to interfere in the affairs of men or demons, except under certain conditions, which are not met here."

"I do not ask you to find Azzie," Ylith said. "I'll do

that myself. But it will take time. And meanwhile his actors, those who will play Prince Charming and Princess Scarlet, remain in their coffins unanimated. And since the glacial ice has run out and the ichor is nearly gone, and Azzie not at hand to call up more, they run the risk of decaying in the warmth of Earth's springtime and thus rendering Azzie's grand scheme inoperable."

"That's sad, no doubt," Poldarge said. "But why tell us? We have no glacial ice here."

"Of course not," Ylith said. "But you are beings of the air, well accustomed to towing helpless creatures from Earth to their damnation."

"True. But what has this to do with your Prince and Princess?"

"I thought," Ylith said, "that you might lend a hand in the preserving of their bodies. It is cold that is needed, the cold of the upper reaches of the atmosphere."

The Harpies conferred among themselves. Then Poldarge said, "Very well, sister, we will take care of these bodies for you. Where did you say they were?"

"In the mansion of the demon, in Augsburg. The way to find it—"

"Don't worry," Poldarge said. "Harpies can find any place on Earth. Sisters, come with me!"

Poldarge spread her dark wings and sped into the upper atmosphere. Two more Harpies followed.

Ylith watched them go. Harpies were known to get easily bored. She had no assurance they wouldn't abandon their charges, and return to the river and their eternal mah-jongg game. But they had a tradition of honor among peers. She just hoped they felt her a member of that select group.

Ylith went aloft now. She had an idea where Azzie might be.

# Chapter 9

When the Harpies went off to carry back the bodies, no one had thought to notify Frike. The first thing he learned of the new arrangement occurred when a pair of Harpies burst through the window. He was sitting on a low stool in Azzie's laboratory, listening to the drip-drip of melting ice and waiting for Ylith to return. Suddenly there was a great fluttering and a bad smell.

For the purpose of efficient flight the Harpies had retracted their legs, so their wide, brazen wings supported only a trunk with prominent breasts and a head. They cawed in loud grating voices and voided themselves over everything.

Frike yelped and ducked under the table. The Harpies spun around the room, buzzing and shrieking. When they spotted the coffins, they flapped over to them. "Stay away, you wretches!" Frike shouted. He went after them with a set of fire tongs. The Harpies turned and attacked him, driving him from the chamber with their steel-tipped wings and green-tipped nails. Frike hurried after a bow and arrow. Before he could fetch them, the Harpies had lifted the Prince and Princess and, flapping heavily now, rose into the air. Frike at last located the weapons and hurried back. But the Harpies were gone, risen high into the sky, and vanishing into the crack between the real and the unreal. Frike shook his fist and then sat down. He hoped Azzie wouldn't ask him to explain too much. He had very little idea what had happened.

But for that matter, where was the master?

# Chapter
# 10

Azzie had been working in his laboratory when he felt the familiar psychic tug which tells you that you are being conjured. It is a sort of pull that starts from the inside of your stomach. Not unpleasant, but always an unwelcome signal of what lies ahead. It would be all right, perhaps, to be conjured when you were just sitting around without anything much to do. But people tend to call you up just when you are most heavily engaged in something delicate.

"Damnation!" he said. Everything was off schedule, and there was no way of telling how long the castle would stand unattended, its obsolescent spells running down. And his young people, the Prince and Princess, had to be animated as soon as possible, before they could deteriorate.

And here he was flying through the air, unable to recite his counterveillance in time to prevent what was happening. Not that it necessarily would. These general spells often fail in specific situations.

Azzie passed out during this transition. When he recovered, he had an ache in his head. He tried to stand up, but he seemed to be on some slippery surface. Every time he rose, he fell down again. He was also a little sick to his stomach.

He was lying inside a pentagram. You can't get any more conjured than that.

This was not the first time he had been conjured, of course. Every demon who wishes to lead an active life among mankind must become accustomed to being conjured many times, since mankind plays tricks on demons just as demons do on people. There never has been a time when men and women did not conjure up demons. There are many folktales to that effect, telling of the triumphs and failures of the humans who have trod such a path. What is not told is how often sensible arrangements are arrived at, since even souls are commodities that can be purchased fairly. It is an ancient arrangement: the demon furnishing various kinds of work in return for a soul. Kings are good favor granters and many of them have had demon servants. But it is not a one-sided situation. Many demons have had kings as servants.

"See, Father, I told you he'd come!"

That was the voice of Brigitte. A triumphant voice. And there she was standing in front and above him, a dirty-faced little girl who had used the promise she had wrung from him to call him up now.

"Looks like you did, all right," a man's heavy voice said. It was her father, Thomas Scrivener. The fellow seemed to have regained his senses. But, of course, he lacked his memory of the Pit and of his meeting with Azzie. Azzie was thankful for that. Once humans got too much knowledge, they became dangerous.

"Oh, it's you," Azzie said, remembering the little girl who had caught him with a spirit-catcher back when he was shepherding her father. "What do you want?"

"My promise!" Brigitte said.

Yes, it was true; Azzie owed her a promise. He would

have dearly loved to forget it. But the world of magic registers promises between humans and supernatural creatures as facts of physical import. It was impossible for Azzie not to deal with this.

"Well," Azzie said, "open one of the sides of the pentagram and let me come out and we'll discuss it."

Brigitte leaned forward to rub out a line, but her father seized her and pulled her back. "Don't let him out! You'll lose all power over him!"

Azzie shrugged. It had been worth a try. "Master Scrivener," he said, "tell your little girl to be reasonable. We can clear this up quickly and I can be on my way."

"Don't listen to him!" Scrivener said to his daughter. "Demons are rich. You can ask for anything you want! Anything at all!"

"I'd better explain about that," Azzie said. "That is the popular superstition, but I can assure you it is not true. Demons can only fulfill wishes within their individual powers. Only a very high demon, for example, could grant you great wealth. I, however, am a poor demon working on a government grant."

"I'd like a new doll," Brigitte said to her father. Azzie tensed and leaned forward. It didn't quite constitute a wish, since it hadn't been directed to him. But if she would say it again . . .

"A doll, Brigitte?" he asked. "I can get you the most wonderful doll in the world. You've heard of the Queen of the North, haven't you? She has a special little toy house with tiny figures that do the work, and pet mice that run in and out, and other things besides, I don't quite remember what. Shall I fetch it for you?"

"Wait!" Scrivener shouted, still drawing Brigitte back. "He's trying to cheat us, daughter. This demon has wonders at his fingertips. He can make you rich, can make you a princess—"

"No, nothing like that," Azzie said.

"Ask for something big!" Scrivener said. "Or better yet, give your wish to me, and I'll wish for enough to make us both rich, and then I'll get you all the dollhouses you could ever dream of."

"Will I still have to clean up after meals?" Brigitte asked.

"No, we'll hire a servant," Scrivener said.

"And will I have to milk the cows and feed the chickens and the rest of the household chores?"

"Of course not!" Scrivener said.

"Don't trust him, Brigitte!" Azzie warned. "I'll tell you what would be better. Just ask me to bring you something nice and I'll surprise you. What about that, eh?"

"Don't listen to him," Scrivener said. "You must wish for a large estate at the very least."

"Don't listen to him," Azzie said. "He always bullies you, doesn't he? But I remember when he was mighty glad to have my help."

"What are you talking about?" Scrivener asked. "I never saw you before."

"That's what you think," Azzie said. "Brigitte, what color do you want your dollhouse?"

"Where did we meet?" Scrivener asked.

"What I really want," Brigitte said, "is—"

"Wait!" Scrivener cried. "If you ask for something insignificant, I'll tan your hide, young lady."

"I wish you'd stop shouting at me!" Brigitte cried.

"I can take care of that for you," Azzie said, and made a gesture.

Thomas Scrivener opened his mouth but no words came out. He strained, his tongue waggled, his cheeks puffed in and out, but he could form no sound.

"What have you done?" Brigitte asked.

"Fulfilled your wish," Azzie said. "He'll not shout at you again. You or anyone."

"That wasn't fair!" Brigitte said. "I was talking to my daddy, not to you! You still owe me a wish!"

"Come on, Brigitte," Azzie said. "Make a wish, then. I have to get out of here."

Thomas Scrivener tried to speak. His face was purple, and his eyes bulged like hard-boiled eggs. He was one hell of a looking sight, and Brigitte started to laugh, then stopped abruptly. Something had appeared in the air.

It solidified.

And there was Ylith, appearing from nowhere, looking disheveled, with smoke coming out of the end of her broom.

"Azzie!" she cried. "Good thing you told me of this wish situation—and I remembered. Is there a problem?"

"It's obvious, isn't it?" Azzie asked. "I'm still trying to get this kid to name a wish so I can grant it and get out of here. But she and her father keep arguing about what it should be."

Thomas Scrivener made pleading gestures to Ylith.

"What have you done to him?" Ylith asked.

"Well," Azzie said, "Brigitte here said she wanted him to shut up, so I shut him up for her."

"Oh, Azzie, stop playing around. Little girl, what do you want to be when you grow up?"

Brigitte considered. "When I was little I wanted to be a princess."

"I don't know whether Azzie can handle that," Ylith said.

"I don't want that now," Brigitte said. "Now I want to be a witch!"

"Why do you want that?"

"Because you're a witch," Brigitte said. "I want to be like you and ride a broomstick and enchant people."

Ylith smiled. "Azzie, what do you think?"

"One more witch, what does it matter?" Azzie asked. "Is that it, kid? You want to be a witch?"

"Yes!" said Brigitte.

Azzie turned to Ylith. "What do you think?"

"Well, I *do* take on apprentices from time to time. Brigitte is a little young, but in a few years . . ."

"Oh, yes, please!" Brigitte said.

"All right," Ylith said.

"Okay," Azzie said. "You got it, kid. Now let me out of here."

"First give my father his voice again."

Azzie did as was requested of him. Thomas Scrivener went to give Brigitte a good slap alongside the head. He found his arm held by an invisible force.

"What did you do?" Brigitte asked Ylith.

"It's simple enough magic," Ylith said. Turning to Scrivener, she said, "Be good to your little girl. In a few years she will be able to make mince pies of you. And you'll have me to reckon with, too."

# TERCE

YLITH

# Chapter
# 1

After Brigitte released Azzie from his captivity, Ylith tied together two of her broomsticks with a stout straw rope and, with Azzie clinging behind her, rode them back to Augsburg. The sensation of the virile young demon clinging to her was very sweet to Ylith. She felt a frisson of delight when his claws, gripping her shoulders, accidentally brushed her breast. What bliss it was to ride with the beloved high above the clouds! For a while all thought of sin or sinner was forgotten, all question of good and evil put aside as she cavorted in the high blue of the sky, through violet-tinged clouds formed into fantastical shapes, melting and re-forming before her eyes. Azzie liked it, too, but urged her to hurry home. They had to recover the young couple from the Harpies.

Back at the mansion, Ylith had a chance to wash her hair and pin it up securely. Then she was ready for the journey.

Using a freshly charged broomstick, Ylith mounted the heights, flying alone now, darting and sweeping with quick control. The earth fell away, and soon she was in the sparkling realms of the sky. There she searched and searched, but not a sign of the Harpies could she discover. She circumnavigated the world by its outer edge and still did not find them. But then a slow-moving pelican appeared and told her, "You're looking for the Harpies with the two stiffs? They told me to tell you they got bored and have parked the couple in a safe place and gone back to rejoin their sisters."

"Did they say anything else?" Ylith asked, making slipstream movements to keep her speed down to that of the slow-moving pelican.

"Just something about a mah-jongg game," the pelican said.

"Didn't they say where this safe place was?"

"Not a bit of it!" said the pelican. "I thought about reminding them, but they were off, and there was no way I could overtake them. You know how fast they go with those newfangled brazen wings."

"In which direction did they fly?" Ylith asked.

"North," the pelican said, motioning with his wing tip.

"True north or magnetic?"

"True north," the pelican said.

"Then I think I know where they are," Ylith said.

She turned her course to the north and piled on the speed, even though she knew the wind force would make her eyes red and unattractive. She overflew the land of the Franks in no time, then passed the deep fjord-pierced coast where Northmen still worshiped old gods and fought with hammers, axes, and other farm tools. She went past the lands of the Lapps, who sensed her passing as they trekked over the snow with their reindeer herds, but pretended not to see her since the best thing to do with ambiguous phenomena was to ignore them. And at last she came to the North Pole, the real one which existed within the imaginary point of true and absolute north and could not be reached by mortals. Slipping through the fold of reality in which it lay, she saw, below her, Father Christmas' Village.

It was built upon the solid sheet of ice with which the North Pole was capped. The buildings that had been set up here were very fine indeed, being half-timbered and wainscoted. Over to one side Ylith could see the workshop, where Father Christmas' gnomes made gifts of all sorts for mortals. These workshops are well known. What is less well known is the fact that there is a special room at the back where essences of good and evil are received from the secret storage places of Earth. In each gift, a bit of good luck or a bit of bad luck was inserted. Exactly who got what kind of luck was a matter no one could tell. But it seemed to Ylith as she strolled through the workshop, watching the little men with their hammers and screwdrivers, that the process was more or less random. There was a hopper in the center of the big worktable, and into it fell glistening bits of good or bad luck, each of them like a little bouquet of herbs. A dwarf would reach in and insert the luck into the Christmas gift without even looking to see what it was.

Ylith asked the dwarves whether a pair of Harpies had come by recently carrying two frozen people. The dwarves shook their heads irritably. Making and stuffing Christmas presents is precision work, and if people talk to you, it spoils the rhythm. One of them jerked his head toward the back of the workshop. Ylith went that way and saw, at the end of the long room, a door with an inscription on it: SANTA'S OFFICE. She went there, knocked, entered.

Santa was a big, fat man with the sort of face that smiled easily. But looks don't always tell the story. Santa was frowning, and his face was long and drawn as he talked into a magical seashell.

"Hello, is this Supply? I need to talk to someone."

The answer came out of a baboon's head, stuffed and mounted on the wall.

"This is Supply. With whom am I speaking?"

"Claus here. Santa Claus."

"Yes, Mr. Claus. Are you authorized to speak to us here in Supply?"

"I guess you haven't heard of me," Santa Claus said. "I'm the one who brings presents around every December twenty-fifth by the new calendar."

"Oh, *that* Santa Claus! When do you start bringing presents for demons?"

"I'm overworked enough bringing presents for humans," Santa Claus said. "I've got this problem—"

"Just a minute," the voice said. "I will connect you with the problems clerk."

Santa Claus sighed. He was on hold again. Then he noticed Ylith, who had just entered the room.

He blinked three times rapidly behind his little rectangular spectacles. "Goodness gracious! You're not a dwarf, are you?"

"No," Ylith said, "and I'm not a reindeer, either. But I'll give you a clue. I got here on a broomstick."

"Then you must be a witch!"

"You've got it."

"Are you going to bewitch me?" Santa asked, slobbering slightly as he perceived Ylith's charms, which had been brought into prominence by her windblown clothes. "I wouldn't mind being bewitched, you know. Nobody ever thinks of bewitching Santa Claus. As if I don't need a little cheering up from time to time, eh? Who brings Santa Claus presents, eh? Ever think of that? It's give, give, give all the time around here. But what do I get out of it?"

"Satisfaction. You bask in everybody's love."

"It's the presents they love, not me."

"The giver is part of the given," Ylith said.

Santa Claus paused and considered. "Do you really think so?"

"How could it be any other way?"

"Well, that's better, then. Might I inquire what you

are doing here? There's never anyone but dwarves and reindeer around here. And me, of course."

"I came," Ylith said, "because I need to pick up some packages that were left for me here."

"Packages? What kind of packages?"

"One male, one female. Both humans. Both frozen solid. The Harpies brought them here."

"Oh, those terrible Harpies!" Santa said. "They've left the snow yellow for miles around!"

"What about the frozen people?"

"They're out in back, in the woodshed."

"I'll pick them up now," Ylith said. "Oh, and one thing more. There's a little girl on Earth named Brigitte Scrivener."

"Little dirty-faced kid with a saucy manner?" Santa always remembered the children.

"That's her. What I'd like you to do is bring her a dollhouse this year. The sort you usually only give to princesses. Filled with moving figures, wallpaper, radios, and other magical things."

"This kid was real good, eh?"

"Goodness had nothing to do with it," Ylith said. "She got a promise from a demon and this is part of the pay-off."

"Why isn't the demon himself here to get it?"

"He had other stuff to do. You know how demons are."

Santa Claus nodded. "Okay, she'll get the present. Do you want me to take special care to make sure it gets a bit of good luck in it?"

Ylith thought it over carefully. "No, just give her whatever comes up. The dollhouse is enough. She'll have to take her chances on the luck it'll bring her just like anyone else."

"Sagely put," Santa said. "Now, before you go, let me give you a present."

"What are you talking about?"

"This!" Santa cried, tearing at his nether clothing.

"Thanks all the same," Ylith said, fending him off easily, "but I really don't need your gift now. Keep it for some other lucky lady."

"But no one ever comes this way!" Santa said. "It's only elves and reindeer!"

"Tough!" Ylith went to the woodshed. She carried out the bodies of Charming and Scarlet. They were both frozen stiff as logs and heavy as sin. Ylith had to call on all her witch strength to lift them.

"Send me one of your witch friends!" Santa shouted. "Tell her I give presents!"

"I'll tell them," Ylith said. "Witches love presents." And then she rose into the air, bearing Scarlet and Charming, heading for Azzie's mansion in Augsburg as fast as she could fly.

# Chapter
## 2

Azzie was pacing nervously in the back courtyard when Frike said to him, "I think that's her, master!" He was pointing into the eastern sky.

As Azzie watched, Ylith appeared, flying slowly with four broomsticks, and carrying the two frozen bodies by ropes suspended from them.

"Careful how you put them down!" Azzie shouted as she soared in for a landing.

"Don't tell a witch how to ride a broomstick," Ylith said, elegantly setting down her burden near the door to the alchemical laboratory.

"At last!" Azzie said, hurrying over to look at the couple. "Took your time about getting here, didn't you?"

"Thanks a lot!" Ylith said. "Go fetch your own bodies next time. And get your own eyes!"

Azzie instantly changed his manner. "I'm sorry, Ylith, but I really have to hurry up or I'll never get these two set up and rolling by contest time. I've gotten some more ichor. Let's stow Charming for the present and get Scarlet to the castle and animate her."

"Just as you wish," Ylith said.

"That's great," Azzie observed when they were done with the Prince. "Now I just hope everything is ready at the castle. We'll go there at once."

And so they did. Ylith carried Scarlet, still rigid with cold, and Azzie, utilizing his considerable flying powers, followed carrying Frike and a sack of provisions and spells he thought he'd need.

"Get that fire going!" Azzie said to Frike, later, when they had taken up residence in the enchanted castle. They were in an upper story, where a chamber had been prepared for Princess Scarlet. First, of course, they had to animate her.

"Have you got the eyes?" Azzie asked.

"Right here," Ylith said. "I got this set from Chodlos, the artist who painted her as the Magdalene."

"And for Prince Charming?"

"The eyes of Skander, the dragon."

"Very nice," Azzie said. "Why is it still so cold in here?"

Frike had been stoking the big fireplace in the bedchamber for over an hour, and the place was still cold. The stone walls seemed to absorb the heat. At this rate they'd never get Scarlet thawed out. They could see her in a rather distorted fashion through the bluish ice. Her features seemed to be at repose. Frike's stitches were not too noticeable. The dancer's legs he had attached to the trunk of the Magdalene model were stitched around the mid-thighs, but the stitching looked like a garter. Frike had some surprising skills.

But why did she take so long to thaw out? Was there a magical spell on this ice? Azzie poked at the ice with his claws and found that it had barely softened.

The fire still wasn't hot enough. Azzie had requisitioned room-warming spells quite a while ago, but they still hadn't come through. He repeated his request now, using the unlimited credit card to ensure instant delivery. In a moment there was a soft explosion in the air and a brand-new warming spell fell into the room, neatly encased in its opaque eggshell.

"At last!" Azzie said, cracking the shell. The spell whooshed silently out and the room warmed up ten degrees almost at once.

"Now for the animating procedure," Azzie said after some thawing had occurred. "Quick, Frike, the ichor."

The servant hunched over the recumbent Princess and splashed ichor on her face.

"Now the animating spell," Azzie said, and recited it.

The composite creature whom they called Princess Scarlet lay still as death and as pale. Then a faint tremor passed over her cheek. Her finely shaped lips moved and parted, and her little tongue came out to taste the ichor. Then her delicate nose widened, her body stirred, relaxed again.

"Quick," Azzie said. "Put in the eyes!"

The eyes fit into place easily. Another spell was necessary now, a vision-start-up spell, quite rare, but Supply had managed to find one. As Azzie chanted Princess Scarlet's eyelids flittered, fluttered, then lifted. Her new eyes, of deepest sapphire, gazed out at the world. Her face took on expression, animation. She looked around and gave a soft moan.

"Who are you all?" Scarlet said. Her voice was loud and snappish, and conveyed in addition a sense of peevishness. Azzie didn't like the sound of that. But luckily he didn't have to love her. That was Charming's task.

The Princess, a newly created being, had no memory. Now it was necessary to explain matters to her.

"Who are you?" Scarlet exclaimed again.

"Your uncle Azzie, of course," Azzie said. "You remember me, surely?"

"Oh, sure," Scarlet said, though of course she didn't. Death had wiped her mind of its memories, the good and the bad alike, and returned her to the world a tabula rasa.

"What's going on, Uncle Azzie? Where's Mummy?"

That had been an expected question. All living creatures assume they had a mother and never take it into their heads that someone might have sewn them together out of a collection of parts.

"Mummy and Daddy," Azzie said, "which is to say, Their Royal Highnesses, are under an enchantment."

"Did you say 'Royal Highnesses'?"

"Yes, my dear. You, of course, are a princess. Princess Scarlet. You want to release your parents from their spell, don't you?"

"What? Oh, sure," Princess Scarlet said. "So I'm a princess!"

"They can be released," Azzie said, "only after you have been rescued from your own enchantment."

"I'm under an enchantment?"

"That is correct, my dear."

"Well—take it away, then!"

"I'm afraid I can't do that," Azzie said. "I'm not the right person."

"Oh. What sort of a spell am I under?"

"You are under a sleeping spell. You spend twenty-some hours a day either sleeping or napping. They call you the Napping Princess. Only one man can break the spell. That is Prince Charming."

"Prince Charming? Who's that?"

"Nobody you've met before, my dear. Prince Charming is a fine, handsome young man of noble family who has just recently heard of your plight. He is on his way here to awaken you with a kiss and take you away to a life of bliss."

Scarlet considered. "It sounds good. But are you sure I'm not dreaming this?"

"This is not a dream, except in the sense that all experience, waking or sleeping, living or dead, is possibly a dream. But leaving metaphysics aside, this is real and you have been enchanted into sleeping. Believe me, trust me on this. Obviously you aren't asleep at the moment, because I need to talk to you and advise you on a few things."

"Maybe the spell isn't working," Scarlet said.

"I'm afraid it is," Azzie said, surreptitiously taking out the sleep spell from his pouch and pressing the little pin that activated it.

Scarlet yawned. "You're right, I *am* sleepy. But I haven't even had dinner!"

"We'll have it ready for you when you awaken," Azzie said.

The Princess' eyes closed and soon she was in a sound sleep. Azzie, under the watchful eye of Ylith, carried her to her bedroom and tucked her in.

Over the next few days it became apparent that Princess Scarlet was going to be difficult. She didn't want to listen to Azzie. Not even Ylith, with her calm and intelligent ways, could get through to the girl, not even in the guise of her aunt. That Scarlet was beautiful, there was no doubt. Not least of her charms was the fact that her long dancer's legs, olive brown and shapely beyond measure, carried an alabaster-white body topped with a blond head. Her dark legs gave Princess Scarlet the look of wearing silk stockings. This did nothing to harm her beauty.

But those long legs were a problem in themselves, and seemed to carry their own karma. The Princess was caught up with a dancing mania. Azzie had to try a number of spells before he could quench this.

But even under the napping spell, Princess Scarlet walked in her sleep, her long legs guiding her to the great downstairs ballroom, where she danced to flamenco music heard only by herself. Azzie had to take into account the Princess' peregrinations during sleep.

"Ylith," he asked, "will you stay and look after her? I'm afraid she's a bit unstable. She might fall and do herself harm. But she has spirit, and I'm sure she'll do what we expect of her."

"I suppose so," Ylith said. "By the way, I asked Santa Claus to give Brigitte a fancy dollhouse for Christmas."

"Oh. Thanks."

"I just told you in case you had forgotten you'd promised her one."

"I hadn't forgotten," Azzie said, though he had. "But thanks anyhow. Take good care of her, okay?"

"I'm doing this for you, Azzie," Ylith said, in a melting voice.

"And I really appreciate it," Azzie said, in a voice which expressed the opposite. "Gotta go get Charming up and moving. Catch you later, okay?"

Ylith shook her head as her demon lover departed in a flash of showy fireworks. Why had she ever fallen in love with a demon? And if a demon, why this particular demon? She didn't know. The ways of fate were inscrutable, to say the least.

# Chapter 3

I just hope we don't have any trouble with this one," Azzie said. "You got those dragon eyes ready, Frike?"

"Yes, master," Frike said. He opened the waterproof deerskin bag in which the dragon's eyes soaked in a solution of ichor, salt water, and vinegar. He lifted out the eyes, first remembering to wipe his hands on his smock, for hygiene in those days, while still rudimentary, seemed important in this situation.

"Beautiful, aren't they?" Azzie said, inserting them into Charming's eye sockets and applying ichor around the edges.

And indeed they were handsome eyes—colored like smoky topaz, with a deep glitter to them.

"They worry me, these eyes," Frike said. "I believe that dragon's eyes see through falsehood."

"Just what a hero needs."

"But won't he see through *this* falsehood?" Frike asked, indicating, with a sweep of his arm, Azzie, the mansion, and himself.

"No, my poor Frike," Azzie said. "Dragon's eyes cannot see through the falsehood in their own situation. They can detect the flaw in others, but not in themselves. He won't be easily led astray, our Prince Charming, but he won't be wise enough or sufficiently farseeing to discover his own situation."

"Ah!" said Frike. "He stirs!"

Azzie had already taken the precaution of assuming his kindly-uncle disguise. "There, there, lad," he said, smoothing back the youth's golden hair.

"Where am I?" Charming asked.

"You might better ask who you are," Azzie said. "And then you should want to know who I am. *Where* you are comes a distant third on the list of vital questions."

"Well, then . . . Who am I?"

"You are a noble prince whose original name has been lost but who is referred to by everyone as 'Prince Charming.'"

"Prince Charming," the youth mused. He sat up. "I suppose that means I'm of noble blood, doesn't it?"

"Yes, I suppose so," Azzie said. "You are Prince Charming, and I am your uncle Azzie."

Prince Charming accepted that readily enough. "Hello, Uncle Azzie. I don't remember you, but if you say you're my uncle, that's fine with me. Now that I know that, can I ask where we are?"

"Certainly," Azzie said. "Augsburg."

"That's nice," Charming said, a little vaguely. "I've got a feeling I've always wanted to see Augsburg."

"And so you shall," Azzie said, smiling to himself to think what a docile creature he'd created. "You'll get a good look at it during training, and again when you ride out of town on your quest."

"My quest, Uncle?"

"Yes, lad. You were a famous warrior before the accident that took away your memory."

"How did I come by this accident, Uncle?"

"Fighting bravely against many foes. You slew numbers of them—you're very good with a sword, you know —but one of the caitiffs sneaked up behind you and hit you over the head with a broadsword when you weren't expecting it."

"That hardly seems fair!"

"People are often unfair," Azzie said. "Though you're too innocent to realize that. But never mind. Your pure heart and lofty spirit will win you golden opinions wherever you go."

"That's nice," Charming said. "I want for people to think highly of me."

"And so they shall, my boy, when you have performed the great deed for which you are destined to be renowned."

"What deed is that, Uncle?"

"Winning through the various dangers that stand between you and Princess Scarlet, the Napping Beauty."

"Princess who? What are you talking about?"

"I'm talking about the great deed that will make you world-famous, and give you happiness beyond human measure."

"Oh. That sounds good. Go on, Uncle. You mentioned a sleeping princess?"

"Napping, not sleeping. But it is a severe disability all the same. My boy, it is written that only a kiss from your lips can awaken her from this spell. When she awakens and beholds you, she will fall madly in love with you. You will also fall in love with her, and everybody will be very happy."

"She's good-looking, this princess?" asked Charming.

"You better believe it," Azzie said. "You will awaken her with a kiss. She will open her eyes and look at you. Her arms will close softly around your neck, she will lift her face to yours, and you will know bliss of an order seldom experienced by mortal man."

"It'll be fun, huh?" said the Prince. "Is that what you mean, Uncle?"

"Fun is too mild a word for the pleasure you will feel."

"Sounds great," Charming said. He got up and tried a few steps around the room. "Let's go do it now, okay? I'll kiss her and then she and I can start having fun."

"It can't be quite as fast as that," Azzie said.

"Why not?"

"It is not easy to reach the Princess. You must fight your way through many perils."

"What sort of perils? Dangerous ones?"

"Yes, I'm afraid so," Azzie said. "But don't worry, you'll win through after Frike and I have supervised your training in arms."

"I thought you said I was already trained."

"Well," said Azzie, "a brushup will do no harm."

"Frankly," Charming said, "this whole thing sounds dangerous."

"Of course it is," Azzie said. "That's how it is with perils. But that doesn't matter, you'll be fine. Frike and I will give you instruction in weapons, and then you will set forth."

"Weapons are dangerous. Other people can kill you with them. I remember that much."

You would, with your coward's heart, Azzie thought. Aloud he said, "You'll have superior weapons which none can oppose. And magical spells. And, most important of all, a magic sword."

"Swords!" Charming said, with a disgusted expression. "*Now* I remember swords! Horrible pointed things people use to open up great cuts in each other."

"But think of the cause," Azzie said. "Think of the Princess! You will fight, of course, but I assure you, you will prevail."

"I couldn't do it," Charming said. "No, I'm sorry, but I just couldn't."

"Why not?" Azzie demanded.

"Because I remember now, I'm a conscientious objector," Charming said.

"The hell you say! You've just been reborn! That is,

brought out of the deep sleep caused by your wounds. How can you suddenly be a conscientious objector?"

"Because I know very well," Charming said, "that if I were in a situation where violence was imminent, I would simply faint dead away."

Azzie looked at Frike, who looked vacantly at a spot on the wall. Even this innocent-seeming movement was capable of interpretation. Azzie knew that Frike was secretly mocking him because he had gone to all this trouble to create a Prince Charming and he had had the bad sense to give him a coward's heart.

"Now, get this straight," Azzie said to Charming. "You are going to get some training. Then I'm going to get you an enchanted sword that will do away with everything it encounters. And then you are going forth on this quest."

"What if I get hurt?"

"Prince Charming," Azzie said sternly, "you had better master this fear of yours. I assure you, you are going to go out of here with a magic sword and see what you can do with it; or you are going to get it from me. And since I have demonic friends, getting it from me is apt to be more painful than anything you can imagine. Now go to your room and wash up. It is almost time for dinner."

"What are we having?" Charming asked. "Something French with plenty of sauce, I hope."

"Beef and potatoes," Azzie said. "We're building fighting men here, not dancing masters."

"Yes, Uncle," Charming said, and walked away. There was a pronounced slink to his walk. Azzie glared at Frike, daring him to comment. The servant lurched away. Azzie found a chair in front of the fire and sat. He stared thoughtfully into the fire. He was going to have to come up with something extra. Prince Charming was sure to cut and run the first time he was in peril. And that would make Azzie a laughingstock everywhere in the three worlds. And that Azzie was not going to take.

# Chapter
## 4

The next morning, Azzie began Prince Charming's training. First, there were exercises in swordplay. For a young man about to face dangerous enchantments, the sword was the great all-purpose weapon. Properly used, a sword can kill just about anything. Prince Charming showed considerable natural talent with the blade. His trunk and right arm had been the property of a swordsman who had been highly skilled. This skill showed when Charming lunged and parried, advanced with stamping right foot, retreated with his sword swinging a windmill of flashing steel. Even Azzie, no mean swordsman himself, was hard-pressed by Charming's impetuous advances and cunning ripostes.

But the Prince seemed constitutionally unable to press his advantage once he had won one. Azzie, clad in an old exercise tunic and wearing only a mild sword-turning spell on his upper body, worked with him over and over on the basic maneuvers.

"Come on!" Azzie said, panting as the two went at it

in the shadowed exercise yard behind the mansion. "Get your back into it! Attack me!"

"I would not want to hurt you, Uncle," Charming said.

"Believe me, you won't touch me. Come on now, go for me!"

Charming tried, but his native cowardice prevented him. Whenever he got close enough to Azzie to perform a killing stroke, he faltered, and the lithe demon was able to batter aside his guard and touch him.

Worse than that, when Azzie attacked, shouting fierce words and stamping his foot, Prince Charming's skill fell apart and he had to turn and run.

Frike, watching, shook his head. Who would have thought that one little part of Charming's body, a coward's heart, would expand and suffuse his entire frame?

Azzie tried the various spells at his command, hoping to enchant the Prince into courage. But something obdurate about him seemed impervious to exhortation and spell alike.

When they were not fencing and exercising, Prince Charming went off to a little gazebo in the far end of Azzie's estate. Here he kept his collection—because, despite his promising appearance, he was given to playing with dolls, dressing them up, and setting them out for high tea. Azzie thought of taking the dolls away until the Prince could attack properly, but Frike advised him against it.

"Oftentimes," he said, "the removing of a childish pleasure can drive a young man into a decline. Charming is uncertain enough as it is without you taking his dolls from him."

Azzie had to agree. It was obvious to him that something had to be done. But first he had to get the Prince's enchanted sword.

Supply had been promising one for what seemed like ages, but still hadn't been able to come up with the genuine article. They had plenty of Fairly Lucky Swords, of course, but none that was truly enchanted, with the ability to pierce any guard, to cut through dragons' scales, to plunge deep into the heart of an enemy. All the magic swords they knew of were already in use by other heroes, since Azzie's was by no means the only quest going on at this time. Azzie pleaded that his contest was special, since its winning or losing involved no less than the fortunes of evil for the next thousand years. "Sure," the supply clerk said, "that's what they all say. Important, crash priority, believe me, we've heard it all before."

"But in this case it's really true!"

The clerk smiled unpleasantly. "Sure it's true, same as all the rest."

Azzie decided to leave Charming's training in the hands of Frike, who seemed to frighten Charming just a bit less than did Azzie himself. Azzie betook himself to Princess Scarlet's castle to see how the preparations were going there.

He came down on the outskirts of the enchanted forest. He had spent a lot of time and thought on this, and Supply had been pretty good about getting him what he wanted.

He stood at the edge of his forest, peering in. It was green and bosky, just as a forest should be. Azzie advanced into it. No sooner was he within the green confines than the trees began to move, and their limbs swung down slowly to grasp and seize him. Azzie eluded them with ease. The forest hadn't really received its full complement of fabulous animals and other strange creatures. And the branches moved so slowly that even a dimwit like Charming could avoid them without difficulty. Damn it, he thought, why was Supply holding out on him?

Angry, he flew back to Augsburg to see how Frike was proceeding with the training. He found his servant sitting on the front stoop eating an apple.

"What's the matter?" Azzie said. "Why aren't you exercising him?"

Frike shrugged. "He said he'd had enough. He said

that he had decided to take a vow not to kill any living thing. Would you believe it, he's turned vegetarian and is considering joining a monastic order."

"Now that is entirely too much," Azzie said.

"Agreed, sire," Frike said. "But what can you do about it?"

"I need some expert advice on this one," Azzie said. "Go prepare my magic powders and the Amulet of Expedition. It's time for me to do some conjuring."

# Chapter
# 5

At first Azzie thought his spells weren't working because Hermes didn't appear no matter what he did. He tried again, with the big candles made from deadman's wax that he saved for really difficult occasions. This time he could feel the spell working. He projected power into it and felt it racing through the aether, spinning through the crack between the worlds, nosing around like a questing bird dog. Then Azzie heard a grumpy voice saying, "All right, I'm awake now." And a few moments after that, the heroic marble-white body of Hermes appeared before him. The god was still combing his long brown hair, and he seemed more than a little annoyed.

"My dear Azzie, you should know better than to use a peremptory spell to call me like that. We spirit-advisers have our personal lives, too, you know. It's not nice to have to drop everything and get conjured up by some young demon like yourself."

"I am sorry," Azzie said. "But you've been so generous to me in the past . . . and my problem now is very dire."

"Well, let's hear it," Hermes said. "I don't suppose you have a glass of ichor around."

"Of course I do," Azzie said. He poured the ichor into a goblet carved from a single amethyst. While Hermes sipped at it Azzie explained his difficulty with Prince Charming.

"Let me see. . . ." Hermes said. "Yes, I remember some old writings on the subject. What your Prince Charming is doing is known classically as the Hero Refusing the Quest."

"I didn't know heroes could do that," Azzie said.

"Oh, yes. It's quite common. Do you know anything about your hero's family?"

"He doesn't have any family!" Azzie said. "I created him all by myself!"

"Yes, I know you did," Hermes said. "But recall what we learned of his legs. All his body parts have remembrances, especially the heart."

"He has a coward's heart," Azzie admitted. "I never looked into the rest of the family."

"I'll check it out for you," Hermes said. He vanished, not in a cloud of smoke as common demons vanish, but in a great flash of fire. Azzie admired the exit. It was something he would really like to learn.

Soon Hermes returned. "It is as I suspected. Your cadaver with the coward's heart was the middle of three sons."

"So? What does that mean?"

"In the Old Lore, the middle son is usually the worthless one. The eldest son inherits the kingdom. In the ordinary course of things, the youngest son goes out on the quest and wins a kingdom. The middle son just hangs around and never does much. It's nature's way of balancing the qualities."

"Hellfire!" Azzie said. "I'm stuck with a middle son who's a coward! What am I to do?"

"Since he is still unformed, there's hope of changing his mind. Perhaps you could convince him that he's a younger son. Then he will be more fit for the quest."

"Will that stop him from being a coward?"

"I'm afraid not," Hermes said. "It will help, of course, especially if you tell him stories of how fierce his ancestors were. But his cowardice is an innate tendency not to be cured by exhortation."

"What do you suggest, then?" Azzie asked.

"The only known cure for cowardice," Hermes said, "is an herb known as gutsia sempervirens."

"Where does it grow?" Azzie asked. "And does it really work?"

"Its efficacy is unquestioned. Gutsia, or the nerve plant, as it is also known, imbues a man with rashness and blindsightedness. You must administer it in small doses, otherwise courage turns into foolhardiness and the hero is killed before he ever gets properly started."

"It's hard to imagine Charming being foolhardy."

"Give him a dose of gutsia about the size of his smallest fingernail, and you will see results that will surprise you. But remember, it's always best to balance it off with something else, like coolandria, the herb of careful forethought."

"I'll remember that," Azzie said. "Now, where am I to find this gutsia?"

"That is the real problem," Hermes confessed. "Back in the Golden Age there was a lot of it about, and no one bothered to eat it, since courage wasn't needed in those days, only capacity for enjoyment. Then came the Age of Bronze, when men fought each other, and the Age of Iron, when they fought not only each other but all other things as well. In those days, men consumed the herb in great quantities. That is one of the reasons why the men of old had such prowess. But the race of humans almost died away from too much warfare pursued too courageously. With the climate change that the new age brought, the gutsia plant died off. And now it is to be found in only one place."

"Tell me where that is," Azzie said.

"It is on the back shelves of Supply," Hermes said, "where the remaining plants were dried and then put into tinctures of ichor for eternal preservation."

"But I already asked Supply for something of that sort! They said they had never heard of such a thing!"

"That's very like them," Hermes said. "You must find some way to get them to make a really exhaustive search. I'm sorry, Azzie, but there's nothing else I can think of that will suffice."

This was a problem, because Supply was acting less and less cooperative. In fact, Azzie had the impression they had written off his quest and were now taking long naps and waiting until something else came up. Azzie knew he was in trouble. He talked to the Prince, recounting to him the heroic deeds of his imaginary ancestors and urging him to copy them in all respects. The Prince wasn't interested, however. Even when Azzie brought him small portraits of Scarlet, done by demon artists who could be counted on not to leave out any pulchritudinous feature, the young man still seemed uninterested, and talked about opening up a dress shop when he was a little older.

# Chapter
# 6

It was early evening. The August sun had been beaming down all day on the mansion in Augsburg. Azzie was sitting in the big roughhewn easy chair, reading one of the fliers that the Department of Internal Affairs put out from time to time. It was the usual thing, an exhortation to everyone to do bad for the common cause, and a list of infernal activities around the nation. There was a calendar of birthday announcements for changelings who had been put into human cradles while the real human babies had been taken away to be remodeled and sent to populate the tribe of Aztecs in the New World, whose blood sacrifices had aroused general admiration. There were house-burning celebrations and Pit sales. All the usual sorts of things, with a few snippets of news here and there. Azzie read, though he was not really interested. Sometimes you found something useful in these homely items, more often not.

Then, as his eyes grew heavy, as he began to drowse in front of the fireplace, there came a vast knocking at the

high main door of the mansion. It boomed so loudly that
Azzie half jumped from his chair. Prince Charming, who
was copying Greek dress patterns from a clay tablet onto
parchment, was up and gone before the last clap had ech-
oed away down the bosky glen. Only old Frike main-
tained his imperturbability, though this was not courage
on his part: the sudden heavy noise had frightened him
into immobility, as the rabbit is said to freeze when the
falcon thunders down on him with angry wings and
grasping talons.

"Pretty late for a caller," Azzie mused.

"Aye, sire, and pretty loud, too," Frike said, unfreez-
ing enough to tremble all over.

"Pull yourself together, man," Azzie said. "It's probably some traveler who has lost his way. Put up a big
kettle of water and I'll see who it is."

Azzie went to the door and threw back its massy
bolts, twice-forced of vulcanite steel.

Standing in the doorway was a tall figure dressed in
white. He wore a simple golden helmet with dove's wings
fastened to each side. He was clad in snow-white armor,
and from his shoulders a white ermine coat depended.
The figure was handsome in an insipid sort of way, with
large, well-formed features and big blue eyes.

"Hello," the figure said. "I think I have the correct
address. This is the residence of the demon Azzie Elbub,
is it not?"

"You got that part right," Azzie said. "But whatever
you're selling, I don't want any. How dare you intrude on
me in my hour of rest?"

"Terribly sorry to impose, but they told me to get here
as quickly as I could."

"They?"

"The steering committee of the Powers of Light
Council on the Millennial contest."

"You're from the Powers of Light?"

"Yes. Here are my credentials." He took out a scroll
tied with a scarlet ribbon and handed it to Azzie. Azzie

unfurled it and read, in the heavy Gothic print used by the council, orders to permit the bearer, Babriel, an angel of the second order in the forces of Light, the right to go wherever he pleased and to observe all things that took up his interest; and that this general privilege also specifically applied to the demon Azzie Elbub, to whom he was now seconded as an observer.

Azzie glared at him. "By what right do the Powers of Light send you here? This is strictly a Powers of Darkness production, and the other side has no right to interfere."

"I can assure you, I have no intention of interfering. May I come in and explain further?"

Azzie was so taken aback by the Creature of Good's effrontery that he made no complaint when the tall, golden-haired angel stepped inside the mansion and looked around.

"What a nice place this is! I especially like the symbols on your wall." He indicated the right, or west, wall, where, set in niches, were a series of demons' heads done in black onyx. The demons had various aspects, including ape, falcon, asp, and from the New World, a wolverine.

"Those aren't symbols, stupid," Azzie said. "Those are busts of my ancestors."

"What about this one?" the angel asked, indicating the wolverine head.

"That's my uncle Zanzibar. He emigrated to Greenland, arriving with Erik the Red, and stayed on to become a graven image."

"What a far-traveling family you have!" said the angel, with an expression of admiration. "I do so admire evil for its dash and vigor. It's wrong, of course, but fascinating all the same. I'm Babriel, by the way."

Frike now spoke up. "If you're an angel, where are your wings?"

Babriel unbuckled his armor, beneath which, much cramped, was a pair of wings which unfolded to reveal themselves colored a beautiful palomino.

"What do you want?" Azzie asked. "I'm doing important work, I have no time to hang around and chat."

"I told you, the Powers of Light sent me. It was decided by the high council that your entry in the Millennial contest was of great interest to us. Since it is so important an occasion, it seemed only fitting that we should dispatch an observer to make sure that you didn't cheat. Not that we are accusing you of that, of course. It just seemed businesslike of us to keep an eye on what you were up to, no offense intended."

"I haven't got trouble enough," Azzie remarked. "Now I got to have an angel looking over my shoulder."

"I just want to watch," Babriel said. "We hear a lot about evil where I come from, but I've never seen any close up."

"It must be pretty dull where you come from," Azzie said.

"It is, of course. But it's good, so of course we like it anyhow. But this chance of seeing a real demon in action —doing bad things—well, I must confess, the idea of evil titillates me."

"You like it, huh?" Azzie said.

"Oh, no! I wouldn't go so far as to say that. But I am interested, yes. And perhaps I can even be of some help."

"To me? Are you kidding?"

"I know it must seem odd. But Good, by its very nature, tends to be helpful, even in an evil cause. Real Good has no prejudice against Evil."

"That's all I want to hear about good," Azzie said. "I hope you're not some missionary type here to convert me to the Other Side. It's no use. You understand what I'm saying?"

"I'm sure I won't be any trouble," Babriel said. "And your own people have agreed to this."

"Your scroll looks official enough to me," Azzie said. "Well, I've got nothing against it. Observe all you want. Just don't try to steal any of my spells."

"I'd rather lose my right arm than steal from you!" Babriel said.

"I believe you," Azzie said. "You really *are* a fool, aren't you? Never mind," he added, seeing Babriel's crestfallen expression, "it's just my way of talking. There's plenty of food in the larder. No, on second thought, you probably wouldn't like that. Frike, get our guest some chickens from the village."

"But I'd be happy to partake of whatever you eat," Babriel said.

"No, you wouldn't," Azzie said. "Trust me on this. So how's Good doing these days?"

"Our entry is coming along well," Babriel replied. "Foundations down and all that. Transepts, nave, choir in place—"

"Entry? What are you talking about?"

"Good's entry in the Millennial contest."

"You're building something for it?"

"Yes. We've inspired a master builder and enspirited an entire village for labor in a massive architectural undertaking. It will be a glorious structure—inspiring humanity to the higher things: truth, beauty, goodness—"

"What do you call the thing?"

"We rather like the term 'Gothic cathedral.'"

"Hmm. And well, well. You guys stuck with an observer, too?"

"Yes. Bestialial is checking it out."

Azzie snorted.

"He's not exactly field personnel," he said. "Desk type. Still . . . Sound, I suppose, when he's paying attention. So you think it's a good entry, huh?"

"Oh, yes. We're happy with it," Babriel said. "And that's what Good is doing. But you know the saying, 'It's good, but it could always be better.'"

"That's just how it is with Evil," Azzie said. "Come into the study. I'll pour you a shot of ichor."

"I've heard of it," Babriel said, "but I've never had any. Is it intoxicating?"

"It gets the job done," Azzie said. "Life being what it is, I mean."

Babriel found this last statement opaque, to say the least. But when has good ever understood evil? He followed Azzie into the study.

"Well then," Azzie said, "if you're going to stay, you're going to stay. I suppose you want to live here in the mansion?"

"It would be more convenient for my duties," Babriel said. "I could pay rent. . . ."

"What sort of piker do you take me for?" Azzie asked indignantly, though the idea of charging rent had crossed his mind. "You're a guest. Where I come from, a guest is sacred."

"That's how it is where I come from, too," Babriel said.

"Big deal!" Azzie sneered. "For a Creature of Light to hold a guest sacred is no big matter; but for one of Darkness to do so is remarkable indeed."

"Just what I was going to say," Babriel said.

"Don't try to ingratiate yourself with me," Azzie said. "I know the tricks and I despise you and everything you stand for."

"That's just as it should be," Babriel said, with a smile.

"So you despise me, too?"

"Not at all! I meant that that was how it should be for you. You're what our archangels call a natural. It's a privilege to see you in action."

"Flattery will get you nowhere," Azzie said, and found to his annoyance that he rather liked Babriel. He'd do something about that! To Frike he said, "Show him up to the little room in the attic."

Frike took an oil lamp, and bent nearly double, with his cane tapping ahead of him and his hump standing up

like a whale surfacing, he walked to the stairs, followed
by Babriel.

The stairs went up and up, past the polished corridors
and rooms of the lower floors. As they went higher the
stairs grew steeper and narrower, with here and there a
tread missing. Frike stumped steadily along, and Babriel,
tall and erect, his white cloak glimmering faintly in the
candlelight, followed, bowing his head to avoid the low
beams.

They came out at last on a landing near the top of the
tall, high old mansion. At the end of the short dark hall-
way was a door. Frike opened it and entered with his
lamp. By its flickering yellow light Babriel saw a small
room with a ceiling so low he could not stand erect. There
was a tiny leaded window high up, tilted at an angle to
match the sloping roof. There was an iron cot and a small
wooden nightstand. The room was just a little longer than
the cot. The floor was thick with dust and the place
smelled of cats in heat and ancient moths.

"Very nice," Babriel said.

"A trifle small, perhaps," Frike said. "Perhaps if you
asked the master, he would let you have one of the third-
floor suites."

"No need," Babriel said. "This will do nicely."

Just then there was a knock at the door.

"Who's there?" Frike asked.

"Supernal Delivery Service. Luggage for the angel
Babriel."

"Ah, thank you," Babriel said. He opened the door. A
man of medium height stood there wearing a delivery-
man's cap. He handed Babriel a piece of paper and a pen.
Babriel signed and handed back the paper. The delivery-
man tugged at his forelock and disappeared.

"It's my luggage," Babriel told Frike. "Where should I
put it?"

Frike looked around doubtfully. "On your bed,
maybe. But then you'd have no place to sleep."

"It'll work itself out," Babriel said, and pulled his suitcase into the room. It was a very large suitcase and the only place there was room for it *was* on the bed, since he and Frike between them used up most of the available floor space.

Babriel looked at the room and said, "Do you think it'll go into the corner?"

Frike looked at the acute angle formed where the room's walls met. "You couldn't push a mouse's corpse into that corner, much less a big suitcase like that."

"Let's give it a try anyway," Babriel said. He pushed the suitcase off the bed and toward the corner. Although it was only a few inches from the end of the bed to the corner, the trunk kept moving. The wall, instead of stopping it, bulged outward to make room for it, and the other walls bulged out to stay in proportion. The ceiling lifted, too, and Frike soon found that he was in quite a large room rather than the tiny room he had entered.

"How did you do that?" Frike asked.

"Just one of those things you pick up when you move around a lot," Babriel said modestly.

Aside from growing larger, the room had also grown brighter, for reasons that didn't make themselves immediately apparent. Frike's eyes widened, then widened again as he heard a curious scuttling noise at this feet. He looked down and saw something small, about the size of a rat, scurrying out of sight. Frike blinked, and when his vision cleared he saw that the floor, which had been an inch deep in dust and cat droppings, had been freshly swept and polished. A certain panic gripped him.

"I'll tell the master you're settling in nicely," Frike said, and departed.


Five minutes later Azzie came up to Babriel's room. Azzie looked at it, twice as big as when he'd seen it last, brilliantly illuminated, nicely furnished, clean, fragrant with frankincense and myrrh, and with a small door at one side opened to reveal a fine tiled bathroom Azzie knew damned well hadn't been there before.

There was a standing closet, too, and its door was open, revealing dozens of Babriel's uniforms, of every cut and description, some with medals, and many with exaggerated collars and huge cuffs. Babriel had changed into one such. It was white and silver, and came with a peaked cap. Azzie thought he looked so ludicrous as to appear sinister.

"Glad to see you're making yourself to home," Azzie said.

"I took the liberty of fixing the place up a little. I'll gladly restore it to original condition when I leave."

"Don't worry about it," Azzie said. "If I'd known you wanted fancy, you'd have gotten fancy. What's that?"

He pointed to a rectangular blob of nacre and ormolu that swung from Babriel's waist.

"Oh, that's my telephone," Babriel said. "So I can stay in touch with headquarters."

Azzie glared at the handset. "They haven't even issued ours yet!"

"You'll love them when you get them," Babriel said.

# Chapter
# 7

It was fine September weather. Azzie became more accustomed to having Babriel living in his house. His room continued to expand, and Azzie had to ask the angel to do some shoring up because it was threatening to capsize the house with its weight and top-heavy leverage. And the training of Prince Charming went on. The young man seemed to be gaining confidence. Azzie had been feeding him a variety of herbal extracts, as well as other exotic ingredients such as powdered unicorn horn, dried banshee shit, and distilled corpse sweat. Charming was now able to hold his own against Frike with the wooden swords, even though Frike fenced with his lame left arm to make the contest more equal. There was definite progress, though it was difficult to say when the young Prince would be ready to face a real foe.

These were quiet days and nights. Azzie regretted only that Ylith was not present. It had been necessary to leave her in the enchanted castle to look after Princess

Scarlet, whose rebellious ways were still something of a problem.

One evening, as Azzie was sitting in the living room smoking his pipe and feasting on a small plate of wolverine hearts with teriyaki sauce, there was a great commotion overhead. Babriel, who was reading one of his interminable books on how to be good, looked up startled as he heard the sound of hooves on the roof. Then there came a scraping sound mixed with swearing. They advanced to the chimney. Azzie could hear a loud grunting and moaning now, and at last something large worked its way down.

It was lucky that, it being a mild September night, no fire was going. Santa Claus emerged, some dark stains on his red suit, tasseled cap askew, a scowling expression on his smudged face.

"Why," Santa Claus demanded, "did you close the flues? It makes it very difficult getting through. And your chimney hasn't been cleaned in ages."

"Sorry, Santa," Azzie said. "I wasn't expecting you this time of year. Not that you come often to us demons, anyhow."

"That's because our charter says we are to bring presents first to humans. And there are more of them every day."

"I quite understand," Azzie responded. "In any event, we demons have our own ways of giving and receiving. But why have you come? If it's a social visit, you could have come in by the front door."

"It's business, not social," Santa Claus said. "I have a rush order here for a young lady witch who gave this as her address. Ylith is her name. Is she around?"

"She's off at my other place," Azzie said. "Can I be of help?"

"You can accept this delivery for her." Santa took a large, gaily wrapped package out of his pack.

"Sure. Glad to."

"You'll make sure she gets it?" Santa said. "It's for a

little girl, Brigitte is her name, to whom Ylith promised it."

"I'll see that she gets it."

"Thank you," Santa said. "I mentioned to Ylith how lonely it gets at the North Pole. She said she'd send some witches my way and I'd give them presents and a good time."

"Witches are overrated. You won't like them."

"You think not? Try a steady diet of elves before you knock witches. Well, must be off."

Azzie walked Santa to the front door. He watched as Santa, moving nimbly for so large a man, scrambled up the trellises to the roof. Soon there was a clatter of hooves and the rest was silence.

Azzie went back inside and opened the package. Within was a miniature mansion and farmyard. It was all nicely detailed with little people dolls, animal dolls. There were tiny windows, mirrors, tables, chairs.

"Could use a little guillotine," he mused aloud. "I had one here someplace. . . ."

# SEXT

BABRIEL

# Chapter
1

Over the next few days Charming continued to progress in the art of fencing. But he did well only when everything went according to form. Unusual things startled him, interrupting his coordination. And he was very distractible. At every birdcall or slammed door he jerked his head around. Irregularities in the ground upset his balance. Every footstep he took forward had a look of retreat to it. Sudden gusts of wind caused him to close his eyes.

But it was mostly his cowardice that bothered Azzie, who knew it to be the real reason for the other signs of ineptitude.

Babriel watched for a long while without comment, though he winced at the young man's awkwardness and the way he flinched whenever Frike lifted his sword.

"What, exactly, is wrong with him?" Babriel finally asked.

"It's the coward's heart I gave him. Instead of imbuing him with basic prudence, as it's supposed to do, it's filling his entire system with fear."

"But if he's so fearful, how will he go out for his quest?"

"I doubt he'll go at all," Azzie said. "I'm trying to motivate him, but nothing is working. It looks like I'm licked before I even get started."

"Oh, dear," Babriel said.

"Yeah, well, you might say that, and a lot else."

"But your contest—the fairy tale you're planning to present—"

"Finished, over with, shot down, *connsumatus est,* and all that."

"It hardly seems fair," Babriel said. "But why throw in the sponge so soon? I mean, heck, hang it all, isn't there something you can do?"

"I need to get some gutsia for him. But my Supply people can't seem to find any."

"Can't they, now? Bunch of slackers, unless I miss my guess. Let's see what my fellows can do."

Azzie stared at him. "*You* are going to get me gutsia?"

"That is what I propose," Babriel said.

"But that won't do *you* any good!"

"Let me worry about that," Babriel said. "You've been such a nice host, I feel I owe you something. And anyhow, the show must go on, eh?"

Babriel stood up, ducking his head because it was a low grape arbor in which they stood, and reached into one of his pockets and withdrew a plastic credit card. It was very much like Azzie's, only white instead of jet black. It bore on one side a golden representation of a constellation moving toward the position it would occupy at the Millennium's end. Babriel looked around for a place to insert it, but couldn't find one.

"Let's take a walk," Babriel said. "Maybe there's something out here. . . . Ah, here's a bay tree, they're always good." He found a slit in the bay's bark and inserted the card.

"What's supposed to happen now?" Azzie asked.

"Give them a moment to respond," Babriel said. "This is an unusual location for a transmission from an angel of Light, you know."

"How's the Gothic cathedral coming?" Azzie asked.

"The walls are a lot higher," Babriel responded.

In a moment there came a soft explosion, then the sound of a carillon, followed by a fanfare of trumpets. The supply clerk of Light appeared before them. She was a young blond woman who wore a plain white gown which did not prevent Azzie's noting that she looked pretty good and might be fun to cavort with. He began to hum the ancient melody called "The Night a Sinner Met an Angel" and edged toward her.

The angel slapped him sharply with the small order book she was carrying. "Don't be crude," she said in a nice voice that showed that although she meant it, she didn't hold his attitude against him. Then, to Babriel: "How may I help you?"

Azzie started to tell her how she could help *him*, but Babriel frowned and said, "What I need, dear person, is a quantity of the herb gutsia, which is used by mortals for the acquiring of courage."

"I knew you wanted it for a mortal," the supply clerk said. "I can tell at a glance that there's no lack of courage in *thy* makeup."

"It is dear of thee to say so," Babriel said. "Praise the Lord!"

"Praise Her!" said the clerk.

"What?" Azzie said. "I had always been led to believe—"

"We use 'He' and 'She' interchangeably when speaking of the Supreme Principle of Good."

"Sometimes we even call her 'It,'" the clerk said. "Not that we believe that She is an It, but we try to show no prejudice."

"Can't you make up your minds?" Azzie asked.

"It makes no difference," she told him. "Supreme Good is beyond sexuality."

"That's not what we're taught," Azzie said. "According to our experts, sexuality is the highest expression of evil, especially when it's good.

"As it could be between you and me, babe," Azzie ended, his voice going husky and a disturbing odor of musk emanating from him.

The clerk frowned and patted her hair and turned to Babriel. "Canst thou not restrain this ill-visaged specter of evil who leers at me with unveiled meaning?"

"Oh, hey," Babriel said, "that's just Azzie. He's a demon, you know. They're supposed to act that way—irreverent and sexual. Poor soul, he knows no better. But not even demons are utterly beyond redemption."

"Praise the Lord!" the clerk said.

"Aye, praise Him," Babriel said.

Azzie said, "Hey, look, can we dispense with the hosannas and get on with the stuff I need? You two can go courting on your own time."

"What a hateful thing to say!" the clerk said, blushing and looking away. "I'll check on the gutsia. Wait right here."

She vanished in a beguiling manner.

"You've got cuter supply clerks than we have," Azzie said.

"That's because under the rule of the Good all creatures are equal. Perhaps, since we have to wait, I could explain to you some of the more basic points of our doctrine."

"Don't bother," Azzie said. "I'm going to take a nap."

"Is it so easy for you to do that?"

"Evil is known for its eternal vigilance," Azzie said. "Except when it gets fed up."

He closed his eyes. Soon the even rhythm of his breathing gave evidence that he was either sleeping or doing a good job of faking it.

Left to his own devices, Babriel said a longish prayer

for the salvation and regeneration of all beings, even demons. By the time he had finished, the clerk was back.

"I have the extract of gutsia," she said, handing Babriel a small flask in which colors of red, violet, yellow, and blue could be seen coruscating softly.

"Great," said Babriel. "We thank you. You have been most unfailingly courteous, helpful, kind—"

"Let's get on with it," Azzie said. "Thanks a lot, babe. If you ever want to change your luck—"

The supply clerk vanished in a cloud of indignation.

Azzie went to the kitchen to give Frike instructions in how to mix the gutsia with Charming's cream of leek soup. Grateful as he was to Babriel for procuring it for him, he was deeply suspicious. Why had the angel been so helpful? Pure generosity didn't seem a sufficient motive. Were angels capable of double-dealing? What was Babriel up to?

# Chapter
# 2

Azzie administered the gutsia that evening, and Charming showed a remarkable improvement. Over the next few days, his fencing skill and aggressiveness picked up. He was no longer interested in his dolls.

All in all, it seemed a good time to Azzie to bring up the subject of his quest.

"I've been meaning to speak to you again about your future," Azzie said one quiet afternoon when he and Prince Charming were together in the big common room of the castle.

"Yes, Uncle?"

"You remember the things I told you about the Napping Princess?" he asked. "It's about time to head off in her direction."

"I wouldn't mind hanging around court," Charming said.

"Forget it. It's a great adventure that's in store for you."

"That's nice, Uncle. But, you know, I've been wondering why I'm supposed to find her and kiss her and all, anyway."

Azzie took on a tone of deepest portent. "My boy, it was written long ago that only a kiss on the lips from her true love would awaken the Princess from the sleep."

"Hope that works out for her," Charming said.

"Of course it will! You, Prince Charming, are the destined lover and husband of this fair maid."

"Are you sure it's supposed to be me, Uncle? I mean, how do you know it's not some other fellow's quest?"

"Because it is so written."

"Written where?"

"Never mind where," Azzie said. "Just take my word for it, if I tell you it's written, it's written. My boy, you are a very lucky youth. Princess Scarlet is the most beautiful of maidens, and she comes with a rich dowry. It will be difficult and dangerous getting to her, but I know you will do fine."

"How difficult? How dangerous?"

"There is an enchanted wood to pass through," Azzie explained. "You must fight the various denizens of the wood. Then there is the glass mountain which you must somehow climb."

"This sounds extremely difficult," Charming said. "Glass mountain, eh? Perhaps I could manage it. I don't know, though."

"I'll see that you come to no harm," Azzie told him. "Trust your old uncle Azzie. Never set you wrong, did I?"

"You won't get a chance this time either," Charming said. "I'm not going."

"At least look at her picture. What do you think?" Azzie asked, showing Prince Charming the miniature.

"She looks all right," Charming said, in tones of profound disinterest.

"Pretty, huh?" Azzie said.

"In a common sort of way."

"Fine bright eyes, eh?"

"Astigmatic, no doubt."

"And the mouth!"

"A regular sort of mouth," Charming said.

"Tiny! Dainty!"

"Smallish," Charming conceded.

"She's lovely, is she not?"

"She's okay, I suppose," Charming said. "But I'm too young to have a princess of my own forever and forever. I haven't even dated yet."

Charming's lack of interest was dismaying. Azzie had not expected this. As a fairly typical demon, he was usually in a state of concupiscence. The very idea that this Prince could be so blasé about the beautiful Princess astounded him. It irritated him also, and when he thought about it further, it worried him.

If Prince Charming evinced no more than a polite interest in Scarlet, how could he be expected to go through hell and high water to reach her bedside and awaken her with a kiss? With his attitude, he'd be more likely to send her a letter saying, "Time to wake up now, miss."

In vain Azzie pointed out the Princess' charms. Charming met them with a devastating indifference which hurt Azzie's feelings, since the Princess was his creation. But he couldn't be too angry since he had created the Prince as well, and thus was more or less responsible for his attitude.

This was a turn of events Azzie had not expected. It had never occurred to him that his Prince would not fall instantly in love with Scarlet. Now that his cowardice seemed somewhat under control it seemed he was romantically sluggish.

"Damn!" Azzie observed, gnashing his teeth. "Oh, damn! Another design flaw!"

It was a hellish situation.

# Chapter
# 3

In the evening he put Charming out of the way with a magic sleep. Then he headed for his conjuring room. Frike was there, humming to himself as he topped off vials of agius regae, bloodswart, hellbane, and other herbs and simples which wizardly demons find useful.

"Put that crap away," Azzie said. "I need to do some conjuring. Bring me ten cc's of bat's blood, some demonswart, and a half gill of black hellebore."

"We're all out of black hellebore," Frike said. "Would toadswart or anything else do?"

"I thought I told you to keep the stock up."

"I'm sorry, master. I developed a taste for it."

Azzie snorted.

"Stuff'll stunt your growth," he observed, "and make your palms hairy. Bring me some heliogabulus root then. It will have to suffice."

Frike brought the root and, following Azzie's directions, arranged it around a pentagram which was set into the stone floor with mother-of-pearl. He lighted the black candles, and Azzie intoned the invocation. The words employed many double glottal stops, a common feature of the ancient language of evil. Presently, a wisp of gray and purple smoke appeared in the circle. It expanded, filled out, grew larger, taller, thicker, and finally resolved into the tall figure of Hermes Trismegistus.

"Hail, Great One," Azzie said.

"Hi there, Little One," Hermes said. "What seems to be the trouble?"

Azzie related his difficulties with Charming. Hermes said, "You made an error in telling him about the Princess, Azzie. You assumed that things happen in real life as they do in fairy tales, and that Prince Charming would fall madly in love with Princess Scarlet from one look at the miniature."

"Isn't that how it happens?"

"Only in fairy tales."

"But this *is* a fairy tale!"

"Not yet it isn't," Hermes said. "After it is all over and retold by a bard, *then* it becomes a fairy tale. But for right now, that condition has not been met. You can't simply show a young man a picture and expect him to fall in love with it. You must use psychology."

"Is that a special spell?" Azzie asked.

Hermes shook his smoky head. "It is what we call a science. It is the science of human behavior. There's nothing like it in the world yet. That's why everyone is so wonky. No one knows why they do what they do because there's no psychology."

"Well, what do I do?"

"The first thing is to wipe out Charming's memories of your telling him about Scarlet. A small dose of Lethe water ought to do the trick. Not a great deal, just enough so that he will forget your recent conversation with him."

"And then?"

"Then I will tell you what to do next."

There was no trouble procuring Lethe water. Hermes brought it in a small crystal flask, and Azzie administered it to Charming. That evening, Azzie and Prince Charming dined together in the big walnut-paneled dining room. Frike served, splashing the soup as usual because of the way he lurched when walking. When the smoking joint had been taken away and the cream tarts eaten, Azzie said, "By the way, Prince, I shall be going out of town for a while."

"Where are you going, Uncle?"

"I have some business to attend to."

"What business, Uncle?"

"My business is none of your business. Frike! Bring me the keys!"

Frike scuttled off and crabbed back with a big bunch of keys set around an iron ring.

"Now pay attention, Prince. I am leaving the keys of the manor in your keeping. This big one is for the front door. The small one opens the back door, and the other small one opens the stable. Here is the key to the cellar where we keep the wine, the beer, and the preserved meats. The one with the curlicues opens my chest of spells. You can play with them if you like; they're not currently armed."

"Yes, Uncle." Charming took the keys. One caught his eye, a small silver key with elaborate arabesques around its haft.

"What about this one?" Charming asked.

"Ah," Azzie said, "that one. Did I leave that on the key ring?"

"Yes, you did, Uncle."

"Well, don't use it."

"But what is it?"

"It opens the small door at the far end of my sleeping chamber. And then, using the other end, it opens a small brass-bound oaken chest in that room. But you must not go through that door and you must not open the chest."

"Why not, Uncle?"

"It would take too long to explain," Azzie said.

"I have time," Charming said.

"Of course you do. You have nothing but time, have you? But I do not have any time. I must be off immediately. Just take my word for it, there will be a bad result if you open that door. So don't do it."

"Yes, Uncle."

"Scout's honor?"

Charming held up his right hand in the salute of the Scouts of Knighthood, a new organization for young knights in training. "I swear, Uncle."

"Good boy. And now I must be off. Farewell, lad."

"Farewell, Uncle."

Charming accompanied him to the stables, where Azzie mounted a fiery Arabian.

"Softly now, Belshazzar!" Azzie cried. "Farewell, nephew. I'll see you in a couple of days, a week at the outside."

Charming and Frike both waved until Azzie was out of sight.

An hour later (a short hour, since the glass ran fast) Charming said to Frike, "I'm bored."

"Another game of Rheumie?" Frike asked, shuffling the cards.

"No, I'm tired of card games."

"What would you like to do then, young sir? Lawn tennis? Quoits? Push and shove?"

"I'm sick of all those namby-pamby pastimes," Charming said. "Can't you think of anything interesting?"

"Hunting?" Frike suggested. "Fishing? Kite flying?"

"No, no . . ." Prince Charming narrowed his eyes, then looked up. His features took on a look of animation. "I know!"

"I await your pleasure, sire."

"Let's go peek in the room I'm not supposed to look into."

Frike had been well schooled. Concealing the smile that threatened to break out, he said, "We couldn't do that!"

"Could we not, now?"

"Certainly not, sire. The master would be dreadfully cross."

"But he wouldn't have to know, would he?"

Frike's expression revealed that he had never thought of that. "You mean . . . not tell him?"

"That is precisely what I mean."

"But we always tell the master everything!"

"Let's make an exception this time."

"But why?"

"For a game, Frike, that's why."

"Oh . . . A game." Frike seemed to ponder. "I suppose that would be all right, if it's only a game. Are you sure it's a game?"

"Frike, I swear to you, it is only a game."

"Well then," Frike said, "so long as it's only a game."

"Let's go!" Charming cried, bounding up the stairs four at a time, the keys jingling in his hand.


Outside the manor house, Azzie, who had parked his horse in the wood and returned on foot, or rather, on wing, since he had fully operational wings beneath his resplendent tunic, hovered above the high bedroom window and smiled to himself. He had never heard of this psychology stuff Hermes had spoken about, but it was going all right so far.

# Chapter
# 4

Ylith was just tucking a blanket about Princess Scarlet, who had dropped off to sleep in mid-conversation with her, when the knocking occurred upon the castle gate. It was not like Azzie to knock, and Ylith could not imagine any other visitor, there atop the glass mountain. Leaving the girl in the leather arms of the huge chair, she moved quickly out of the sitting room and headed for the castle's main hall. The sound came again as she traversed the high-ceilinged stone room.

She unlatched the normal-sized postern door beside the big gate, opened it, and looked outside. A tall, not uncomely figure, clad in white and gold, returned her gaze and smiled.

"Yes?" she said.

"Am I correct in assuming this to be the castle of the Napping Beauty, Princess Scarlet?" he inquired.

"You are," she replied. "But you can't be Prince Charming, can you? It's a little early, and those aren't the right eyes—not that I have anything against big blue ones, mind you."

"Oh, no," he answered. "My name's Babriel. I'm the observer for the Powers of Light. I'm a guest of Azzie's and I just thought I'd pop over and check out this end of the operation. Is everything proceeding in good fashion?"

"Why, yes," she said. "Won't you come in?"

"Thank you, I will," he replied.

"I'm Azzie's—associate," she said, "in this matter. My name's Ylith. Glad to make your acquaintance."

She offered a hand. He raised it and pressed it to his lips.

"Oh," she remarked, staring at her hand after he released it. "Uh, come this way. I'll take you to see the lady. She's napping now, of course."

"Of course," he replied, seeming to realize suddenly that he was still holding her hand and releasing it quickly, "if it is convenient."

"Certainly, certainly."

She turned and led him across the hall.

"Nice hall," he observed.

"Thanks."

"You and Azzie been together long?"

"Oh, we go way back. But we're not exactly—to-gether—right now. Except on this project, I mean."

"Clever entry you have."

"I suppose so. It's all Azzie's idea. I'm just helping him out, for old times' sake."

"I see. Brotherhood of Evil and all that," he said. "Sis-terhood, too, of course," he corrected quickly.

"Sort of. This way," she said, leading him out of the hall and into the sitting room. "There she is. Napping Beauty. Pretty, huh?"

"Lovely," he remarked.

Ylith blushed as she realized he was looking at her. Immediately, he suffered a coughing spell.

"May I get you something to drink?" she offered. "A little ichor, perhaps?"

"Please."

"Have a seat. Be comfortable."

She hurried off, returning in a few moments with a pair of drinks.

"Here. Thought I'd join you," she said.

"Thank you."

He sipped it slowly. She seated herself nearby.

"I take it the project goes well," Babriel repeated after a time.

"Oh, Azzie has his problems, I understand," she answered.

"You must be a great help and comfort to him."

"I wouldn't know," she replied. "He's been somewhat uncommunicative."

"I don't understand."

"The last time we talked he was a trifle—cold. It may be he has more problems than I realize, or it may just be—"

"What?"

"That he's just that way—to me."

They sipped their ichor in silence for a time. Then: "It is in the nature of evil to be nasty, I guess," Babriel observed. "Even to its friends and allies."

Ylith looked away.

"He wasn't always like that, to me."

"Oh."

"Your side is nicer about these things, I suppose."

"I'd like to think so."

"But then you have to be. . . . The nature of things."

"I suppose. But I like to think that we do it because we really want to. It just makes us *feel* good."

"Hmm." She turned toward Princess Scarlet. "Look at her," she said. "Poor thing has no notion that she's only a counter in a game."

"But she wouldn't exist, save for that."

"Still, it might be better than being used."

"An interesting theological point."

"Theological, hell! Excuse me. But people aren't things, to be manipulated that way."

"No, they have free will. So she's still her own person. That's what makes this whole thing interesting."

"Free? Even when the choices are artificially narrowed?"

"That's another interesting theological point—that is, yes, I suppose it isn't very nice. Still, what's to be done? She really is something of a game piece."

"I guess so. I can't help feeling a bit sorry for her, though."

"Oh, I do, too. We're big on sympathy."

"Is that all? I mean, it doesn't help her much."

"But we're not allowed to help in this. Though now you mention it, I suppose I could recommend her for some grace."

"Wouldn't that be cheating, helping her?"

"Not really. Grace sort of helps without helping, if you know what I mean. It kind of helps you to help yourself. I can't see that as cheating. Yes, maybe I should. . . ."

Another sip.

"Have you always been that way?" she asked.

"What way?"

"Kind."

"I suppose so."

"How refreshing. It makes it easier having you as the observer."

"Have you always been a witch?"

"It was a career choice, a long time ago."

"Enjoyable?"

"Most of the time. What sort of entry does the Power of Light have going?"

"Oh, we're calling it a Gothic cathedral—a radically new concept in the architecture of devotion and goodness."

"How does it differ from the regular variety? Here, let me freshen your drink."

"Thanks."

When she returned, he began explaining Gothic cathedrals. She smiled and nodded regularly, fascinated.

# Chapter
# 5

Scarlet paced before Ylith.

"I'm getting so sick of napping," she said. She continued to pace.

"I'm never fully awake, it seems, and I can't get a good night's sleep either. I need to do something more than stay here in this stupid castle waiting for some guy to come along and wake me up. I want to get out of here! I want to talk to someone!"

"You can talk to me," Ylith replied.

"Oh, Aunt Ylith, you're very nice. I'd be completely out of my mind if you weren't here. But I'd like to talk to someone else. You know . . . a man."

"I wish I could help you," Ylith said. "But you know you're not supposed to have any company. You're just supposed to sleep until Prince Charming gets here."

"I know, I know," Scarlet said. Tears filled her eyes. "But it's so boring, just sleeping all the time. And not even sleeping well. Napping! Oh, please, Aunt Ylith, isn't there some way you can help me?"

Ylith considered. She felt more irritated with Azzie than before. She should have known better than to trust him again. Still, there was nothing she could do about it now.

The following day, there came a knocking at the gate: it came during one of Scarlet's rare moments of wakefulness, and she rushed down to open it herself.

Standing at the door was a six-foot frog dressed in footman's livery, with a white peruke slightly askew on his warty green head.

"Hello," Scarlet said calmly. She was getting quite used to enchanted visitations. After talking with Azzie — who was very strange, in his puff-of-smoke comings and goings — and Ylith, who spent considerable time before a magic mirror, observing the townspeople at the foot of the mountain, as well as points distant (including the nether regions and lower astral realms) — nothing could surprise her. "Are you the Prince who's supposed to awaken me?"

"Heavens no!" the frog said. "I am a messenger."

"But underneath the frog disguise you're really a handsome young man, aren't you?"

"Afraid not," he replied. "I've been enchanted to possess the power of human speech and made to be six feet tall."

"What are you like when you're not enchanted?"

"I'm six inches tall and I croak."

"What do you want?"

"I have an invitation for you."

He held out a square of cardboard upon which letters had been embossed:

*YOU ARE INVITED TO A CELEBRATION*
*MASKED BALL IN HONOR OF*
*CINDERELLA AND HER PRINCE*
*MUSIC BY ORLANDO AND THE FURIOSOS*
*GIORDANO BRUNO AND THE HERMETIC*
*TRADITION*

*SPARTACUS AND THE REVOLTING SLAVES*
*CHARADES, DOOR PRIZES*
*TASTEFUL REVELRY*

"Oh, thank you!" Scarlet said. "But why did Princess Cinderella ask me? I don't even know her."

"She heard that you are alone here and is sympathetic to your plight. She's had her own problems, you know."

"I'd love to go! But I have no ballroom gown."

"Surely you can get one."

"And transport . . . How would I get there?"

"Merely contact Enchanted Ball Caterers, and at the proper time they will dispatch me with a coach fashioned out of a pumpkin."

"Oh. But won't I get pumpkin juice on my gown?"

"Not a chance of it. The interior is upholstered in rarest watered silk."

"Watered?"

"It's dry, don't worry."

"Thank you! Thank you!" Scarlet rushed off to tell Ylith about the wonderful invitation.

"Faith, child, Azzie has a spell over this whole place," Ylith replied. "It would take a plenipotentiary pass to get you out of here. And that, only the Powers of Darkness can supply."

"But what can I do?"

"Nothing, poor dear," she mused. "Though if you had Azzie's unlimited credit card, then a lot would be possible. And he keeps it so carelessly, too, in the upper pocket of his waistcoat. You'll just have to hope that he drops it when he visits you next, and that you can pick it up before he misses it."

"But what if he doesn't drop it?"

"Your own hands can help you," Ylith said. "Especially the left one."

Scarlet looked at her hands. The left one, the pickpocket's hand, was slightly smaller than the right one, and looked, she didn't know how to say it, somehow more *sly* than its near mate.

"What is it about my left hand? I can see it's small and I suppose dainty. But what of it?"

"That hand has a skill for getting what you need."

"And if I had the card?"

"Why then," Ylith said, "you could call up a ballroom gown and get an order through to the Enchanted Ball Caterers. Then you could go to the ball, so long as you came straight back."

"Why are you telling me these things?"

Ylith looked away.

"Anger and pity, my dear," she said at length. "The first is a strength and the second a weakness. So think of it mainly as the first. And it is time that you learned about balls. And free will."

She patted Princess Scarlet's hand, which half succeeded in removing a jeweled ring as she was about it.

"Yes," she continued. "The hell with Azzie." And she smiled. "That's grace for you."

# Chapter
# 6

The next time Azzie came to call, Princess Scarlet was all smiles. She chattered about her dreams, which were the only interesting things in her daily life. She showed Azzie dance steps she remembered from before her death. She danced tempestuously, her little feet stamping on the floor in the figures of the Seguriyas, and she ended in a whirl of movement as she pirouetted across the room and collapsed into Azzie's arms. "Let me embrace you, Uncle, you have done so much for me!"

Azzie felt her small pointy breasts pressing into his chest, and thought not at all of what her clever little fingers were doing.

Ylith said, once she was alone with Scarlet, "Do you have it?"

Scarlet smiled, showing her even little teeth and the dimples in the corner of each cheek. She held up the black card. "Here it is!"

"Well done," Ylith said. "Now you have only to use it."

"Yes," Scarlet said, trying to stifle a yawn. "But what will I do about this damnable napping spell?"

"Have a good stiff slug of ichor," Ylith replied. "I'll add a spell. You'll sleep three or four times longer than usual, then be awake another three or four times as long afterward."

Scarlet brightened.

"Hurry," she said.

# Chapter
# 7

The pumpkin coach glided up to the canopied reception area, moving silently on its radish wheels. The frog footman hopped out and opened the door for Scarlet. She stepped out, taking care not to mess her gown. It was a beautiful thing, pink tulle with a sprig of hyacinth, created especially for her by Michael of Perugia and charged to Azzie's account.

Uniformed attendants welcomed her and led her inside. The ballroom was a blaze of color and light. At the far end was the orchestra. Princess Scarlet was dazzled. Never had she seen a spectacle such as this. It was like something out of a fairy tale, and the fact that she herself was something out of a fairy tale made it no less wonderful.

"You must be Princess Scarlet!" Scarlet was being addressed by a radiantly beautiful young woman of about her own age.

"Are you Princess Cinderella?" Scarlet said.

"How did you recognize me? Do I have soot on my nose?"

"Oh, no . . . I just assumed . . . having gotten your invitation. . . ." Scarlet was filled with confusion, but Cinderella laughed and put her at ease. "It was just my little jest! I am so glad you could come. I heard you are under a sleeping spell."

"Actually it's a napping spell. But how did you hear about it?"

"Word gets around in the domain of fairy tales," Cinderella said. "If you should need them, we have resting rooms upstairs, and a variety of stimulants if your spell responds to chemical means."

"No need," Scarlet said. "I was able to get a temporary rescindment."

"However you did it, I am very glad you could come. This is the debutante event of the season, you know. We have many eligible bachelors here, mostly of the nobility, but also a few enterprising and famous commoners like Jack of the Beanstalk and Peer Gynt. Come, let me get you a glass of champagne and introduce you to some people."

Cinderella gave Scarlet a foaming glass of champagne and, taking her hand, led her around from one group of gorgeously dressed people to the next. Scarlet's head was awhirl, and the music—loud, rhythmic—was setting her dancer's toes to tapping. She was pleased when a tall, dark, handsome man in a gold lamé suit and crimson turban asked her to dance.

They whirled around the dance floor. The turbaned man introduced himself as Achmed Ali. He was a fine dancer, conversant with the newest steps. Scarlet had a dancer's quick instinct for dance steps, and so she soon found herself doing the straddle duck, the limping elbow, the pigmy hop, the delirious dogleg, and the double wolverine, all dance sensations of that eventful year of the Millennium. Achmed Ali seemed to float across the floor, matching her consummate skill with his own scarcely in-

ferior efforts. The other dancers moved back to clear a
space for them, so obviously superior were they to the
common lot. The orchestra segued into *Swan Lake*, so bal-
letic was the spectacle before them. Around and around
Scarlet and Achmed whirled while the trumpets blasted
and the steel guitars whined, turning ever more daring
pas de deux, whirling, tapping, stamping, as the applause
mounted. At last, for the finale, Achmed Ali danced her
out of the ballroom and onto a little balcony.

The balcony overlooked a little lake. The moon had
just risen, and little silvery ripples moved slowly toward
the dark shore. Princess Scarlet fanned herself with the
Chinese fan that Supply had provided and, turning to
Achmed Ali, said in formal tones, "Belike, sir, I've not
seen thy match for overall all-in dancing eftsoons."

"Nor I thine," Achmed answered gallantly. His face,
which was spread neatly along either side of his hawk
nose, had firm, finely cut lips of pale pink behind which
teeth of a nacreous white could be seen when he smiled or
lifted his lip in the small sneer with which he expressed
emotion. He told Scarlet that he was a prince from the
court of the Grand Turk, whose lands stretched from the
misty frontier of eastern Turkestan to the sea-shrouded
coastline of hither Asia. He described the splendor of the
Grand Turk's palace, which had so many rooms that they
were uncountable save by those skilled in mathematical
necromancy. He told her of the palace's main features,
the carp ponds, the mineral springs, the great library
where could be found writings from all over the world.
He mentioned the kitchens where delicacies of unusual
splendor were prepared every day for the delectation of
the ensemble of happy and talented young people who
made up the court. He told her how she would dazzle all
of the beauties of that court with the previously unheard-
of splendor of her delicate and finely proportioned features. He declared that he, despite their short acquain-
tanceship, was utterly and entirely smitten with her, and
begged her to accompany him so he could show her the

splendors of the Grand Turk's domain and, if she so desired, stay on for a while. He described the luxurious presents that he would shower on her, and he went on in that vein and similar veins and tendentious arteries of teasing promises for so long that the Princess' head was turned and turned again.

"I would like to go with you and see these things," Princess Scarlet said. "But I promised my aunt that I would return home immediately after the ball."

"No problem," Achmed said. He snapped his fingers. There was a flapping sound in the air, and Princess Scarlet beheld a large and luxurious Persian carpet which had come seemingly from nowhere and hovered now at the level of the balcony.

"This is a flying carpet," Achmed said. "It is a common means of transport in my land, and by utilizing it I can take you to the Grand Turk's court, show you around, and return you to this very spot before the evening is out."

"It is very tempting," Scarlet said. "But I really shouldn't. . . ."

Achmed Ali smiled a subtle smile of incredible attractiveness and stepped from the balcony onto the carpet. He turned to Scarlet, extending his hand.

"Come with me, beautiful princess," he said. "I am crazy about you and I will show you a very good time and respect you throughout and I will have you back here in plenty of time to return to your esteemed aunt as you had originally planned."

Princess Scarlet knew she shouldn't. But the unexpected freedom, the temporary relief from the napping spell, the grandeur of the ball, the mysterious and tantalizing presence of Achmed Ali, the glass of unaccustomed champagne, and the perfume of the Mater Delirium plant that grew beneath the balcony all combined to make her senses reel and cause a feeling of boldness to come over her. Scarcely knowing what she was doing, she accepted Achmed's hand and stepped onto the carpet.

# Chapter
# 8

Cinderella was just about to go to the sumptuous buffet and get herself another glass of champagne, and perhaps a plate of sherbet, too, when a footman came up to her, bowed low, and said, "There is a someone, Princess, who wishes to converse with you."

"A man?"

"A demon, I opine, though manlike for all of that."

"A demon," Cinderella mused. "I don't remember asking any demons."

"I believe he came on his own recognizance, Princess," said the footman, straining to find enough time to mention that he, the footman, was himself a prince in disguise.

"What does he want?"

"I do not know," the footman said, brushing his wrist against his luxuriant mustache. "He claims it is a matter of great importance."

This exchange might have gone on longer if at that

moment Azzie hadn't come striding up with two doormen clinging to his coattails trying to restrain him.

Azzie gave a shrug that sent them sprawling, and said, "You are Cinderella?"

"Yes, I am."

"And this is your party?"

"Yes, it is. And in case you're thinking of crashing it, I have demons of my own whom I can call up at a moment's notice."

"It seems that you invited my niece, Princess Scarlet, to your festivities."

Cinderella glanced around. Several of the guests seemed to be taking an interest in the conversation, and the footman was still hanging around twirling his ridiculous mustache as he tried to insert himself and his bogus credentials into the proceedings.

"Come over here to the secret bower," Cinderella said. "There we can talk quietly."

They walked to the bower.

"You can put your broomsticks in the corner," Cinderella said.

"I think I'll hold on to them. Enough small talk. Where's Scarlet?"

"Are you really her uncle? You shouldn't have left the child alone so long in that enchanted castle. I didn't think it would do any harm to invite her to my party."

"Where is she right now?" Azzie said, his foot tapping ominously.

Cinderella looked around, but she couldn't see Scarlet. She called over a footman—another one, not the one with the mustache—this one had a little goatee—and told him to find Princess Scarlet.

In a moment the footman hurried back. "I am told she left with the turbaned gentleman, Achmed Ali."

Azzie turned to the footman. "How did they depart?"

"By flying carpet, milord."

Azzie rubbed his chin and looked thoughtful. "And in what direction did they head?"

"Due east, milord."

"Do you know who this man is?" he asked Cinderella.

"He's a nobleman from the courts of the Grand Turk, ruler of all Turkestan."

"Is that all you know?"

"Know you something *al contrario*?"

"Did he tell you his court position?"

"No, not specifically."

"He is the Chief Procurer for the Seraglio of the Grand Turk."

"How do you know this?"

"I make it my business to know such things," Azzie said.

"Procurer! Surely you don't mean—"

"I mean," Azzie said, "that Princess Scarlet is at this very moment being transported across international boundaries for purposes of white slavery and imperial prostitution."

"I had no idea!" Princess Cinderella said. "Where is my grand vizier? Strike Achmed Ali's name from the guest list! Put a double line through it! My dear demon, I can't tell you how sorry I am—"

But she was talking to herself. Azzie had already leaped to the rail of the balcony and, pausing only to activate the brooms' drive mechanisms, soared off onto the ambient air, going east, due east.


Flying carpets are swift, powered as they are by the strongest spells of mighty djinns. But they are not aerodynamically efficient and tend to be unstable. The leading edge of a carpet in flight invariably curls up like the front of a toboggan and provides an airfoil that slows flight. Still, Achmed was making good time. As for Scarlet, she had started to think about her situation and found it a little less delicious than she had earlier. As she looked at Achmed, sitting tailor fashion at the carpet's controls, she noticed the cruel lines etched down his face, which some-

how she had overlooked earlier, and the angry way his
black mustache curled down and then back up again, ter-
minating in needle-sharp waxed points. It occurred to her
that she had been just a touch precipitous when she had
accepted this invitation. It was only then that she thought
about Prince Charming, her intended. He might even
now be entering the enchanted castle. What if he arrived
and didn't find her and went away and found someone
else? Would she be doomed to live alone under the napping spell for the rest of her life? Was there any salvation
for Napping Beauties who have the bad luck not to be
found by their Prince Charmings? And anyhow, what
was she getting herself into and was this Achmed really
sincere?

"Achmed," she said, "I have changed my mind."

"Indeed?" Achmed said, in an offhand way.

"I want to go back to Cinderella's party now."

"The Grand Turk's court is just a little way from
here," Achmed said.

"I don't care! I want to turn back right now!"

Achmed turned to her, and now his face was ugly
with machismo, self-pride, hatred, bad faith, as well as a
touch of pusillanimity. "Little Princess, you have chosen
this adventure, and now there is no turning back."

"Why are you doing this?" she asked. "There comes a
time when only the truth will suffice.

"It is my job," he replied, "and my master, the Grand
Turk, will reward me well for adding you to his seraglio.
Need I put it any clearer?"

"I'm not going to any seraglio! I'll die first!" Scarlet
said. She moved to the edge of the carpet. Peering over,
she saw, far below, the isles of Greece, dark lumps in a
milk-white sea. She decided that things weren't so extreme as to warrant suicide, at least not yet.

She shrank back to the middle of the carpet, already
mourning the handsome young prince who she seemed
destined now never to meet. She brushed back her long
hair, which was getting ratty from the wind, and saw,

behind her—for that was the direction in which she turned in order to ease a crink in her neck—a tiny speck in the sky moving directly toward them. The speck grew, and hope blossomed in Scarlet's heart, and she turned away so as not to betray her emotions or her discovery to Achmed.

Azzie, driving the two broomsticks at full throttle, saw the flying carpet ahead of him, outlined fantastically against the full moon, and he closed in, his eyes slitted against the airstream. His rage seemed to power the broomsticks even faster. He gained rapidly on the flying carpet, and then, coming up behind and above it, nosed the broomsticks over into a power dive.

The first thing Achmed Ali knew about this was when he heard a great sound that surpassed even the roar of the slipstream and, turning, saw a fox-faced demon astride two blazing broomsticks, diving down on him from above. Achmed threw the carpet into a sideslip, hanging on to Scarlet with one hand as the carpet fell through the sky. Scarlet shrieked because they seemed certain to crash. But Achmed pulled out only a few feet above the shining sea. He turned the carpet to bring its spell-powered thunderbolts into play. Not for the first time did he wish he had the new super thunderbolts, but the Grand Turk, profligate in matters concerning his seraglio, was stingy when it came to updating the armament of his flying carpets.

Before Achmed Ali could bring his standard-issue weapons to bear, Azzie was firing at him with jagged lightning bolts, the short, explosive, painful kind. Achmed dodged and swerved, but the bolts of lightning came closer and closer, singeing the edges of the carpet and spoiling its meager airflow characteristics. Achmed found that no matter how hard he tugged, the web and woof lines would no longer control the craft. The carpet tilted precipitously and Achmed had to grab an edge with both hands. Released from his grip, Princess Scarlet slid to the edge of the carpet, now tilted almost to the perpendicular, over the side, and into the air.

She fell, and so great was her terror that not even a scream could come out of her paralyzed lips. The sea came up fast, and there was a steep little island in the middle of it rising at her with incredible rapidity.

Death seemed certain. But at the last possible moment, as the needle-pointed rock pinnacles were reaching for her with hard granite fingers, Azzie swooped beneath her and scooped her up, draping her over the broomsticks like a sack of flour on a terrestrial pack animal. Scarlet could feel the g-forces build as Azzie barrel-rolled around the mountain and tried to break out of the dive that seemed sure to take them into the white-mouthed sea. And then he had pulled them out of it, and they were soaring into the air again, safe!

"Oh, Uncle Azzie," Scarlet said, "I'm so glad to see you! I was so frightened!"

"You were very naughty," Azzie said. "If it weren't so late in the game, I'd let you go to the Grand Turk's seraglio and make myself a new Princess Scarlet. My young Prince deserves a faithful heart!"

Scarlet said, "I'll never run away again, I promise. I'll nap quietly in my chamber and await his coming."

"At least a moral point about obedience has been made from all this," Azzie said, and turned the broomsticks in the direction of the enchanted castle.

# Chapter
# 9

After recovering his credit card and putting Princess Scarlet back where she belonged, Azzie continued on to Paris, long one of his favorite cities. He had decided to stay away from Augsburg for a few days in order to give Prince Charming a chance to moon over the miniature of Princess Scarlet which he had been forbidden to touch, and so fall in love with her according to the rules of psychology.

What better way to pass some time than in riotous living in one of the satanic clubs that Paris was famous for even then?

The one he chose, the Heliogabulus Club, was in a cave under Paris. After going down an endless flight of stone stairs, he came out in a grotto furnished with skulls and skeletons. Torches flamed in their iron wall-holders, casting gloomy shadows here and there. The tables were sarcophagi brought in by some ingenious entrepreneur from Egypt, where they have a never-ending supply of them. Coffins of the more ordinary sort served as chairs.

Drinks were served by menials dressed in priests' cassocks and nuns' habits. These wretches also served as complaisant bodies for the orgies that climaxed most evenings' entertainments. Sex and death: it was one of Europe's first theme bars.

"What'll you have?" a heavyset man in priest's garb asked Azzie.

"Give me an expensive imported beer," Azzie told him. "And do you have anything to eat?"

"Nachos," the servitor said.

"What are they?"

"Something which François the Expeditious brought back from the New World."

So Azzie had the nachos, which turned out to be oat chips covered in a smelly Camembert with tomato sauce over them. He washed them down with a piggard of dark ale imported from England and started feeling better at once.

As Azzie was eating he had the feeling that someone was watching him. He began looking around the room. There was a table in a far corner which was dark, unlighted even by a candle. He could perceive movement in the gloom. The sense of being watched seemed to emanate from there.

Azzie decided to ignore it at first. He ordered up another plate of nachos and switched to wine. After a while he began to grow tipsy. Then, as the evening rollicked on, Azzie became drunk. Not just pig drunk, but demon drunk. That was very drunk indeed. He began to sing a little song that demons from Canaan sing when they are having a good time. The lines went:

> Oh, I am feeling no pain
> And I haven't any name
> For the fine old fun
> That often doth come
> When I'm drunk and feeling no pain.

The song had several other verses, but he was having difficulty remembering them, or, indeed, anything else. It was very late. He had the feeling he'd been in this place a long time. Looking around, he saw that the other patrons had fled. What had they put into his wine? He was dizzy now; far more than tipsy, he was staggering drunk. There was an odd feeling in the pit of his stomach, and he wasn't sure he could stand up. Finally, with great deliberation, he brought himself to his feet. "Who's doing this to me?" he said, but the words came out all garbled.

"Hello there, Azzie," a voice said behind him.

Azzie had the feeling he'd heard this voice before. He tried to turn around. But just then something heavy crashed into the back of his head, near the left ear, always a delicate spot in demons. Normally he could throw off the effects of a blow like that. You don't put a demon down easily. But this time, combined with the strong spirits and with whatever somebody may have mixed into the drink, he had no resistance. Damnation! He had gotten himself into a spot. And that was all he thought at the moment, because he passed out so quickly he wasn't aware of doing so until much later.

# Chapter 10

Azzie awoke some undetermined time later. He came back to consciousness groggily and not too happily. He had a hangover which was monumental in its size and extent. He tried to roll over to ease the aching in his head and found that he could only move slightly. His arms seemed to be tied. Also his legs. And he himself was strapped to a very large chair.

He opened his eyes two or three times, experimentally, then opened them definitively and looked around. He was in a sort of underground grotto. He could see the walls of the cave, shining with phosphorescence from the mica in the rocks.

"Hello!" he called. "Is anyone there?"

"Oh, yes, I'm here all right," a voice said.

Azzie strained and after a while perceived a figure in the gloom. It was a small figure, and it had a beard. He recognized the features, such features as were visible under all the facial hair.

"Rognir!" For it was indeed the dwarf whom he had gotten to give him the felixite and his treasure.

"Greetings, Azzie," Rognir said. His voice was bright with malice. "Not feeling too good?"

"Not exactly good, no," Azzie said. "But never mind, I've got great powers of recuperation. I seem to be entangled in something that is holding me to this chair. If you would kindly release me, and give me a drink of water, I think I'd be quite all right."

"Release you?" Rognir said. His laughter was scornful, as the laughter of dwarves so often is. Others joined in, following it up with mutterings.

"Who are you talking to?" Azzie asked. Now that his eyes were growing more accustomed to things, he could see that there were other figures in the cavern with him and Rognir. They were small men, dwarves all, and their eyes glittered as they stood in a ring, peering up at him.

"These are dwarves of my tribe," Rognir said. "I could make introductions, but why bother? You aren't going to be here long enough for small talk and amusing conversation."

"But what is this all about?" Azzie said, though he had a pretty good idea.

"You owe me, that's what it's about," Rognir said.

"I know that. But is this any way to discuss it?"

"Your servant wouldn't allow us in when we came to talk to you about it."

"That Frike," Azzie said with a chuckle. "He's so protective."

"Perhaps he is. But I want my money. And I'm here to collect. Immediately. At this moment."

Azzie shrugged. "You've probably already gone through my pockets. You know I don't have anything on me but small change and a spare charm or two."

"You don't even have that anymore," Rognir said. "We took them away."

"Then what more do you want?"

"Payment! I want not only the profit you promised me on my treasure, but the treasure itself back."

Azzie gave a small, amused laugh. "My dear fellow! There was no need for all this. As a matter of fact, I'd come to Paris for the purpose of finding you and telling you how well your investment was doing."

"Hah!" Rognir said, an expletive which could have meant anything but probably implied disbelief.

"Come now, Rognir, there's no need of this. Release me and we'll talk it over like gentlemen."

"You are no gentleman," Rognir said. "You are a demon."

"And you're a dwarf," Azzie said. "But you know what I mean."

"I want my money."

"You seem to have forgotten that the deal was for a year," Azzie said. "The time's not up. You're doing well. When the time runs out you'll get your capital back."

"I've been thinking this over, and I've decided that I don't trust the notion of putting one's capital out to work this way. It seems it might do something terrible to the working classes—like us dwarves. You know, a jewel in the sack is worth two or three on some foreign market that might go bust."

"A deal's a deal," Azzie said, "and you agreed to let me have it for a year."

"Well, I'm disagreeing now. I want my poke back."

"I can't do anything for you tied up like this," Azzie said.

"But if we release you, you'll pop out a spell and that'll be it for us and our money."

That was exactly what Azzie had been planning. To turn attention away from it, he said, "What is this 'us' stuff? Why are these other dwarves involved?"

"They're my partners in this venture," Rognir said. "Maybe you can talk around me, but you won't get around them so easily."

One of the dwarves came forward. He was short even

for a dwarf, and his beard was white except around the mouth, where it was stained yellow from chewing tobacco.

"I am Elgar," he said. "You have hoodwinked this simpleminded dwarf Rognir, but you're not going to get away with that with us. Give us back our money immediately. Or else."

"I told you," Azzie said. "I can't do anything with both my arms tied. I can't even blow my nose."

"Why would you want to blow your nose?" Elgar said. "It's not running."

"It was a figure of speech," Azzie said. "What I meant—"

"We know what you meant," Elgar said. "You're not going to put anything over on us. We have plans for you, my fine friend, since you can't pay."

"I can pay, but not trussed to a chair like this!" He smiled in a winning manner. "Untie me and give me a chance to go after some funds. I'll come right back, and I'll swear any oath you please to that effect."

"You're not going anywhere," Elgar said. "If we give you an inch, you'll be all over us with your damnable enchantments. No, you have a count of three to produce everything you owe to Rognir. One, two, three. No money? That's that, then."

"What do you mean?" Azzie asked. "What's what?"

"You're for it, that's what's what."

"For what?"

Elgar turned to the others. "Okay, boys, let's take him to the Wheel of Labor."

That was something Azzie had never heard of before. But it looked as if he were going to learn soon what it was. Small horny hands, lots of them, lifted the chair with Azzie in it and bore it deeper into the cavern.

# Chapter
# 11

The dwarves sang as they went down the tunnel, deeper and deeper into the bowels of the earth, around doglegs and over camelbacks, skirting cul-de-sacs and precipices and wading across icy streams. It was so dark that Azzie's eyes began to ache from trying too hard to see something. They went on, and they sang other songs after a while, songs in a language Azzie did not understand, and at last they came to an opening which let out onto a large underground plain.

"Where's this?" Azzie asked. They ignored him. Many little hands held him tight as they untied him from the chair and tied him to something else. By touch Azzie thought it was a framework of some sort, made of metal and bits of wood. When he tried to take a step, something moved under his feet. He realized after a few moments that he had been tied securely to the inside of a big wheel, like a waterwheel. His feet were free, but his hands were securely bound to handles that came out of the wheel's sides.

"This," Rognir said, "is a work wheel. You walk inside it and it turns, and through a series of gears, it moves a wheel that turns rods and finally operates machinery in one of the upper chambers."

"Interesting," Azzie said. "But so what?"

"You are expected to walk on the wheel, thus turning it. You will thus help us work and you will pay off your debt that way. It should only take a few hundred years."

"Forget it," Azzie said.

"Suit yourself," Rognir said. "All right, boys, open the sluice gate."

There was a grinding sound from overhead. Then something started falling from above him. It was a rain of excrement, as Azzie's nose quickly told him. But it was not ordinary human or demonic excrement. Azzie had spent plenty of time handling that. This was excrement of an orduosity so extreme that his nasal receptors tried to commit hara-kiri.

"What is that stuff?" he cried.

"Aged fermented dragon shit," Rognir told him. "We're close to a dragon's lair, and we've tapped it from the bottom as an incentive for you to go to work."

Azzie's feet started moving of their own accord. The wheel turned. After a moment, the rain of dragon shit stopped.

"The way it works," Rognir said, "the dragon shit starts when you stop treading, and continues until you start up again."

"But what about rest periods?" Azzie asked.

"We'll tell you when you can rest," Elgar said, and the other dwarves laughed.

"But listen to me! I've got important things to do! You must let me out of here so I can make arrangements! I'll pay you back—"

"You will indeed," Rognir said. "In kind or in labor. Check with you later, demon."

And so the dwarves departed. Azzie was left alone, pumping and thinking desperate thoughts.

# Chapter
# 12

Azzie walked, turning the wheel, annoyed at himself for not telling Frike where he'd gone. He'd simply left the house, not giving his servant any instructions. And now, just when there was great need for haste, because it was time and past time for the adventure of Prince Charming to begin, he was caught in the darkness beneath Paris and condemned to turn a wheel for a bunch of stupid dwarves.

"Hi, there," a voice said. "Are you a demon?"

"Who's talking to me?"

"Look down near your right foot and you'll see me."

Azzie looked down and saw a worm about six inches long.

"You're a worm?"

"Yes, I'm a worm. You're a demon?"

"That is correct. And if you can help me, I can offer you a deal you can't turn down."

"What is that?" the worm asked.

"If you'll help me get out of here, I'll make you king of the worms."

"Actually, we worms don't have a king. We have district leaders, and a high council."

"I'll put you in charge of the council."

"First I have to become a district leader in order to become eligible."

"So all right, I'll make you a district leader. What's your name?"

"Elton Wormbrood. But my friends call me Tom."

"Okay, Tom, what about it? Will you help me?"

"I might. It's been pretty quiet down here. I just might help you in order to relieve the tedium. Then again, I might not."

"Well, which is it going to be?"

"I'm not sure. Don't rush me. We worms are kind of sluggish thinkers."

"Sorry. Take your time. . . . Have you had enough time yet?"

"No, I haven't even begun to think about it."

Azzie controlled his impatience. "All right, take all the time you want. Call me when you've decided."

The worm didn't reply.

"Is that all right?" Azzie asked.

"Is what all right?"

"That you'll tell me when you've made up your mind."

"That sounds all right," the worm said. "But don't get your hopes up."

"Don't worry about it. I'll wait."

And so Azzie began to wait and continued turning the wheel. He could hear the worm moving very softly about the chamber, now on the surface, now burrowing under the earth and rock. Time passed. Azzie couldn't tell how much time. It felt like an awful lot of it. What was annoying was that Azzie's chest itched. An itch is a most uncommonly irritating thing when your hands are tied to a wheel. Azzie found that by arching backward, he could just reach around to the front with his tail. Carefully now, since his tail was very sharp-pointed, Azzie scratched himself.

It felt wonderful. But annoyingly enough, there was something which blocked a really satisfying scratch. He worked the end of his tail carefully up and around it. Yes, there it was. Clenching it in his tail, he brought it out farther where he could see it. It was a couple of inches long and seemed to be made of metal.

"I'm still thinking," the worm said.

"That's good," Azzie answered. He lowered his head and got the cord from which the object hung up and over it. He lowered the object and touched it with his fingertips, first retracting his claws for better tactile contact. It seemed to be a key. Yes, it *was* a key! Azzie remembered now. He had kept a spare key to the castle hanging about his neck, where it would be safe no matter how many times he changed his clothing. It was a common sort of key, and it had a small red gem set into its handle. And inside the gem, he remembered now, there was a small spell that he had put there and forgotten about.

He said to the spell, "What is your name and what do you do?"

A tiny voice from the red gem said, "I am Dirigan. I open doorways."

"Gee, that's great," Azzie said. "How about getting these bindings off me?"

"Let me take a look at them," Dirigan said.

Azzie passed the key over his manacled hands. The light within the jewel pulsed softly, throwing out a ruddy glow.

"I think I can do something about this." The jewel glowed more fiercely, then died out. The manacles fell open.

Azzie's hands came free. "Now, guide me out."

The worm lifted his blunt head and said, "I'm still thinking."

"I wasn't talking to you," Azzie said.

"Oh. Just as well. Because I still haven't made up my mind."

"What mind?" Azzie muttered. With his hands free he felt strong, capable of action again. He moved away from the wheel. Let the dragon shit rain down now! He was out of its way!

"Now," he said, "to find the way out. Spell, give me some light."

The jewel pulsed more brightly, throwing shadows across the cavern walls. Azzie walked until he came to a branching of the ways. There were five different directions he could go in. He asked the jewel, "What way should I head now?"

"How should I know?" said the jewel. "I'm just a minor spell. And now I'm used up."

The light faded out.

Azzie had heard about these underground branchings of the dwarves. They held great menace, for often the tunnel floor was undercut so that someone passing over them would fall through. Down below there were pits, noisome places filled with nasty things. If he fell into one of those, he might never get back up. And the worst of it was, Azzie, like many other demons, was virtually immortal. He could stay in the deepest pit for ages, perhaps forever, alive but bored, if no one came to bring him out. There were stories of demons who had been buried by some misadventure or other. Some of them were said still to be trapped underground, where they had been since earliest times.

He moved forward. He heard the worm rustle, then say, "That's not the right way."

Azzie stepped back. "What way should I go?"

"I still haven't made up my mind whether to help you or not."

"You'd better decide pretty soon," Azzie said. "The offer isn't open indefinitely."

"Oh, all right," Tom Wormbrood said. "I guess I'll help. Take the tunnel on the farthest right."

Azzie did so. As soon as he entered it the ground gave way beneath his feet. He was falling. He just had time to scream, "But you said this one was safe!"

"I lied!" the worm cried. "Ha-ha!"

Azzie was falling, falling.

But it was only a short drop. Five feet perhaps. And to his right was a metal door, marked with a faintly phosphorescent EXIT.

Cursing, he pushed through.

# Chapter 13

In Augsburg, Frike was wringing his hands, pacing up and down the front yard, watching the sky for a sign of the return of his beloved master. Then he saw a tiny dark speck, which resolved itself quickly into Azzie.

"Oh, master, at last you have returned!"

"As quickly as I was able," Azzie said. "I was detained by a family of dwarves, a load of dragon manure, a work wheel, and a schizophrenic worm. I hope you have had as pleasant a time and kept a watch on Prince Charming."

Frike's face twisted in sorrow. "I watched out for him, sire, as well as I was able. Dragon manure?"

"Dragon manure. Did he break my stricture and go to the locked room upstairs?"

"That he did, master."

"And once within it, did he find the small locked casket in the upper drawer of my bureau in the closet?"

"He went to it at once, master," Frike said.

"And opening it, did he find the little miniature of the Princess Scarlet?"

"That he did, sire, that he did."

"Then why don't you tell me in your own ill-chosen words what transpired next?"

"Well, sire, the Prince looked upon the visage of the Princess, then looked away, then looked again. Holding the miniature in his left hand, he tugged at his lip thoughtfully with his right. He cleared his throat, going 'ahem, ahem,' like a man who knows not what to say yet feels under a compulsion to say something. He set the miniature down very gently and turned and walked a stride or two away. Then he returned and raised it again. Then he put it down, looked away, and with his left hand this time, pulled gently at his upper lip."

"This is a wonderful detailing, Frike," Azzie said. "But could you get to the nitty-gritty, as the heart of the matter is sometimes described?"

"Most certainly, sir. After bemusing himself with repeated looks, or I could more properly call them glances, at the portrait of the young lady in question, he turned to me and said, 'Frike, this girl is a corker.' "

"Those were his words, eh?"

"His very words, sir. I didn't know what to respond to that, master, so I made a low bestial noise deep in my throat, figuring the young man could interpret it in any way he pleased. Was that all right, sire?"

"Very judicious, Frike. And what happened?"

"Why, master, he paced around a time or two, and then he turned to me and said, 'Why has Uncle Azzie been keeping this from me?' "

"A-ha," Azzie said.

"Beg pardon, sir?"

"Never mind, it was a meaningless interjection. What did you say to him?"

"I said, 'For reasons best known to himself, young Prince,' and again made the low bestial noise in my throat."

"That was well done, Frike. And what happened after that?"

"After more staring at the painting, and fumbling with his lip, and various other movements which I leave out for the sake of brevity, he said, 'Frike, I must have her.'"

"I knew my scheme would work!" Azzie said. "What else did he say?"

"That was all for the first day," Frike said. "By the second, he was getting impatient. He wanted to know where you were. Since he is a dutiful lad, he wanted your permission before he set forth after her."

"Good lad," Azzie said. "Where is he now?"

"Gone," Frike said. "Soon after, he decided he couldn't wait."

"But where did he go?"

"Why, after the Princess Scarlet, of course. Just as you wanted him to. He waited five days, master, and longer he could not abide due to the fever of passion her picture had inspired in him. Was that not how you wished it, master?"

"Of course. But he needed to have instructions first and the special quest hunting equipment. What did he take?"

"He went into the heavy-equipment closet and selected a sword and armor from the equipment hanging on the wall. And then he took some money you had left in the chest of drawers and said he was on his way and to tell you he'd be back with the Princess and hoped you wouldn't be annoyed with him."

"Damnation!" Azzie cried. He stamped his foot and sank into the earth up to his waist. He extricated himself with difficulty.

Babriel had wandered out of the house upon Azzie's arrival. He had listened and now said, "What's the matter? He's doing what you want him to, isn't he?"

"Yes, but he shouldn't have left yet," Azzie said. "I've set up this quest to be difficult and dangerous. It's the only kind that will get the attention of the High Powers. He is going up against dangerous matters of magic, which common men had best leave alone. And he has none of the magic protection I have been collecting for him."

"What, then?" Babriel asked.

"I must get the things that he needs to him," Azzie said. "And I need to do this quickly, quickly! Did he tell you where he planned to begin his search?"

"Not a word of it, sire."

"Well then, which way did he go?"

"He went straight ahead that way," Frike said, pointing. Azzie looked in the direction indicated. "North," he muttered. "He went north. A bad omen. Frike, we must find him before it's too late."

# NONES

# Chapter
1

Prince Charming rode alone into the great green forest, beyond the familiar fields and hills, into the terra incognita that lay beyond. His way took him into the north, and as he rode he thought about swords. He knew that a Fairly Lucky Sword was not as good as a Truly Enchanted Sword, but it was a lot better than an ordinary sword. He held up the Fairly Lucky Sword and looked at it. It was an exceedingly handsome weapon, with its nicely curling pommel and the tassels around the grip. This was one of the loveliest swords he'd ever seen. It was considerably smaller than the big broadswords that were in vogue in those days, and it was a straight sword, without a curve, none of your Turkish curlicues, thank you very much. It was double edged, sharpened on both sides, and it had a needle point. This would be enough in itself to establish it as one of a special class of sword, since most ordinary swords were only edged on one side and were hardly ever pointed.

The Fairly Lucky Sword was a nice weapon, but it

had its problems. There is a general class of Enchanted
Swords, and Azzie, in haste to find a magical weapon for
his protégé, didn't look at the bin he took it out of. He
might have thought all Enchanted Swords were the same.
He didn't realize that "enchanted" was a generic term for
a certain type of sword; that is to say, swords with enchantments of one sort or another upon them.

Enchanted Swords differ greatly in efficacy. There are
(or used to be) Unbreakable Swords, and those that
never lose their temper. Swords that unerringly kill their
opponents are exceedingly rare, although that is the quality every sword-builder tries to get into his blade. All-
Conquering Swords can be found from time to time, but
these puissant blades generally don't outlast the life of
their owner, who, since he can't be overcome man to man
in swordsmanship, is typically poisoned by a close friend,
a wife, or a wife of a close friend. Even with a perfect
sword, humans don't get out of this world alive.

Prince Charming rode through the tangled forest. It
was, of course, an enchanted forest. Magical trees just
stood there, dark and gloomy, a green world with black
shapes flitting across it. This was like the ancient wood of
the Old World, concealing hordes of monsters.

Charming came at length into a clearing, in a bright
little meadow surrounded on all sides by darkness and
menace. At the far end Charming could see a pavilion
made of green and orange cloth. A large black horse was
tethered to a tree nearby, tall and fine, a proper battle
horse.

Charming walked forward and approached the pavilion. There were arms piled outside it: heavy, black armor,
splendidly made, encrusted here and there with pearls.
Whoever it belonged to, he must be wealthy and doubt-
less powerful.

Charming saw that there was a slughorn hanging
from a standard outside the tent. He raised the horn and
blew a loud blast. Before the echo had faded, there was a
stirring within the pavilion. Then a man emerged. He was

large, black-haired, and scowling. He dragged beside him a fair maiden in a swooning mode.

"Now who is this blows my slughorn?" the knight said. He was clad in brightly striped smallclothes. Seeing Charming, he scowled more deeply.

"La, sir, I am Prince Charming," Charming said. "And I ride forth to rescue the Princess Scarlet from her sleeping spell."

"Ha!" said the knight.

"Why do you say 'ha'?" asked Charming.

"Because it behooves me to make a scornful sound on hearing of this slight and utterly insignificant quest of yours."

"I suppose your quest is more important?"

"Of a surety it is!" the man replied confidently. "For know, young man, that I am Parsifal, and I quest after no less a thing than the Holy Grail."

"The Grail, huh?" said Charming. "Is it really in these parts?"

"Of course it is. This is the enchanted forest. In it subsist all things, and the Holy Grail is sure to be found here."

"What about the woman?" Charming asked.

"Beg pardon?"

"That woman you're holding by the hair."

Parsifal looked down. "Oh, her. She signifies nothing."

"But what are you doing with her?"

"Must I spell it out?"

"Of course not! What I mean is—"

"I know what you mean," Parsifal said. "She is here for me to toy with until the Grail is in sight."

"I see," said Charming. "By the way, do you need that horse?"

"My horse?" said Parsifal.

"Just thought I'd ask. Because if you don't, I could sure use him. He's a lot bigger and stronger than mine."

"This is the weirdest thing I've heard in a long time,"

said Parsifal. "This child knight scarcely dry behind the ears comes riding into my camp and he wants to know do I need my horse. Why, no, certainly not, fellow. You can have him if you want him."

"Thanks," Charming said. He dismounted. "That's really uncommon kind of you."

"But first," Parsifal said, "you will have to fight me for him."

"I was afraid there'd be a condition attached."

"Yes, there is. I see you have a Fairly Lucky Sword."

"I do," Charming said, drawing it and holding it out. "Nice, isn't it?"

"Nice," Parsifal agreed, "but of course it's not an Enchanted Sword like mine." He drew his own and showed it to Charming.

"I don't suppose," Charming said, "a sword like mine would be much good against a sword like yours."

"No, in all honesty, I don't think so," Parsifal said. "Fairly Lucky Swords aren't bad, but you can't expect much of them against a real Enchanted Sword."

"I didn't think so. Look, do we really have to fight?"

"I'm afraid we do," Parsifal said, and attacked.

Prince Charming jumped out of the way and swung his Fairly Lucky Sword. The two swords clanged together with an uncanny sound. This was succeeded by an even more uncanny sound when Prince Charming's blade broke.

"I win!" cried Parsifal, swinging up his Enchanted Sword for the death stroke. "Gawg!"

Charming thought he was finished, so he used his final seconds to think over his memories, which in his case didn't take very long.

But Charming's time on Earth was not quite up. Since his sword had been Fairly Lucky, and a very good example of its kind, it happened that when it broke, a single bright shard of metal had flown upward, penetrating Parsifal's throat, where the gorget revealed a fraction of an inch of flesh.

This was the cause of the "Gawg!" Parsifal voiced, before he fell to the earth with a thunderous sound.

"Sorry, but you asked for it," Charming said. He turned and moved away, figuring that someone else would be along after a while to bury the man.

"Take the handsome sword," a voice recommended.

"Who said that?" Charming asked.

"Me," Parsifal's sword explained. "Take the horse, too."

"Who are you?" Charming asked.

"They call me Excalibur," the sword said.

"What do they say about you?"

"Read my runes," the sword answered.

Charming took up the sword and looked at its gleaming blade. Sure enough, there were runes engraved there, though he couldn't understand them. He looked at the sword with respect and said, "Why did you speak to me?"

"I'm not supposed to," the sword admitted. "But I couldn't just let you walk away and leave me. I'll be out of work, and I love my work. You'll find me very useful. If anyone gives you trouble, they'll have me to answer to."

As Charming turned toward the horse, "Hold, sir!" cried the maiden, rising from her semirecumbent position upon the earth. "I beg thee succor me, by thy knightly oath."

Not recalling any oaths of a knightly sort, Charming nevertheless replied, "What sort of succor did you have in mind?"

"I am a Valkyrie," she explained, "and this man overpowered me on a battlefield by feigning death to lure me near. I can only go home to Walhall now if I summon the Rainbow Bridge and have a suitable trophy to take with me. Can you help me locate my horn, which he appropriated?"

"That seems easy enough," Charming replied, "especially if it's the slughorn I blew on my approach. Is that it hanging from the standard by the tent?"

"Indeed it is," she replied, crossing to it, raising it to her lips, and winding it in an eerie fashion.

Instantly, the end of a rainbow fell from the sky, barely missing Charming.

"Thank you, good sir," she stated, commencing to gather Parsifal's armor.

"Don't you want the dead knight?" Charming asked. "I thought you ladies collected them."

"I've no use for a knight who can't keep his myths straight," she observed. "Good armor, on the other hand, is hard to come by." She dinged the breastplate with a sharpened fingernail, carried the pieces to the rainbow, blew him a kiss, called, "Be seeing you," and vanished in a flash of light.

Charming rode off on the charger through the forest with the sword Excalibur strapped to his shoulder, leading his original horse. It was wonderful to feel the sword there. After a while he heard a low murmur beneath his right ear and realized that it was Excalibur, muttering to itself.

"What is the matter?" Charming asked.

"Nothing much. A touch of rust."

"Rust!" Charming drew Excalibur and examined the shining blade. "I do not see it."

"I can feel it coming on me," said the sword. "I need anointing."

"I have no oil."

"A bit of blood or ichor will do very well."

"I have none."

"Then forget about it, laddie, and let me nap and dream of the old days."

That seemed to Charming a very strange thing to say. But he let it pass. He continued on.

Presently, the sword seemed to sleep, because a low even snoring sound came from it. Charming had no idea that talking swords could also snore. He tried to ignore it, and rode along until he passed a man in a friar's cowl.

The friar greeted Charming, and they went their respective ways. But Excalibur said, "Did ye see the sly-naughty look of him?"

"I didn't notice anything of the sort."

"He was planning your destruction," the sword said. "Such insolence! And such malevolence!"

"I didn't think it was like that at all," Charming said.

"Are you calling me a liar?" the sword asked.

"Certainly not!" Charming said, since it is natural to use caution when talking to a talking sword, especially one with runes.

"I hope we meet that friar again," Excalibur said, and rattled up and down with low, sinister laughter.

Later that day they passed a group of merchants. They were civil enough, but no sooner were they out of sight than the sword told Charming that the merchants were actually thieves who were planning to knock him, Charming, over the head, and steal him, Excalibur. Charming said he didn't think so, but the sword would not listen. He finally pulled himself out of Charming's belt, said, "I'll be right back," and flashed off into the forest. He came back an hour later, bloodstained and wobbling.

After that, the sword swore and sang like a drunken person, and finally began to accuse Charming of planning some evil against him, such as melting him down when he came to the next foundry. It was obvious that the sword had a problem.

That evening, when he lay down for a little rest and the sword had gone to sleep, Charming got up and ran away from Excalibur as fast as he could.

# Chapter
# 2

Relieved of the sinister company of Excalibur, Charming continued his search for Scarlet's castle. He moved silently through the forest, huge trees on all sides, vines and creepers using up whatever space was left. It was an undersea kind of landscape, green and wet, with odd noises coming from all around him.

Prince Charming walked. Unfortunately, Parsifal's big black horse had run off with his first horse when he abandoned Excalibur.

Meanwhile Azzie, in Augsburg, was rushing about his mansion frantically, trying to put together the things he needed to give to Charming once he found him.

"Quick, Frike, better put in a bottle of magic wound ointment."

"The edged-weapons kind, sire, or the clubbed-in-the-head kind?"

"Better pack in both, we can't tell what he's gotten himself into."

"Lady Ylith is back, m'lord," Frike advised him.

"Oh? I thought she was keeping an eye on Scarlet. . . . More bandages."

"That she is, sir. Though in your absence she's felt obliged to maintain the agreement on your behalf by reporting developments to the observer on a regular, daily basis."

"The observer? That being Babriel? Of course. Good girl. Where is she now?"

"In the parlor, I believe, conferring with the observer over tea. . . . Here are the bandages."

"I'd best stop by and say a quick hello before we leave. Thanks, Frike."

Ylith and Babriel were stealing glances at each other over tall flagons of wine and exchanging glances through the haze of burnt mist which surrounded the smoking crumpets. They seemed to have developed a taste for each other's company. You could tell by the way Ylith arched her back at every opportunity. As for Babriel, it seemed that some heavenly analogue to desire was working itself out in him.

Azzie bounded into the room, grinning or grimacing as the case may be, causing Ylith to spring to her feet.

"Azzie, dear, I'd thought you still far gone," she announced, rushing toward him, embracing him. "I was just taking advantage of the opportunity."

"Opportunity for what?" Azzie asked.

"Why, to see how things are going on your end of the business," she stated. "How fares the project?"

"The moment is crucial," Azzie observed, disengaging himself, "and my presence is required on the scene. I think you'd better get back to Scarlet's castle to watch developments on that end. Hi, Bab. How's Good doing these days?"

"Why, uh. We've just come up with a very interesting and inspiring touch for our entry. We're calling them stained-glass windows. I'd really like you to see them sometime."

"Sorry, I'm in a hurry right now. Stained glass?"

"Yes. Beautiful and morally instructive."

"Ugh! Sounds terrible. Sorry I can't stay and chat. Have another drink. It's good for you. Frike! Have we got everything we need?"

"Here, master, is the final thing!" cried Frike, stumping into the room. He was holding in his hand two long horseman's boots made of limp red leather. There was nothing unusual about them except for the small dials set into the heels.

"My Seven League Boots!" Azzie cried. "Frike, you're a genius!"

Azzie put them on, hefted the sack containing spells, extra swords, and other odds and ends. He tapped the heels of the boots twice, activating them.

"I'm off!" he cried.

Azzie went through the front door in a single stride and took to the air.

Babriel and Ylith rushed to the windows to watch, for they had never seen Seven League Boots in operation before. Azzie's pair was not new, but they worked perfectly. Off he went, just clearing the houses of Augsburg but gaining altitude, and climbing steadily.

The Seven League Boots took him high into the air, and Azzie could see the great forest below him, stretching to every horizon in a boundless sea of green. Every once in a while a clearing broke the uniformity and showed a settlement below. This went on for a long time. Azzie didn't know where he was and decided to ask directions. He tried to get the boots to take him down. The boots refused to vary from their previous course. That was the trouble with Seven League Boots. They were very literal, taking you exactly seven leagues at a step, not an inch more or less. He reached down and hammered at them.

"I want to go down right here!" But the boots ignored him, or at least didn't register his complaint. Straight and true they carried him, above the forest and its several rivers, coming down at last outside a town.

Amazed peasants in the village of Vuden in eastern

Wallachia watched as a demon made a perfect landing in the middle of the weekly fair.

"The enchanted forest!" Azzie cried. "Where is it?"

"Which enchanted forest?" the villagers cried back.

"The one with the enchanted castle with the Sleeping Princess in it!"

"Back that way about two leagues!" the villagers cried, pointing the way Azzie had just come.

Once again Azzie soared into the air. And once again the Seven League Boots took their full seven-league stride.

Now began a nerve-racking contest in which Azzie tried to estimate what direction to take in order to reach his destination in exact increments of seven leagues. It took a while to figure out the appropriate zigs and zags.

There it was ahead, the peak of the magic mountain, recognizable by the haze of obfuscation which hung over it. But now, where in its vicinity was Charming?

# Chapter
# 3

Prince Charming walked all day through the forest. The ground was fairly even, there were numerous sparkling streams, and from time to time he would pass a fruit tree and pick his lunch. The sun slanted in, gilding the leaves and branches. After a time, he came to a glade where he rested.

When he awoke, the woods were gloomy with evening light and something was passing near him. He scrambled to his feet and moved off into the underbrush, reaching for his sword before recalling he had abandoned Excalibur. Drawing a knife then, he peered out from behind a blackberry bush. He saw a shaggy little pony enter the clearing.

"Hello, young man," the pony said, halting, and staring at the bush.

Charming was not surprised that the pony could speak. After all, it was an enchanted forest.

"Hello," he said.

"Where are you going?" asked the pony.

"I'm looking for an enchanted castle that is supposed to be somewhere nearby," Charming said. "I am to rescue a maiden named Princess Scarlet, who lies there in an enchanted sleep."

"Oh, the Napping Princess thing again," the pony said. "Well, you're not the first who has been through these parts in search of her."

"Where are the others?"

"They've all perished," the pony said. "Except for a few who are still striving onward, and who are destined to perish soon enough."

"Oh. Well, I'm sorry for them, but I guess that's how it should be," Charming said. "It wouldn't do to have the wrong fellow awaken her."

"So you're the right fellow?" the pony inquired.

"I am."

"What's your name?"

"Charming."

"Prince Charming?"

"Yes."

"Then you're the one, all right. I was sent out here to find you."

"Who sent you?"

"Ah," said the pony, "that would be telling. All will be revealed to you at some later time. If you live long enough, that is."

"Of course I will," Charming said. "After all, I'm the right one."

"Get up on my back," the pony said. "We can discuss it as we go along."

# Chapter
## 4

Prince Charming rode along on the pony, until at last
the woods opened and he could see a field in which
many tents were pitched. Strolling among them were
knights in holiday armor, eating barbecue and flirting
with damsels in tall pointed hats with flimsy veils who
went back and forth carrying wine, mead, and other
drinks. There was even a little orchestra playing a
sprightly air.

"Looks like a goodly bunch over there," Charming
said.

"Don't you believe it," the pony replied.

"Why shouldn't I?"

"Take my word for it."

Charming knew, in the part of his mind which housed
ancient wisdom, that shaggy little ponies who appeared
mysteriously in the woods could be counted on to give
good advice. On the other hand, he also knew that men
were not supposed to follow this advice, since if one al-

ways listened to the voice of reason, one would never do anything interesting.

"But I'm hungry," Charming responded. "And perhaps those knights know the way to the enchanted castle."

"Don't say I didn't warn you," the pony said.

Charming kicked the pony in the ribs and it ambled forward.

"What ho!" cried Charming as he rode into the midst of the knights.

"What ho to you!" the knights called back.

Charming rode closer. "Art thou a knight?" the foremost of them called out.

"Indeed I am."

"Then where is thy sword?"

"That's quite a story," Charming said.

"Tell it to us, then, will thee?"

"I met this sword named Excalibur," Charming said. "I thought it was a proper blade, but no sooner had we started traveling together than it opened on me a mouth such as you would not believe. And it grew passing strange, till finally I had to escape it lest it kill me."

"That's your story, is it?" a knight asked.

"That's not my story, it's what *happened*."

The knight made a gesture. Two knights came out of a white pavilion carrying a baby-blue satin pillow between them. Lying on this pillow was a sword. It was dented, covered with rust, and its tassels were frayed, but it was recognizably Excalibur.

"Is this your sword?" the knight asked.

"Yes, though that's not how it looked when last I saw it," said Charming.

Speaking in a thin shaky voice, Excalibur said, "Thanks, fellas, I believe I can stand on my own."

The sword rose off the pillow, almost fell over, then balanced steadily on its point. The bright jewel in its pommel looked at Charming without winking.

"It's him, all right," Excalibur said. "He's the one who abandoned me on the field of battle."

The knights turned to Charming. "The sword asserts that you abandoned it on the field of battle. Is that true?"

"It wasn't like that," Charming said. "The sword is raving."

The sword swayed, then regained its balance. "My friends," it asked, "do I look deranged? I tell you, he threw me away for no reason at all and left me to rust on the hillside."

Charming made a gesture of finger to the temple, denoting that the thing referred to was crazy.

The knights didn't seem convinced. One said to another, in a clearly audible voice, "A little weird, perhaps, but definitely not crazy."

One of the knights, a tall gray-bearded man with the eagle-eyed look and thin lips of a spokesperson, took out a sheet of ruled parchment and a stylus.

"Name?"

"Charming."

"First name?"

"Prince."

"Occupation?"

"Same as first name."

"Present assignment?"

"Mission."

"What type of mission?"

"Mythic."

"Nature of mission?"

"Awaken Napping Princess."

"By what instrumentality?"

"A kiss."

After completing their questions, the knights retired to a quiet part of the field to consider what to do next, leaving Charming trussed hand and foot with silken cord and rolled under a hedge.

It seemed to Charming that these were not the ordinary run of knights. Their line of questioning was unexpected. Their faces, bony pallidities half-hidden behind moldering iron-and-wood casques, were unprepossessing. Charming overheard them talking as they moved off:

"What'll we do with him?"

"Eat him," came a reply.

"That goes without saying. But how?"

"Fricasseed is nice."

"We just had fricasseed knight last week."

"Then let's do the pony first."

"How?"

"What about roasted with fines herbes? Did anyone see any fines herbes around here?"

Charming immediately decided (a) knights didn't speak as he had supposed they did, or (b) these fellows were not knights at all but actually demons in knights' clothing.

A general consensus was reached on the fricasseeing. But they had some difficulty getting a fire going. It had rained recently in this part of the forest and there wasn't much dry wood to be found.

Finally, one of the knights caught a baby salamander. Piling moist kindling against it and rapping its nose sharply when it tried to escape, they soon had a good blaze going. Two more knights turned to the creation of the sauce, and another pair made the marinade while the rest sang.

Charming knew he was in deadly peril.

# Chapter
# 5

Azzie was under way again, having given up the
Seven League Boots in favor of his own demonic
flying abilities. He flew and scanned the woods, noting a
fire in the distance. He went to it, circled overhead, adjusted his vision, and saw Charming, trussed like a capon,
awaiting fricasseeing aux fines herbes while the pony
cooked and screamed.

"You can't do this to me!" it cried. "I haven't finished
briefing him."

The demon knights kept on singing.

Quickly Azzie set down in the bushes nearby. He was
considering things he might do to harass the knights and
free Charming when, of a sudden, Babriel appeared beside him, resplendent in white armor, his dazzling white
wings fluttering.

"Come to brag about your cathedral?" Azzie asked
him.

Babriel looked at him sternly. "I hope you're not
thinking of wading in there yourself, old man."

"Of course I am," Azzie said. "What do you think, I'm going to let my hero be eaten by renegade demons?"

"I didn't mean to intrude, but it is my duty to keep an eye on you. I can see that your Prince is in trouble. But you know the rules as well as I do. You mustn't help him. Not directly. You must not try to influence matters by your own actions."

"I've just got a few things for him," Azzie said. "A dagger. An invisible cloak."

"Let me see them," Babriel said. "Hmm. Dagger seems all right. Can't tell much about this cloak, though."

"That's because it's invisible," Azzie said. "But you can feel it, can't you?"

Babriel felt it all over.

"I guess it feels okay," he finally acknowledged.

"Even if it didn't," Azzie asked, "who'd know the difference?"

"I'd know," Babriel said. "And I'd tell."


Prince Charming lay trussed up and feeling foolish. Why hadn't he paid attention to what the shaggy pony had tried to tell him? Now it couldn't continue the questing lecture. Why hadn't he believed? If you won't believe an oracular shaggy pony, what will you believe? It did smell good, though. . . .

Then he heard a sound. It sounded like someone saying, in a loud whisper, "Hey there!"

"Who is it?" he asked.

"Your uncle Azzie."

"I'm glad you're here, Uncle! Can you get me out of this?"

"Not directly, no. But I do have a couple of things for you."

"What?"

"The first is an enchanted dagger. It will cut your bonds."

"And the second?"

"A cloak of invisibility. You can use that to get out of the mess you're in."

"Thanks, Uncle! I'd do the same for you!"

"I doubt that," Azzie said. Aiming with care, he dropped the dagger. It went point first into a log beside which Charming was propped.

"Got it," Charming said.

"Good boy. Now here's the cloak of invisibility. Be sure to read the instructions. And above all, do not remove them under penalty of law! Good luck! I'll see you a little later."

Charming heard something soft falling, landing near him with a hushed whisper. That would be the cloak. After the enchanted dagger had cut his bonds, he looked for the cloak but couldn't find it. That figured, he realized. It wouldn't be easy to find an invisible cloak, especially on a dark night.

# Chapter
# 6

The demon knights were returning. They were singing,

> Fair is foul and bread is dead
> Put pease pudding in his head
> And stuff his gut with fine persimmons
> Till he looks like Jack Fitzsimmons.

No one had ever explained the meaning of this verse.
It was very old, from a time when men found obscurity a
comforting way of life.

The demon knights sprawled about the campground
then, grunting, stretching, chuttering, yawning. With an
occasional belch and considerable scratching, they settled
themselves quickly.

Charming turned to the cloak. It wasn't there again.
Then he caught sight of the tag, a small square of cloth
with phosphorescent writing on it. It said, DO NOT REMOVE
THIS TAG UNDER PENALTY OF DIVINE PUNISHMENT. PLEASE

READ INSTRUCTIONS ON OTHER SIDE. Charming tried to read the instructions on the other side but they were not illuminated.

He arranged the cloak around himself as well as he could and started walking softly among the sprawled ranks of warriors.

A slight inconsistency in the height of the ground caused him to stumble and brush against one of the figures.

" 'Ere there!" An unsteady hand reached out and seized him. "Boys, ye ken what I've found?"

"Why you got your fist half-clenched like 'at, Angus?" the others cried.

"Because within it, my friends, I've got holt of an invisible spy."

"I'm not a spy!" Charming cried.

"But you *are* invisible, won't try to deny that, will you?"

Charming broke free and ran. The knights got up and chased after, awakening others with their loud hoots.

From behind him came their cries. These were answered by shouts from ahead. At first Charming thought it was an echo. But then the fact that the cries from before him were becoming louder tipped him off to the real situation. There were demon knights ahead as well as behind. They must have moved quickly to cut him off. He saw that he was going to have to pass through their ranks.

Pausing to re-drape the cloak of invisibility, he was fascinated to see his hand disappear as soon as the cloth was passed over it. Charming could look through the cloak and through his hand that it covered and see the ground beneath it.

Of course, the part of his hand that was not covered remained as visible as always. More visible, in fact, since the existence of an arm in which the hand terminated bloodlessly and at a slant did nothing to make it more imperceptible.

Quickly, he draped himself as best he was able and set off running again. He plunged into a broad grassy field. Horsemen appeared by moonlight on the edge of the meadow. Then one of them pointed and waved, saying, "There, where the grass is parted, that's where he must have gone!" Immediately a squadron went out in pursuit.

Charming dodged back into the woods, and there, finding a shallow cave, concealed himself long enough to tear out the cloak's lining. As he had hoped, this material, thin though it was, had the same qualities as the cloak itself. And so Charming could devise a mask for himself, a full-length wraparound mask, and thus even his head was concealed.

He could do nothing about the movements of his passage, however. Every footfall was marked by a bruising of leaves and bending of small boughs and grasses. At least hiding his head was rendering the finding of him more difficult.

He hurried, even knowing that he was kicking up a considerable trail. It occurred to him that he might do better if he could get himself to move slowly and carefully, thus eluding his pursuers while he was among them. That was how a fairy-tale prince might act, he thought, but that was not the way he was at all. He was running, his long legs exulting in stretching and striding, hurrying away from danger. Viewing himself from the viewpoint of his legs, he was a soaring creature proceeding by leaps and bounds. But the fact was the horses of his pursuers were moving faster. They were coming up on either side of him, the riders only slightly impeded by the necessity of having to sight his movement through the bending branches that marked his passage.

They closed in, their steel lance points winking at him. He could see a clearing ahead, but doubted that he could make it. It was all the more tantalizing because it contained a long limestone shelf. The stone would neither retain his footprints nor reveal his passage. It was going to be close.

One of the knights took aim with his lance and came charging.

It was only at this moment of extremity that his salvation came. He did not know whether it was natural, or induced somehow by Azzie. Where before the air had been still, now a wind rose up. Not just a little wind, but a full-blown gale, bearing drops of icy water and a scattering of hail.

On all sides, the foliage blew into wild disarray, making his movements undetectable.

The leading knight missed him by five feet. The second wasn't even close. The knights spread apart, trying to contain him within their circle. But Charming easily slipped between them and hurried down to the limestone shelf. This he was able to traverse without leaving a trace. When he stopped, the wind had died again, and there were no sounds of pursuit. He realized he had eluded the demons.

# Chapter
# 7

$P$rince Charming ran until his legs grew numb and his lungs fiery. At some point, he collapsed and slept.

When he awoke, he saw himself to be in a sunlit meadow. At the far end of it a mountain rose into the sky, a gigantic Matterhorn of the Imagination, a dream mountain of multicolored glass. In front of the mountain, and blocking further access to it, was a dense forest of what looked like metal trees. Charming advanced upon the strange forest and regarded it. The trees were made of thorned stovepipe, and the tallest of them was not over seven feet in height. As he approached, the trees began to emit a yellowish gas which quickly caught fire, sparked by igniters located below-ground.

Prince Charming might not have known what these were, save that he recalled seeing Azzie studying a slip of paper which he later left lying upon his desktop. Curious, Charming had looked at it. It proved a receipt from the All Spiritual Regions Gas Company for payment for gas to power flame trees.

If Uncle Azzie was indeed paying the bill to fuel the trees—and Charming could draw no other inference from the evidence—then the signs of manipulation were unmistakable. He felt strange now when he considered the ramifications. It made him feel as if he were painted cardboard, a cutout figure pinned to the background. This was frightening, but it came at a time when there was an urgent need to get on through the place. So he saved it for later consideration and moved ahead.

If the things could be turned on, they could be turned off. He sought for the better part of an hour before he located the valve in a ditch. The trees went out when he turned it. How very strange, to set up a thing like this in the first place.

He passed among them.

And so he came to Glass Mountain Village, final base camp and source of provender, sustenance, and souvenirs for those who would climb to the sun-dazzled summit of the great mountain, where, it was said, stood the enchanted castle within which lay the sleeping Princess Scarlet.

The principal industry of the town was to serve those who sought to climb the Glass Mountain. Here came explorers and glass-mountain climbers from all over. The lure of the thing was irresistible.

Charming walked down a line of shops on Main Street in Glass Mountain Village. Many of the shops specialized in glass-mountain-climbing equipment. Glass is a tough substance to scale. To hear the townspeople talk you'd think the glass changed qualities every time a cloud came over the sun. The mountain boasted every kind of glass to be found: Swift Glass and Devious Glass, Tricky Glass and Swamp Glass. There was High Mountain Deadly Glass and Low Plain Bed Glass. Each kind of glass (and Glass Mountain was said to be composed of all of these kinds and more) had its own difficulties, and booklets were available at the shops dealing with the remedies for every variety.

Although some believed that this Glass Mountain was the only place of its kind in the world, unique and unduplicatable, there were intellectuals who insisted that the perennial human custom of climbing glass mountains could only be accounted for by deep historical memories, practically universal to the race of man, of doing so countless times and places in the past. These theorists would have it that Glass Mountain was an archetype of human experience whose physical corroboration was always taking place on innumerable levels, from the first moment of the beginning of the past to the last instant of the furthest unrolling of the future.

The bookstores of Glass Mountain Village were also filled with technical books on how glass mountains had been climbed in this year or that. There were histories, guidebooks, books of interviews with climbers and theorists. There were several shops in town that sold nothing but crampons of all types and descriptions, including diamond-studded ones.

The matter of whether or not to use horses to climb Glass Mountain called up some controversy in the town. In general, it is much more difficult for a horse to climb a glass mountain than it is for a man. Horses' legs don't go in the right ways. They are noble beasts, excellent on plains and prairies, agile in forests and pretty fair even in semidense jungle, but just not good at climbing glass mountains. So the custom had sprung up of riding up the mountain on goatback.

To traditionalists, this was unacceptable. Everyone expects Prince Charmings to scale the Glass Mountain on horseback. Generations of illustrators, some of them claiming to be authorized by high spiritual powers, had shown horses climbing glass mountains with Prince Charmings on their backs. The fact is, as learned societies have never tired of pointing out, even if a horse could manage the mountain, it would leave him damaged in spirit and weak in the wind. Despite this, no one liked the idea of goats.

Charming was like everyone else. "Are you kidding?" he said, when told about riding a goat. "No way!"

"In that case," they told him, "you'll have to wear crampons and try to get up the mountain yourself."

"Me wear crampons?" He had the common superstitious awe of these useful objects.

"They are what all the climbers wear."

"No thanks. You're not going to get those things on me."

"If you don't wear them, you'll never get to the top. It's all glass, you know. Slippery."

Charming, like so many young men in those days, had prejudices against both goats and crampons. Sighing, he chose at last what seemed the lesser evil.

"So all right already, saddle me up a goat!"


Not even all the goats make it up Glass Mountain. That must be understood by those who think a goat is all it takes to win a princess. It's just that you need to use a goat even to get into the running. If at the very end, you want to substitute a horse for your goat, after the feat is accomplished, and have your portrait painted that way— well, a horse looks better than a goat, and it can be arranged.

And so it was that at last Prince Charming found himself racing upward on goatback until he came to the entranceway to a great castle whose battlements rose high into the air. Ahead of him was a staircase. He knew he had arrived when he saw the cardboard sign on an iron stanchion. It read, YOU HAVE ARRIVED AT THE ENCHANTED CASTLE. THE SLEEPING PRINCESS IS IN THE FIRST CHAMBER TO THE RIGHT AT THE TOP OF THE STAIRS. CONGRATULATIONS.

With a tremulous feeling in his thumbs, Prince Charming performed the final climb over the barbican, endured the icy swim across the moat, and then, dripping wet, went down the gallery and through the turret passageways, and finally through the outer rooms where ensorcelled servitors snoozed, to the staircase with upward curves of great cruelty, to the flagstones of the outer chamber.

He opened the door and took two steps inside. In the middle of the room he saw the bed, a high four-poster. Lying on it, eyes closed, was the most beautiful woman he had ever seen. She was the one whose miniature he had fallen in love with. But in person she was incomparably more lovely than her painted representation.

# Chapter
# 8

Any eyes would have sufficed to see her beauty. But Prince Charming's dragon's eyes saw something more. They saw through Azzie's scheme and understood the snare that the demon had planned. The dragon's eyes saw that he, Charming, wore the hated face of Scarlet's seducer. What would she do when she saw that face? The dragon's eyes could see the shadow of disaster here. But Charming ignored the warning, bending low over the Princess.

This was the moment Azzie had been working toward since he had thought up the plan in the first place.

The kiss! The fatal kiss!

Azzie had already positioned the poisoned dagger on the little bedstand, close to Scarlet's hand. This was what Scarlet would use when she opened her eyes and recognized who had kissed her—the despised seducer!

Azzie, from behind the curtain where he had stationed himself, addressed the great unseen audience watching the drama unfold.

"Ladies and gentlemen, beings of Light and Darkness, fellow demons, rival angels! I bring you now the conclusion of the most ancient and edifying drama of Prince Charming and Princess Scarlet. Behold, the awakening kiss and its outcome!"

Even while his words died away, Prince Charming, with his dragon's eyes, continued to regard Azzie's scheme, and he spoke of it, thus:

"A-ha," he soliloquized, "it's obvious to me I am a nothing, a mere congeries of disparate parts, and that my so-called uncle Azzie, a demon indeed despite his ingratiating ways, gave me the face of Scarlet's seducer when putting me together, for the purpose of being sacrificed by Scarlet when I awaken her. Well then, if that's so, let it be. Kill me, pretty Princess, if that's what will content you. But though I am a nothing man, constructed of odds and ends and brought to life by a fiend, yet a true heart beats in my breast, and I can only say, I am yours, Princess, do with me what you will."

Scarlet felt the touch of a man's lips. Her eyes opened, but at first she saw nothing due to the nearness of the young man kissing her. Her first thought was, What bliss to be so awakened!

Then she saw his face. That face! O Gods! She recognized it instantly. This was the face of the man who had seduced her and abandoned her.

Her eyes widened. One white hand fluttered to her breast like one of the lost doves of Hera. He! It is he! Her hand groped behind her and encountered the haft of the dagger lying on the little nightstand. She lifted it. . . .

Azzie had calculated this part with precision. He knew how the dagger would slide into her hand as if of its own volition. The audience, invisible but present, would lean forward. The members of the Awards Committee would see Scarlet's hand pull back, then plunge the dagger into his back, through to the heart! And then, with Charming expiring on the floor of her chamber, Azzie himself would step forward. "Alas, little princess," he would say (the speech long rehearsed), "you've killed the only man you could ever love, the man in whom was bound your salvation!" And after that, Azzie thought it would make a pretty ending if Scarlet turned the dagger on herself, thus ensuring herself an eternity of pain in the Pits of deepest Hell. He had even considered bringing Charming back to life long enough to watch Scarlet die, in order to tempt him into uttering blasphemies so great as to ensure his own eternal damnation. A good ending for one who likes to tie up loose ends.

So sure of all this was Azzie that he appeared before Scarlet now, saying, with heavy irony, "Heaven finds means to kill your joys with love; but the world is not thy friend nor thy world's law."

People argued for a long while afterward as to why this plan was not successful. In Azzie's opinion, simple reciprocity should have guided Scarlet's fingers to the dagger, and the dagger to the unprotected back of the young Prince. But life, with its healthy habit of indeterminacy, would not have it so.

Azzie had miscalculated the effect of Scarlet's eyes. Though they had not the ability to see the truth, as had those of Charming, yet the eyes could see triviality and artifice, and these they perceived as she considered the tableau she made, she and Prince Charming, and the poisoned dagger. Her artist's eyes saw the artificiality of it: this was not a good subject for one who paints from life. She rebelled for artistic reasons from plunging home the knife, and then, later, her sensibilities followed her aesthetic judgment.

Scarlet said, "What are you talking about?"

"You shouldn't have killed him," Azzie said. "You've doomed yourself to an eternity of infernal torments, young lady."

Scarlet burst out laughing.

"Laugh at me? I'll show thee—"

Another voice joined in the laughter. It was Charming, standing beside her, his arm around her waist.

Charming, undead! The dagger had not been employed for its fell purpose! Azzie stepped back in confusion.

They were alive, those two, and somehow love had won out over the ancient predestination of Azzie's curse. Seeing these beautiful young people together, the audience of angels and demons was moved; there wasn't a dry eye in the place.

"This isn't what I meant!" Azzie cried. "This isn't what I meant at all!"

But this was what he had produced: a merry little tale of love and redemption which caught everyone's fancy and ensured that Good, not Evil, would win the destiny of men's souls for the next thousand years.

# VESPERS

THE OWL OF HERMES

# Chapter 1

Ylith's slim fingers went *tap tap tap* on the door that led into Azzie's alchemical lab.

"Azzie? I know you're in there."

No answer. Babriel, standing at her side, said, "I guess we'd better try again." Ylith did so.

"Azzie! Come on! Let me in! It's me and Babriel here. We know you had a serious disappointment. We're your friends. We want to be near you."

There was a harsh grating sound. The steel rod that served as the door bolt was withdrawn. The beamed wooden door of the alchemical lab opened a few inches. Frike's long-nosed face appeared.

"Is the master here, Frike?" Ylith asked.

"Oh, yes, miss. He's inside. But I wouldn't go near him right now. He's in a rather foul mood. It's not impossible he would do somebody a mischief at this time."

"Nonsense!" Babriel said. "Let me speak with him!"

He pushed his way in through the door.

Azzie was seated on a little throne he had set up in

one corner of the laboratory. He lounged there in his purple cloak, with an orange tam o'shanter pulled over one eye. He looked like hell. His eyes were bloodshot. Tankards and bottles of ichor were strewn around the floor. There were other bottles on nearby shelves, jocund in their fullness, within easy reach.

"Come now, Azzie!" Babriel said. "You've put up a very good contest. Remember, it's not winning or losing that counts, it's how you play the game."

"You've got that entirely wrong," Azzie said. "What counts is winning. How you play the game counts for nothing."

Babriel shrugged. "Well . . . Different rules, different divine imperatives, I suppose. But you really should stop drinking now, old man. Here, let me help you up."

He extended an arm to Azzie. Azzie gripped it with one hand and tried to claw it with the other. Babriel deftly fended him off and helped him to his feet.

"After all, old man," Babriel said, "what does it matter who wins, really?"

Azzie stared at him. "Am I hearing you correctly?"

"Well, yes, of course. I mean, as Creatures of Light and Darkness we must take the long view. We all serve life and death, intelligence, and all the other supernal forces."

"I shouldn't have lost," Azzie said. "It's because I got no cooperation from the Powers of Darkness. You yourself, Babriel, my opponent, were more help than people on my own side. That's the trouble with evil. It's not cooperative, not even with itself."

"Don't take it so hard," Babriel said. "Come with us, Azzie. We'll all go to the Awards Dinner and have a few laughs."

"Oh, yeah, sure," Azzie said. "The damned Awards Dinner. All right. I'll be there in a bit. You go on ahead, though. I've got a few little things I have to do first. How's the Gothic whatchamacallit coming?"

"They're just finishing the bell tower," Babriel replied.

As they departed Babriel said to Ylith, "You know, we really ought to do something nice for Charming, for the wonderful way he managed his part."

"What a fine idea," she replied.

Azzie gnashed his teeth.

When they were gone, he summoned Frike.

"Did you ever hear anything like that?" he asked him.

"Like what, master?"

"Like those two sappy-faced so-called friends of mine. Did you hear them talking on the way out? Such nonsense! Can you imagine? They want to reward Charming for a job well done."

"Yes, master," Frike said. "Very funny, ha-ha."

"I thought so, too," Azzie said. "Well, I think we will give Master Charming a little acknowledgment of the part he's played in screwing up my drama by taking from him the life that was my gift to him. I can't kill him myself, though. Not directly. There are rules. Stupid rules, but rules all the same, that prohibit a demon from savaging and killing a human being for no reason at all."

"Oh, that's too bad, master," Frike said.

"Yes, I've always thought that, too," Azzie said. "But I believe we can get around it."

"Oh, master, how will we do that?"

"Frike," Azzie said, "how would you like to be an avenging warrior for a change instead of a cringing servitor?"

"Sounds nice," Frike said. "How do we do that, master?"

"We've got plenty of body parts left over," Azzie said, "and I'm a master at the art of human sculpture. Come with me. Lie down on yonder marble slab."

"Master, I'm not sure this is such a wonderful idea."

"Shut up," Azzie said. "Don't argue with me. Remember, I can replace your personality as easily as I can change your body."

"Yes, master, of course." Frike lay down on the table. Azzie found a scalpel and sharpened it on his heel.

"Will it hurt?" Frike asked.

"Of course it will hurt," Azzie told him. "Anesthesia hasn't been invented yet."

"What did you say hasn't been invented yet, master? Ana-something?"

"Never mind. Bite down hard on your lip. I'm going to begin cutting."

# Chapter 2

P rince Charming was leaning out of one of the high windows of the Enchanted Castle. He was in a good mood, lazy and well pleased. Love does that to a man, at least for a while, and Charming was in the first rush of it.

Still, it was disconcerting to see, as he watched through the window, bits and pieces of the Enchanted Castle disappearing.

He looked again, toward the stables. Half of them had disappeared while he was looking the other way. He reminded himself that they'd have to get out of here soon. This castle wasn't going to last long, the way the power of its protective spells was running down.

"Darling! Come down! Our guests want to meet you!"

Scarlet's voice floated up the staircase to the bedroom where Prince Charming was supposed to be arranging his tunic. He liked to have his clothes look good. He knew this party was a big occasion for Scarlet, because this was the time she was bringing over Cinderella and other storybook friends. Charming wasn't completely sure how he liked having all his friends imaginary beings from folk-lore, but it seemed to be working out all right.

He was interested in the way the Enchanted Castle worked. As he stood there, watching, he could see a piece of the entrance road which led under the castle wall. Sud-denly a section of the wall vanished. A stone gargoyle on one of the battlements disappeared.

"Charming!" Again, Scarlet's voice. "Where are you?"

A slight petulance to the voice . . . It occurred to Charming that he didn't know his sweetheart very well. He had assumed that the eternal happiness promised to them in the fable was of the self-creating, self-adjusting kind, not meaning he had to do adjustments himself. All right. . . .

With a final glance at his appearance in a tall mirror, he departed and went down the stairs. Below him, in the great ballroom, an orchestra in black tie and white pe-rukes was sawing away at something polyphonic. The guests stood about, under the great crystal chandeliers, sipping champagne and nibbling canapés.

There was Scarlet, arm in arm with Cinderella, who had become her greatest friend. It had been Cinderella's idea to have a waking-up party for Scarlet. It would also serve as an engagement party for Scarlet and Prince Charming.

Prince Charming recognized two famous Irishmen among the guests. They were Cuchulain and Finn Mc-Cool. Looking around, he saw other heroes from France, Germany, from the Orient—Roland, Siegfried, Aladdin.

They saw him, and a round of applause went up. There were exclamations of "Well done, old man!"—the words one wants most to hear after having awakened the Napping Princess. They sang a rousing chorus of "For He's a Jolly Good Hero."

Yes, moments didn't get much better than this, Charming decided. Even if bits of your enchanted palace are breaking away, even if Princess Scarlet has a bit more of a whine than you might have wished, his moment of triumph was sweet.

So he felt all the more trepidation when there came a loud pounding on the gate. It reverberated through the castle, and every guest stood still and gazed at the doorway.

Prince Charming said to himself, Rats! Good events don't usually introduce themselves so emphatically.

"Who is it?" he called.

"One who would crave a favor," came a muffled voice from outside.

Charming was about to say no, but then he realized that on this day of his triumph he had to face up to what came along. Storybook heroes who are about to marry the Napping Princess don't refuse to answer the door of the Enchanted Castle to anyone, no matter how bad the premonitory vibes.

"Well," Charming said, "I really don't have time for a big favor, but maybe a little favor . . ."

He unbarred the door. The man who entered reminded him of someone. But where could he have met this tall, grim-faced warrior with the brazen helmet pulled down about his ears?

"Who are you?" Charming asked.

The warrior pushed back his helmet. Charming found himself looking into the bearded half-mad face of Frike.

"Frike!" Charming said. "It's you! But there's something different about you . . . let me think a moment. . . . I've got it! You used to be rather small and hunchbacked, and now you are quite tall, well muscled, and with no indication of a limp."

"You are observant," Frike said, smiling in a bloodthirsty manner.

"To what do I owe the pleasure of this visit?"

"As for that," Frike said, "my master, Azzie, sent me."

"I hope he is well."

"He is fine. He has sent me here to fetch him something which I shall put in here."

Frike opened a leather satchel he carried. Within it was a sharp odor.

"Vinegar!" said Charming.

"Ye say true," said Frike.

"And why bearest thou a satchel filled with vinegar to this enchanted castle?"

"The vinegar is for the purpose of preserving that which I would bring away with me."

Charming did not much like the way the discussion was going, but he said, "And what would you bear back from here in vinegar, Frike?"

"Ah, lad, it's thy head I've come for."

"My head?" cried Prince Charming. "But why should Uncle Azzie want that of me?"

"He's angry at you, boy, because Princess Scarlet didn't kill you when she was supposed to. Thus he lost the contest between Darkness and Light which is played out on the eve of each Millennium. He's decided you're sly and unreliable and he wants your head."

"But it was not my fault, Frike! And even if it had been, why should Azzie hold a grudge against me merely for trying to preserve my life?"

"It's illogical, I'll grant that," Frike said. "But what can you do? He's a demon, and he's bad, very bad. He wants your head and I'm here to take it to him. I hate to tell you this, for it is your wedding day. But I have no choice over timing. Say good-bye to your Princess. It is to be hoped you have enjoyed her favors betides, because there'll be no aftertides when I've taken your head ensor."

"You're really serious about this, aren't you?" Charming said.

"Better believe it. I'm sorry, kid, but that's how it goes in fairyland. Ready?"

"Wait!"

"Nay, I wait for nothing!"

"But I have no sword!"

"No sword?" Frike said, lowering his blade. "But you must have a sword! Where is your sword?"

"I need to get it."

"You're supposed to have a sword on your person at all times."

"Give me a break, it's my wedding day."

"Well, go get your sword, but be quick about it."

"Frike, you were practically a father to me. How can you do this?"

"Well, I'm playing a pretty traditional role," Frike said. "The crippled servant who is slightly sympathetic but still has a fatal bias toward evil. Nothing personal, but we must fight it out with swords."

"Well, rats," Charming said. "Wait right here. I'll be back with my sword."

"I'll be waiting," Frike said, and went over to sample the buffet.

When Prince Charming had been gone almost half an hour, Scarlet went to look for him. She found him in what remained of the stables. He had just finished saddling up the swiftest goat he could find.

Scarlet said, "What do you think you're doing?"

"I don't know how to tell you this," Charming said, "but I think I've got to get out of here."

"Coward!" Scarlet said.

"Bitch," Charming said.

"But our new life together has hardly begun!"

"What matter a new life if I'm too dead to enjoy it?"

"Maybe you could defeat him!"

"I don't think so," Charming said. "Frankly, though, I'm not happy about running out like this. I sure need the advice of some wise spirit."

There was a flash of light. A voice said, "I thought you'd never ask." It was Hermes Trismegistus.

# Chapter
# 3

Never had the demigod looked handsomer. His dark cloak, draped artfully over his massive white marble body, looked miraculously beautiful. Every strand of his hyacinthine hair was in place. A faint Oriental tilt to his eyes gave him a look of unutterable beauty and wisdom. The blankness of his eyes, which, in the classic statuary mode, were without pupils, made him seem preternaturally wise. Even his sandals gave off an air of sapience.

"O Hermes," Charming said, "what Azzie is doing isn't fair, sending out Frike to take my head, and all because I haven't fallen in with his scheme of having Princess Scarlet murder me."

"It does seem unfair," Hermes said. "But who ever said demons were otherwise?"

"Has he even the right by divine law to send his servant to take my head?"

"Let me see," Hermes said. He removed from a fold of

his cloak a thick scroll. He threw it into the air and it unwound, soaring upward with paper spilling down.

Hermes snapped his fingers and a small spotted owl appeared.

"Find me the relevant passage for laws regulating the actions of demons' assistants," Hermes said.

"You got it," said the owl, and fluttered up into the air, darting close to the endlessly long page of the scroll. Finally it darted in on a section, pinched the parchment in its beak, and brought it back to Hermes.

Hermes read the entry and shook his head sorrowfully. "As I feared. He can do anything he wants with you via a servant, since he created you. Assembled, actually, but it comes to much the same thing."

"But why should that give him power of life and death over me?"

"That's how it goes in the creation game. But you are not without recourse."

"What can I do?"

"Kill Frike."

"You think I might be able to? He looks awfully strong to me."

"Yes, but you're a hero. Maybe if you had a good sword . . ."

"I had Excalibur but we parted ways. It was trying to kill me."

"You must get it back. It will take a magic sword to kill a supernaturally augmented demon's assistant."

"I think I ought to mention, I'm very scared," Charming said.

"That's because you were given a coward's heart. Don't worry about it, though. Everyone's scared."

"Everyone?"

"Those who are too courageous perish too quickly to leave a record. Cowardice is nothing to be ashamed of, Prince Charming. It is like measles—most people get it at least once in their lives. Just ignore it and it'll go away. Carry on without it. The metaphor is unclear, but your path of duty is not. Get out of here, Charming, and find the sword. Tell your coward's heart to stop fluttering and get on with destroying this knave of a Frike and claiming your Princess for forever after. She's very pretty, by the way."

"Yes," Charming said, "isn't she? But I'm afraid she's sulky."

"The good ones always are," Hermes said. "Come on, let's go get that sword!"

# Chapter
# 4

There wasn't much time for Charming and Hermes to find Excalibur. Hermes took them first to the Bureau of Lost Swords. They had the sympathetic vibration print of every sword ever forged, all kept in a central registration point on the planet Oaqsis IV. Hermes found a trace of Excalibur and followed it back to Earth, carrying Prince Charming along with him.

On Earth again, Prince Charming soon found himself in a tavern. Guided by Hermes, he went to the kitchen. There he beheld a sword, all nicked and dented, but unmistakably of fine temper, being used by a scullion to decapitate radishes and turnips, eviscerate cabbages, decorify carrots, and all the rest of the homely life of domestic steel. Yet despite this, the sword recognized Charming as soon as he came in.

"Master, here I am!" it said in a breaking voice. "Your own forsaken sword!"

"What has happened to you?" Charming said. "Did you really have to cut vegetables?"

"It's not my fault," the sword said. "How can I help the base purposes men put me to? Take me back into your employ, master, and I'll show thee good service."

"Come on then," Charming said.

The sword leaped to his hand. One of the tavern drudges looked ready to put up a quarrel, but a single glance, nay, a bare glancelet at the yard of steel gleaming in Prince Charming's hands put a stop to that. And so it was that Charming turned, sword in hand, and through the magical attentions of Hermes was able to return to the Enchanted Castle with Excalibur.

Seeing him, Frike put down the cracker spread with chopped chicken liver at which he had been nibbling whilst awaiting Prince Charming's return, wiped his mouth on his sleeve, and said, "Are you ready?"

"Aye, ready!"

"Then here we go!"

The swords clashed. The fight was on.

# Chapter
# 5

Charming's blade, Excalibur, grunted with the weight of Frike's blow, bent like a willow, and then snapped back. Excalibur beat down hard on Frike's iron casque, forcing him backward. Frike took two steps to recover balance, then stomped forward again, his sword swinging in blinding patterns of advance and foil. Excalibur met the other's thrusts and parries with equal ardor and undaunted skill. The guests, who had gathered on the staircase and on the small interior balcony above to watch the fight, gasped and held their breaths.

Then Frike smiled, for he knew the fatal flaw in Excalibur. It was a demented demon-sword, and upon the signal, it responded to a hellish master. Fitting that description fully, Frike waited until their swords were crossed once again. Then he cried, "Come to thy master, O mighty Excalibur! Come to me!"

"Not likely!" snarled Excalibur, slashing off Frike's right arm.

"I command you!" shouted Frike, his high berserk

temper feeling no pain as he whirled a battle-ax around his head with his good, or rather remaining, hand, the left, or sinister one.

"But you didn't say it in Runic," Excalibur replied, lopping off Frike's other arm in response to Prince Charming's valiant swing.

"Spare me this fuscating of quiddities!" Frike shouted, now attacking with both feet, which were armed with scythes of a wicked temper. "By the arts of the ancient wicked ones, I bespeak thee, come now to me and at once and without further palaverations!"

"Why," Excalibur said, "if you so desire, then so be it!" And the great shining sword sprang from Charming's grasp, described a graceful arabesque in the air, and came to Frike point first, not stopping until it had pierced the man's armor and run him through his deepest extent.

"Alack, I am finished," Frike said.

Charming turned to the Princess. His eyes were ablaze. It was in his mind to end all ambiguity now.

"Give me one final kiss!" Charming said. "And then stab away to your heart's content, if this desire still be present, for no death is as dear as that bestowed by the beloved at the moment which should, if things had worked out otherwise, be that of highest bliss."

"I'll give thee kiss, and kiss for kiss, and then more kisses to repay those kisses betides!" Scarlet said. "Speak not of death. That was the old way. Now shall we go on forever in our pleasures!"

And so it was.

# Chapter
# 6

Moondrench was a young spirit who had not had his sexual awakening. Although he was called "he," he was in fact a neutral in matters of sexuality. Agrippa was an older spirit who had been around for a very long time and was more than a little jaded. He did like fresh young spirits, however, and he may have had something of a sporting nature in mind when he invited Moondrench. He liked the naive responses of young spirits. They gave him something to be superior to.

They arrived at the north entrance to Limbo at the time appointed for the Millennial Awards Dinner. Together they mounted the cloud-staircases that led to the building where the banquet was to be held. Clouds are not easy to walk on, even if you are a demon. In no time at all, Moondrench began complaining.

"I'm sick of walking," he said. "Let's fly."

"It's not allowed," Agrippa said.

"But we always fly! Remember that flying game you taught me?"

"Please, let's not speak of that here. It is said that we walk today in honor of our victim's ancestor, Adam."

"Adam, shmadam," Moondrench said. "I just don't want to get my new outfit sweaty."

"Stop complaining," Agrippa said.

Ahead lay a great cloud-pasture. It seemed to expand like an unbounded metaphor. It had Corinthian columns which added to its classical look.

They walked to the entrance. A demon in a powdered wig and beige silk stockings checked Agrippa's invitation, holding it up to the light to make sure it had the water-mark. The Millennial Awards was such an important event that many spiritual beings tried to lie their way in, or get by with forged credentials. Luckily for Agrippa, his excellent connections with the High Demon Council, for whom he threw parties and literary soirees, had assured him and his friend of places at the banquet.

Agrippa, many centuries old, had the leathery skin and deep wrinkles of a rottweiler.

The attendant verified his invitation and let them continue inside.

Within the banqueting hall they came to a table so long that it disappeared from sight at either end. Luckily, Agrippa and Moondrench's seats were near the middle. They found little name tags in the form of paper pennants stuck into grapefruits.

Taking their places, they nodded to their neighbors on either side. The speeches from the high table had already begun. Agrippa found himself sitting next to a Nubian angel with an ebony halo. Moondrench looked around, still considerably in awe, and saw food being passed.

"Can I eat now?" he asked Agrippa in a loud whisper.

"Yes, but don't make a pig of yourself."

Moondrench snarled at him and speared a turkeydog-leg from a platter as it went by. He followed it up with a glass of mescal ichor. This had the embryonic dragon at the bottom of the glass, identifying it as genuine. He munched and looked around. He stared at the tall blond creature with big blue eyes who sat across the table from him. "Hot damn," he remarked to Agrippa. "That's what I call some kind of sexy."

"Forget it," Agrippa said. "That's an angel and he's not for the likes of you."

It was a fact that demons were always lusting after angels, who, it is said, were flattered by the attention. This occasion of the Awards Dinner was one of the few times they were able to mingle freely with each other.

Waiters hurried back and forth with trays of food and drink. Many of them wore the ethnic masks which were so popular in celestial circles. Their masks matched the type of food they were serving. Italian angels served tiny pizzas, Vietnamese angels had eggrolls and Pho soup, and Arab spirits bore silver trays with kebabs piled high on them.

The food was good, of course, but Moondrench was more interested in strong drink. "Pass the ichor," he told a tall skinny spirit diagonally across the table from him. Agrippa was getting a good start, too. Moondrench considered joining a group of devils off by themselves in a corner, where they drank ichor out of each other's shoes and giggled immoderately. At a different part of the table, a fat demon in a clown's outfit cut into a large pie, releasing four-and-twenty blackbirds, which fluttered around the heads of the guests.

"Having a good time?" Agrippa asked Moondrench.

"It isn't bad," Moondrench said. "But who is that over there waving his hands?"

"That's Asmodeus," Agrippa said. "He's in charge of this section of the banquet."

"And the dark lady beside him?"

"That is Hecate, Queen of Night. If they look in your direction, just smile and raise your glass. They are very important."

"You don't have to tell me how to behave. What is Asmodeus doing? He seems to be reading something. But I didn't know that Lord Demons could read."

"Very funny," Agrippa said. "If he hears you saying things like that, you'll see how humorous he'll feel." Agrippa peered more closely. "He seems to be studying the notes for his speech."

"What speech?" Moondrench asked. "You didn't say anything about the speeches."

"I thought you understood what this is all about."

"Just some sort of big party, isn't it?"

"Rather more than that," Agrippa said. "This is the occasion when they announce the winner of the Millennial contest which determines the quality that will dominate men's lives for the next thousand years."

Moondrench said, "Is it so important, this matter of human destiny?"

"Not to us, perhaps," Agrippa said. "But to them it means quite a lot."

A Nameless Horror stalked by, reeking of deep reptilian musk. Its companion, a model of the Pickman variety, asked, "Did you hear what happened to Good's entry?"

The Nameless Horror grunted in the negative.

"The whole damned thing fell down! Made a beautiful crash—with those stained-glass windows and all. Too bad about the gargoyles, of course."

"How come?" the Nameless Horror growled.

"Something to do with buttressing and flying—I'm not clear on the mechanics. Guess Good wasn't either. Har! Har!"

"I want some more to drink," Moondrench said. "You promised me I'd have lots of fun."

"Here comes the waiter with the ichor," Agrippa said. "Please don't act silly."

"I shall drink as much as I please," Moondrench said, helping himself to a flagon of ichor. "And I shall probably drink a lot. Drinking to excess is never silly."

There was a disturbance at the rear of the hall. A fox-faced demon had entered and was making his lurching way forward, colliding with waiters, bumping against diners, knocking dishes from tables as he passed. Murmurs rose as he went by:

"How rude!"

"Isn't that . . . ?"

"Is that . . . ?"

"Looks like Azzie."

"Didn't he have an entry in the contest?"

"Wonder what happened."

"Hey, Azzie! You okay?"

"I heard he screwed up a big one."

"I thought he was still in the Pits."

"Looks soused to the ear tufts."

"Watch it there, fella!"

"What else can you expect from a drunken demon?"

"What'd he want with a glass mountain, anyhow?"

"Give 'em hell, Azzie!"

"Yeah! Hell! Brimstone and all that!"

Moondrench was being difficult. Agrippa no longer considered him as attractive as he had before. And now the banquet was in full swing. More food kept arriving, brought in on silver platters by demons in black tuxedos. There were some unusual dishes. Suckling chimaera, for example. And there were all sorts of dishes with little handwritten signs on them telling the diner what he was getting into. A few of the dishes were even able to enunciate. "Hello," the stewed turnips said, "we're delicious."

The sound of all those beings conversing was beginning to grow deafening. In order to reach anyone more than two or three seats away, you had to use the seashell telephones located beside each setting.

On a sort of boardwalk which extended over the dining table, a tableau of great hits of the past was being presented, highlights of the macabre and the virtuous. As new guests arrived, each had to have his lineage and accomplishments announced by the white-furred major-domo.

Azzie continued to push his way forward, on the crest of an advancing wave of chaos.

Then Asmodeus got up. He was fat, and his white skin had a greenish cast. His lower lip protruded so far that a saucer could have balanced on it. He wore a bottle-green coat, and when he turned around, his twisted pig's tail was visible.

"Hello, friends," Asmodeus said. "I think we all know why we are here, don't we?"

"To get drunk!" an ugly spirit off to one side said.

"Well, yes, that, of course," Asmodeus said. "But we are getting drunk tonight for a purpose. And that purpose is to celebrate the eve of the Millennium, and to announce the winner of the contest. I know you're impatient to find out who it is, but you'll just have to wait a little longer. First we are going to have some special appearances."

Azzie moved to the front of the hall.

Asmodeus began to call out names, and various spirits got up to take bows. They grinned and smirked, scraped and bowed to the enthusiastic audience. The Red Death was introduced and stood up. He was tall, and wrapped from head to foot in a bloodred cloak. Over his shoulder he carried a scythe.

"Who's that couple over there?" Moondrench asked. "The big blond angel and the dark little witch?"

"The angel is named Babriel," Agrippa told him. "The witch is Ylith—a good friend of Azzie's, one of our more interesting and active demons. I believe he just went by."

"I've heard of him," Moondrench said. "He was doing something special for this year's festivities, wasn't he?"

"So it's been said. There he is now, down front. Looks like he got a head start on the rest of us. I wonder what he's up to?"

Azzie climbed onto a table, to the consternation of the diners who surrounded it. He swayed. He breathed smoke and struck sparks as he moved.

He made as if to say something several times but failed. Finally, he plucked a flagon from a diner's talons, raised it, and drained it.

"Fools! Pigs! Bastards!" he roared then. "Ye less-than-sentient things! I address myself particularly to my so-called brothers of Darkness, whose champion I have been, betrayed utterly by your indifference. We could have won it, boys and girls! We had the chance! My conception was glorious, unprecedented, and it could have worked!"

He paused and coughed. Someone passed him another flagon, and he sipped from it. The hall had grown quiet now.

"But did I get any cooperation?" he went on. "Not a bit! The fools in Supply acted as if I were doing this for my own personal aggrandizement, rather than the greater glory of us all. Why, damn it! I got more help from that fool Babriel, the stupid-faced observer from the Powers of Light, than I got from any of you. And you call yourselves evil! You are living proof, all of you, of the banality of bad! And now you sit here and celebrate and await the announcement. I tell you, friends, Evil has grown boring and stupid in this day and age. We of Darkness have lost the ability to steer the destinies of humanity."

Azzie glared around him. Everyone was silent, waiting for him to continue. Azzie strode across the table, took another swig, swayed again, regained his balance.

"So I say, the hell with all of you! I am going away now to a private place, to think and to rest. This entire event has been very trying. But I want to tell you all, this isn't the end of me. Not at all. I still have a few tricks, my masters! Wait now and see what I bring next for your amusement!"

Azzie threw out a double travel-spell and disappeared in a clap of thunder. The assembled demons and angels glanced at each other uneasily. "What do you think he meant by that?" several were heard to mutter.

They did not have to wait long to see.

Before they could move, a tornado came sweeping in from outer reality. It roared, ripped, and tore at the banquet hall, and it was accompanied by a rising rush of water. The carefully noted speeches of the elder demons

and angels were ripped from their hands and sent flying
to the skies. There followed an infestation of frogs, thousands, millions of them, dropping from out the heavens.
The walls began to sweat blood, while noxious halations
suddenly became the order of the day. And through it all
there was a faint demonic laughter—Azzie's laughter—as
he sent peril after menace after direness after terror into
the banquet hall.

All in all, it proved a most memorable dessert.

# Chapter
# 7

Brigitte was playing with her dollhouse when she heard something behind her. She turned slowly, a question already forming on her lips, a question which was lost due to the moue of surprise she gave when she saw who was standing there, tall, red-furred, with a mean smile on his face.

"Why, hello, Azzie! How are you?"

"I am very well, Brigitte," Azzie said. "And you look well. And I can hear the sound of a pen scratching in an upstairs room, so I suppose Thomas Scrivener is living up to his name and recording something about the events that have befallen him recently."

"Indeed he is," Brigitte said. "But he tells me he doesn't know the ending."

"It may surprise him," Azzie said. "Indeed, methinks it may surprise all of us. Heh, heh, heh."

"What a sinister chuckle you have, Azzie," Brigitte said. "Why have you come?"

"I've brought you a present, child," Azzie said.

"Ooo! Let me see!"

"Here it is." Azzie brought out a box made of diffi-
cult-to-acquire cardboard and, opening it, showed within
the little guillotine.

"How nice!" Brigitte said. "It looks like the perfect
thing for cutting off the heads of my dollies."

"And so it is," Azzie said. "But you really shouldn't do
that, because you love your dolls and would be sad to see
them without heads."

"That's true," Brigitte said, and she began to snivel in
anticipation of her bereavement.

"But how can I play with my new guillotine if I do not
cut off the heads of my dolls?" She looked around.
"Maybe one of the new puppies—"

"No, Brigitte," Azzie said. "I am evil, but I am not
cruel to animals. There's a special Hell reserved for those
who are. You see, my dear, these toys must be used with
care, and played with in due gravity."

"It's no fun if I can't cut off anyone's head," Brigitte
said.

So far his plan, which was of that brand of evil termed
nasty, was proceeding perfectly.

"Stop sniveling," Azzie said. "I am going to bring you
something special."

"What is it?"

"Something whose head can be cut off!"

"Oh, Uncle Azzie!" She ran to him and embraced
him. "When will I get this something?"

"Soon, my dear, very soon. Be a good girl and play
now. Uncle Azzie will return presently with your new
gift."

# COMPLINE

THE NAMELESS HORROR

# Chapter
# 1

Prince Charming and Princess Scarlet set up house-keeping in a modest castle Cinderella had recom-mended, in a region of great natural beauty on the Rhine. Briar roses grew round about it. Charming converted his shield into a planter for sweet herbs. Good spirits danced around their hearth. Sexy spirits inhabited their bedroom.

"Charming! Would you come here a moment?" Scarlet called.

He looked up from the garden, where he was working away among the organically grown vegetables.

"Where are you, love?"

"In the bedroom."

"I'm on my way."

High in the room's northwestern corner, as he held her, kissed her, and caressed her, an eye opened and re-garded them. As they fell upon the big feather bed, watched over by indulgent spirits of the Good who cele-brated their part in the glorious Millennium, the eye re-garded them for a moment. As he unlaced her blouse and drew it up over her head, the eye winked out.

# Chapter 2

Back in his mansion in Augsburg, Azzie turned off his all-seeing eye, one of the last items he'd picked up from Supply.

Suddenly there was a sound from outside. Looking out of the window, he saw a Nameless Horror picking its way up the path. It was vaguely man-shaped, it had one talon in a sling, and it wore an eye patch.

"Hail, Azzie," the Nameless Horror said.

"Hail yourself, Nameless Horror," Azzie said. "You have about five seconds to tell me why you have invaded my awesome solitude before I boot your Shapeless Ass out of here."

The apparition's eye sockets glowed. Its mouth curled into an approximation of a smile.

"Ah, milord Azzie, you talk exactly as I thought you would! I've been so longing to meet you!"

"What the hell is this all about?" Azzie asked.

"I'm your greatest admirer," the Horror said. "I hope to do great things in the world. At present I am only an apprentice demon, and am serving my time doing Nameless Horror work. But I know that will come to an end and I will be awarded full demon status. Then I hope to be just like you!"

"That's a laugh," Azzie said, laughing sardonically, but flattered in spite of himself. "Me, the failure, the loser."

"You are not up on recent events," it said, solidifying slightly to improve its enunciation. "The Powers of Evil have decided to grant you a prize extraordinary." It held out to Azzie a small box. Azzie opened it and found within a small statuette of a stylized demon, done in nasty orange, all except for the eyes, which were colored green.

"What's this piece of rubbish?" Azzie asked.

"It's a special award for Best Evil Deed of the Millennium."

"But what's it for?"

The Nameless Horror took out a scroll from somewhere within its shapeless clothing. It read, "This is in acknowledgment of a masterful performance at the Millennial Awards Dinner, when the said Azzie Elbub did disrupt and confound the proceedings with various Hateful Visitations, thus proving that, even in defeat for the main prize, *viz.*, direction of man's destiny for a thousand years, the said Azzie Elbub has shown the effrontery and sangfroid that marks the true worker in the vineyards of Evil."

Azzie accepted the award and turned it this way and that. It was really very nice. It was not the main prize, which the Powers of Good had won by default, despite the cathedral fiasco, as a continuation of a previous victory. It would look very nice on his mantel.

"Well, thank you, young demon," Azzie said. "It's sort of a consolation prize, I suppose, but welcome nonetheless. You say you admire me, eh?"

"That is correct," the Nameless Horror said, and after that intoned some lines of praise so fulsome in their ingratiation that another being would have been embarrassed.

But Azzie, who was not much bothered by self-doubt—
only the insufficiency of others—was well pleased.

"Thank you, Nameless Horror. I accept this prize,
and please tell the committee that I am well pleased by it.
Now go you and do evil!"

"That's what I was hoping you'd say," it replied, and
took itself away.

# Chapter
# 3

It was very nice getting the prize, but that was not all. Soon after, there was a brightening of light around the Augsburg mansion.

"Now who the hell is that?" Azzie remarked. He didn't appreciate all the interruptions when he was getting ready for a good sulk.

This shape took its time solidifying. Azzie waited, and it finally took on the form and substance of Babriel.

"Hail, Azzie!" Babriel cried, standing tall and blond and as stupid looking as before.

"Yeah, hail and all that," Azzie said. "You want to rub it in, I suppose?"

"Not at all. You know I never gloat."

"That's true," Azzie said, "and it makes you all the more annoying."

"You're a great kidder," Babriel replied. "But let me tell you why I'm here."

"If you wish," Azzie said. "It makes no difference to me."

"By the powers vested in me by the Committee for the Powers of Light," Babriel said, reading from a scroll he had taken out of the white folds of his robe, "we hereby present a special Power of Light award to Azzie Elbub, demon, but not utterly damned, for the good services he did for the Powers of Light in helping us win the destiny of mankind for the next thousand years."

So saying, he removed from his bosom a small effigy of an angel, done in a sickly yellow white, with glinty blue eyes and cutesy little wings.

"Well," Azzie said, pleased despite himself, "that's very nice of the Powers of Light. Very nice indeed." He struggled to find something ugly to say, but for the moment was overcome. He had received awards from both the Powers of Light and of Darkness. He was pretty sure he was the first ever to win both awards.

After Babriel had left, Azzie fell to musing. He set his two awards down on a table and looked at them. They *were* rather attractive things. He was pleased despite himself. Rage still boiled, however, when he considered how near he had come to winning the real one, the big one, the Millennial Award itself. But there was no use brooding over it.

For now, what he needed was a little rest and — strange how the thought should occur to him — some home cooking, before shrinking his enemies and delivering them to Brigitte and her guillotine. His thoughts strayed to Ylith. He hadn't paid much attention to her recently; he'd been too preoccupied with putting together his entry. But now it was over.

He mused. He could use a vacation. There was a nice spot he recalled in India where generations of Assassins had worked, killing their thousands of victims each year as they attached themselves to the great pilgrimages. The Assassins had built a special resort on the flat top of a low mountain somewhere north of the Ganges. He was sure he could find it again. It would be fun to go there with Ylith. He remembered the amusements that had been available last time: bowling with human heads, croquet matches with giraffes' necks, table tennis with eyeballs. Yes, it was time he gave Ylith a break.

# Chapter
## 4

Just then the doorbell rang. It was the postman. He
delivered a huge sack made of horsehide and standing about three feet high. The bag wriggled, and piteous
moans came from it.

"Who's that?" Azzie asked.

"It's me, master," Frike's muffled voice said from
within. "Master, I would really appreciate it if you'd put
me back together again."

"And so I shall," Azzie said. "But first I've got some
work to do. Have you seen Ylith?"

"I can't see anything from in here," Frike said. "Could
you please reconstitute me?"

There came the sound of singing, from upstairs.

"All in good time," Azzie said. "I think I hear her
now."

He hurried up the stairs. Yes, she sang a witching
melody, old when the pyramids were mere foundations.
"Ylith! Are you there?"

"Down the hall," Ylith called back.

He hurried to the spare bedroom from which her voice had come and entered the room. She was packing a small suitcase. She looked radiant. Something about her seemed different, though. Was it her complexion? Yes, it had definitely changed for the paler. And her eyes, night black and deliciously sinister, seemed to have become cornflower blue.

"Ylith! What is come over you?" he cried. "Has an infestation of good gotten to you? I know several charms and simples that could cure it. . . ."

"There's nothing wrong with me, Azzie," Ylith said. "What you see are the visible effects of happiness."

"But what have you got to be happy about?"

"My dear, I don't know how to tell you this. . . ."

"Then don't," Azzie said. "When anyone starts like that, it's sure to mean bad news. I've had enough bad news for a while."

"What are those things you're carrying?" Ylith asked.

"Oh. Some awards. One from the Powers of Light, the other from Darkness. I guess they both thought I should have them."

"Azzie, how wonderful!"

"Yes, it is nice," Azzie said. "But listen, Ylith, I've been thinking. I haven't treated you very well. But you know how it is when you're serious about the service of evil. Always something to do. Well, I've ignored you for too long. I'd like you to come away with me now, to a very fine little hotel I know in India. India's lovely at this time of year, and we'll sport and disport ourselves and have a great time. What do you say?"

"Ah, Azzie," she said, her voice soft and breathy, "if only you could know how much I've longed to hear those words from you!"

"Well, now you've heard them. It's good that you're packing. We can be away at once."

"Darling, I hate to tell you this, but I love another."

"Ouch!" Azzie said, sitting down, then getting up again. "Well, I suppose whoever it is could come with us," he offered. "That's in the nature of evil, isn't it, to share when you don't want to?"

"I'm afraid it cannot be," Ylith said. "Babriel would never stand for it."

"Babriel!"

"Yes, he is the one I love. He has asked me away from here, to a beautiful little place he knows where there are green pastures and lambs frolic and the flowers of spring-time shine everywhere."

"Sounds sickening," Azzie said. "What are you thinking of, Ylith? It is not in the nature of evil to have a taste for lambs, except in the form of chops done with a bit of rosemary and mint jelly."

"Same old Azzie," she said, smiling. "You don't understand. I've converted. I've decided to be good."

"No! Not you, Ylith! You need an exorcism immediately!"

"It's not like that at all," she replied. "I've fallen in love with Babriel. I will go with him, and I will be a person he can love and respect."

Azzie mastered himself for the moment. "Are you sure you want to do this?" he asked.

"Absolutely. Look!"

She turned. Azzie could see the rudimentary wings sprouting from her back. They were whiter than mourning doves, whiter than foam from untrammeled seas. They were tiny now, but they would grow. She had become a Creature of Light.

"That's disgusting," Azzie said. "You'll regret this, I promise you."

He left the door standing open as he stalked away.

# Chapter
# 5

Prince Charming and Princess Scarlet! And their happiness! Azzie was fascinated in spite of himself. He returned to the magic mirror in his workroom. It was large and had a faintly bluish cast. He staggered up to it, a bottle of ichor clutched in one hand, and stood before it.

He stared into the mirror and said, "Show them to me."

"Show who?" the mirror said.

"You know damned well who," Azzie said.

"Just one moment while I make the connection," the mirror replied.

Azzie waited, fuming. Beside him, in the leather bag, the various parts of Frike squirmed. Azzie ignored them. Caught up as he was in a demonic obsession, infused with unholy dynamism, he watched the mirror turn cloudy, then slowly grow clear.

The images of Prince Charming and Princess Scarlet appeared. How pretty they were! In their silken clothing, they seemed a symbol of all that was good with the world.

Azzie could hear them, in their soft, well-modulated voices, making small talk with each other.

"Izzum my woozie baby?" This from Scarlet.

"I am yours forever," Charming said. "I know it is usual in these matters not to look into the denouement. I know that the sour scansions of a later age will say that I bullied you, or that you nagged me. But what care we for such cynical glosses? We are young, we are in love, we are beautiful, and contrary to popular expectations, we are going to stay this way for a long time and love each other faithfully and well."

"How nicely you put it!" Scarlet said, settling back into his arms.

"Happy, are you?" Azzie snarled. "We'll see to that. There must be something I can do."

"Master! There is!" This from the leathern bag.

"What is it?" Azzie asked.

"Ah, master, take a moment to put me back together and I'll be pleased to tell you!"

"This had better be good," Azzie muttered. "Better than the quickness of falling steel."

He opened the bag and spread out Frike's parts. Working swiftly, he joined them together, getting the arms a little wrong in his drunken haste, but doing a creditable job, all in all.

"Thank you, master!" Frike said.

"Now, speak!"

"Oh, master, you can still take your revenge on these despicably pretty and lucky young people. The unlimited credit card, master! You still have it!"

"Oh, good thinking, Frike! I'll soon put paid to their merrymaking!"

He removed the card from his waistcoat pocket and tapped it twice on a convenient nasty surface. There was a very brief hiatus and then the supply clerk appeared before him.

"Yeah, what do you want?"

"I need a special wish," Azzie said. He smiled meanly,

an expression he had often practiced but had never really used before, saving it for a moment like this. The hell with the rules.

"What would you like?"

"First, a nice catastrophe. I want to collapse the castle of Prince Charming and his consort, Princess Scarlet, around their ears. Then I'll need a special Hell to put them in for a few thousand years, to prove to them that it doesn't pay to flaunt your happiness in front of a demon."

"What sort of a catastrophe?" the clerk asked, reaching for his pencil and order form.

"Let's make it an earthquake."

"One earthquake coming up," the supply clerk said.

"And after that I'll show you our collection of special Hells." The clerk opened the big ledger. Suddenly he looked up. A great bell had begun tolling. Azzie could hear it, too. In fact, in the village near Azzie's château bells were tolling, too.

"What is it?" he asked. "It isn't Sunday, is it?"

Frike had rushed to the window. "Nay, master, it is the beginning of the Millennial celebrations. People are dancing in the street! Oh, master, what spectacles of untoward joy open before my eyes!"

"To hell with that," Azzie said. To the clerk: "What are you waiting for? I want an earthquake!"

The clerk smiled meanly and closed his ledger book with a snap. "Sorry, your order is canceled."

"What are you talking about? I'll have your guts for a necklace unless you do as I say!"

"No, you won't," the supply clerk responded. "It is the stroke of high noon. The Millennial contest is over. The Great Powers of Darkness have canceled your unlimited credit card."

"No, they can't! Not yet! I must do this final thing!"

He held up his card, waving it frantically. The supply clerk smiled with sour satisfaction and made a gesture. The card melted in Azzie's hand.

Azzie let out a scream of baffled rage and tangled

madness. Frike lurched away and crouched within an elaborately carved armoire. Azzie stamped his foot. The floor opened beneath him. He sank through it, down, down, down to a remote dark cool underground tunnel where he might wander for a while and regain his composure. Frike rushed to the hole and peered in. He could see Azzie sinking ever downward, still fuming. And outside, from village to village all across the land, the bells of the Millennium went on ringing.

# About
# the Authors

Roger Zelazny is the author of the Hugo Award-winning *Lord of Light* and the bestselling *Amber* series, including the classic *Nine Princes in Amber*. He is a six-time Hugo winner and has won three Nebula Awards.

Robert Sheckley is a novelist and scriptwriter whose short fiction has appeared in *Playboy, Atlantic Monthly,* and *The Magazine of Fantasy and Science Fiction*. One of his short stories was adapted to film as *The Tenth Victim*.

# Available now
# from Roger Zelazny
# and Robert Sheckley:

# IF AT FAUST YOU DON'T SUCCEED

Here is an excerpt from a new novel of devilish fun and frolic by the authors of *Bring Me the Head of Prince Charming*. In IF AT FAUST YOU DON'T SUCCEED, Good and Evil once again duke it out as the fate of humanity hangs in the balance.

The plot is hatched at the Halfway Tavern in Limbo, where the Archangel Michael and Mephistopheles himself meet to discuss the new Millennial Deeds contest. This time humankind's representative in the contest will be the famous alchemist and philosopher Johann Faust . . . or will it? For when Mephistopheles arrives in Faust's workshop to offer him everything mortal man could desire, Faust is not there. Instead a cat burglar named Mack the Club, who is on the scene relieving the good doctor of a few items of value, accepts the offer of money, fame, beautiful women — and takes off with Mephistopheles on a journey through space and time to earn his reward.

In the following excerpt, Mack comes face to face with the *real* Faust during the debut performance of Christopher Marlowe's famous play, *Doctor Faustus*.

Mack approached the London house of Dr. Dee. Mack said, "Are you sure you've got it straight now?"

"I think so," Marguerite said. "But I don't like it."

"Forget about that. Just do what I told you. It'll work out, believe me."

Marguerite looked unhappy, but quite pretty. Her chestnut hair was shining. She had on fresh makeup. Even her gown, of green with panels of spotted dimity, was fresh and shining. Mack had seen to it that she looked her best.

He approached the door of a queer humpbacked old house with shuttered windows that made it look like a cat sleeping. It was in a noxious part of London. On either side were the shadowed headquarters of dubious business enterprises, because this was the notorious Tortingham district, only later to be gentrified to the confusion of cutpurses, mollygaggers, yokers, and assorted cony-catchers. Here was where the famous Dr. Dee now made his home.

In his sitting room, Dr. Dee, tall and angular, clad in

his doctor's gown with a round fur hat on his head pulled down well over his ears, was regarding an ancient volume of curious and forgotten lore. He paused and looked up.

"Kelly!" he cried.

At the other end of the room, a short, broad-shouldered man looked away from a ball of yarn he was untangling. Edward Kelly, medium extraordinary—a fey-eyed Irishman from County Limerick—quirked an eyebrow.

"Yes?" he asked.

"I've a premonition of someone on the stair," Dee said.

"Shall I go and see who it is?" Kelly asked.

"Prognosticate first, for I've also a foreboding or two."

Kelly reached across the table and put a glass of water in front of him. With a moistened forefinger he roiled the surface, then stared into it intently. In its swirling depth he saw strange shapes uncoil, glimpsed the forms and visages of drowned things and the many-colored windings and unwindings of spirits no more palpable than so many twists of smoke. He heard sounds as well, for that was how the gift took him. And he looked into the water and saw a man and a maid. Around them, visible only to his eyes, hovered a nimbus of mysterious events.

"There are two people approaching the door," he told Dee. "They are a strange pair, though it is not easy to say wherein their strangeness resides. The man is tall and yellow-haired, and the woman brown-haired and beautiful. They look decent enough."

"If they look good to you, then we'll see them," Dee said. "It was just a matter of certain feelings that came over me."

"So why ask me?" Kelly said. "Why didn't you look into your magic mirror and learn all about them?"

"The magic mirror is in the other room," Dee said. "And I don't see what you're so cross about."

"Me, cross?" Kelly said, scowling. "What makes you think I'm cross?"

"Well, you look cross."

"Why should I look cross," Kelly asked, "when I have nothing to complain about? Didn't I follow you and your psychic circus across Europe? Am I not the star act in your dog and pony show? Do I not do all the work, the better to give you the energy to enjoy all the credit?"

"Now, Edward," Dee said. "We've been over this ground before. Go see to the arrivals."

Thus grumbling, Kelly went to the door. The servant was never around when you wanted him to do something like this. It didn't take much prognostication to know that the servant was in his room under the eaves, nursing the old war wound he got under the Black Prince, or so he told the tale. Kelly thought about Ireland as he walked to the door, Ireland green and boggy, with the young girls who used to walk by him on their way to sheep flocks they tended on the downs beside the cold and glittering sea. He shook his head irritably. Stop speaking, Memory.

He opened the door.

"Hi," Mack said. "We'd like to speak to Dr. Dee, if you don't mind."

"What do you want to see the doctor about?"

"That's for his ears."

"Give it to my ears or his ears will never hear."

"It's for his ears alone," Mack said.

Kelly shrugged and led them to the dining room.

"Something secret and important, so he says," Kelly told Dee.

Mack nodded to the doctor and smiled.

"We are interested in buying your magic mirror," he told him.

Dee raised his heavy eyebrows.

"Sell you my magic mirror? Sir, you must be daft! A mirror with the power and foresightedness of mine is not sold like a bag of horse feed. This mirror of mine, my dear sir, has been the object of covetousness in royal circles throughout Europe. King Stanislaus of Poland offered me an estate for it on the Wladiwil, complete with servile peasants and wild boars, and the title of duke to go along with it, and to sweeten the deal he threw in the favors of the beautiful young countess of Radwivill whose callipygian accomplishments have caused restlessness and social upset as far west as the Weser. I turned him down with a laugh, a laugh of scorn, my dear sir, for to offer mere worldly goods for my mirror, which presents a view into the unseen kingdom, and can prognosticate future events, is to offer dross for gold."

"I realize that," Mack said. "But I come to you with an offer you can't refuse."

"Can I not, now? Let's hear your offer."

Mack produced the scarlet silk handkerchief Mephistopheles has given him, still enfolding its mysterious prize. History fails to tell us what was involved, or its precise effect on the vain and supercilious Dr. Dee. Only one thing is certain. Some ten minutes later, Mack and Marguerite left Dee's house and were on their way to Southwark, the magic mirror under Mack's arm, nestled in a form-fitting case of chamois.

• • •

At the theater, the crowd was coming in slowly. Although the theater held somewhat less than three hundred persons, thousands were seeking entry, drawn from all parts of the kingdom by news of the first public performance of the first play in English history. These theatergoers were dressed in all their finery. Men and women alike wore long cloaks, since there was a chill in the air even on this fine May afternoon. The audience was a motley bunch. There were many nobles from the court, among them my lord Salisbury, my lord Dunkirk, my lord Cornwallis, my lord High Executioner, and my lord Faversham. Some had come with their wives, others with their mistresses, pert in their paste diamonds, and still others, the very young ones, like my lord Dover, who was only eight, with their parents or tutors, or, as in the case with Viscount Delville, seven years old and sickly, with their bodyguard-doctors. These were the notables; but most of the audience was made up of common people: heavyset cloth merchants from Meaching Row, tall thin apothecaries from Pall Mall and Cheapside, angular feed merchants from Burlington Arcade and Picadilly, and the even commoner sort, sturdy vagabonds who had cadged a ticket and called no man master, soldiers on leave from the Netherlands wars with their fantastical plumed caps and deep-cut sleeves. There were more than a few clerics in the crowd, even a few of the dour puritan persuasion, who had come not to amuse themselves but out of a serious purpose, because *Faust* was supposed to be a sacrilegious play, and they expected to get good material out of it for their Sunday sermons. They all trooped in, jostling and hawking and spitting and buying oranges and little bags of candy from the wenches who provided such things, and gawking around at the theater, which was small and oval-shaped with a row of boxes to either side and a raised stage that extended out over the foremost ranks of the audience. Flambeaux flickered in the din of loud English voices calling to one another. "I say, Harry!" "Oh, there's Saffron!" "Look, here comes Melisande and Cuddles!" And the like.

The admission at the door for those without passes was thruppence ha'penny, for Lord Strange's men didn't do this for free. But they paid anyway and no demurrers were raised in that free-spending easy-thinking crowd, for this was a day of celebration, and the future was uncertain, for if the Spanish Armada landed, as some predicted, and prevailed over the naval forces of the red-haired Queen, your money wouldn't be worth boo anyway. Down near the candled floodlights, the groundlings had assembled in their best piebald hose and multicolored jerkins to talk and carouse and make japes at the actors.

Not only was this the first theater in England; it was also the first use of stage lighting in a building that hired out for performances. Young Shakespeare, sitting in the audience, was thinking about this as, to a flourish of trumpets, Edward Alleyn came out upon the stage. Young Will, already balding, noted for his future use how the chattering young fops and their bright-bedankeled loud-laughing ladies quieted for a moment, as though in unconscious obeisance to the historic importance of the moment. The house lights of magnesia and naptha were set alight in pewter bowls set on top of three-legged standards. They had recently replaced the adamantage, the old rush stage lighting in a copper pot that had served well enough in pre-theater days. Sparks were applied to them and they flared up, calling the audience to attention. The bassoons in the small orchestra took up the *Faust* theme—tee dee dee DUM DUM tee. Soon all London would be whistling it.

The setting on the stage represented the town of Wittenberg in the previous century. It was quite realistic except for the fact that the Draken watchtower where Faust will later meet the Spirit of Earth was leaning somewhat precariously to the left, for stage design was still in its infancy and proper bracing for the sets would only be achieved in the early 18th century. As the curtain went up there was a prolonged clearing of throats, this being the height of the phlegm season, and a rustling of feet which were covered in many different substances, but most of them consisting of an irregular and scratchy surface, the only sort you'd expect in this day of pre-industrial handicrafts, and their roughness accounted for the annoying sounds they made when dragged back and forth through the egg shells and orange peels and the peanut hulls, since in that year of plague the populace was mad for amusements and willing to pay any price for the snacks to accompany them, and whose shells and peels covered the floor of this Ur-theater.

Just as the performance was beginning Mack hurried in late, and slid along a row of seats with murmured "sorry"s and "oh excuse me"s and took his seat somewhat breathlessly, the magic mirror, safe in the chamois case, clutched to his side. Marguerite followed, and took her seat beside him with a giggle of girlish anticipation.

"I've never seen a play before," she confided. "Is it like sitting around telling stories?"

"Very similar," Mack said. "Except that people act out the story instead of someone telling it."

"Or sometimes both," a man sitting beside him remarked.

Mack turned. A man of middle years was sitting beside him, robust of form and ruddy of face, with piercing dark eyes and a look of hawklike intelligence. Mack knew he had seen him somewhere before. But where was it? Then he had it. This was the fellow who had suddenly materialized in Florence and saved the life of Pico della Mirandola.

"You must be—" he said.

"You are correct," the personage said. "I am Johann Faust, and you are a stinking imposter."

"Shush," said a surly voice in a row in front of them. "Can't you see the performance has begun?"

On stage, Edward Alleyn stepped forward, swept off his cap with a flourish, and struck a pose.

"I'll discuss this with you later," Mack said. "But my name's Faust, too."

"Think you can get away with this?" Faust asked. "I'll Faust you! We'll see who's the Faustest with the mostest."

*Shush!* the man in front of them said.

On the stage, the chorus had finished its opening speech. William Alleyn, resplendent in a crimson surplice, with a gilded cross upon his chest, was saying, "Now that the gloomy shadow of Night, eager to spy Orion's drizzling band . . ."

"There's nothing to discuss," Faust said. "Simply begone at once. I'll take over from here."

"Not a chance," Mack said.

"I am the real Faust. You are an interloper. I demand that you stop impersonating me at once."

"Demand all you want," Mack said. "It'll get you nowhere. The fact that your name is Faust has nothing to do with the archetypical drama that I am now acting in, in much the same manner as that actor upon the stage might claim to be Faust, in that he wears the mantle of an attitude."

"This is presumption! How can the story of Faust be told by anyone but Faust himself?"

"How can there be a Faust himself if, as is the case here, anyone who performed certain actions with a certain attitude of mind could have claimed to do that which is the essence of Faust, and therefore tantamount to Faust himself. Faust is not a person. He is many persons. Faust is a set of attitudes and actions. It would be fair to say that Faust is a form of knowing. I should know. I am him myself."

"How silly of you to think so! There's nothing Faustian about you!"

"Yeah? And what makes you think *you're* so Faustlike?"

"But I *am* Faust! Whatever I do is Faustian!"

"Whereas I," said Mack, "am Faustian, so anything I do must prove me to be Faust."

It was clear that the matter was descending into a sort of intellectual shouting match. This was a break for Mack, for when it came to volume and stamina, Mack was second to none in his possession of a loud voice and an aggressive manner. Faust himself also shared those mannerisms, and in this regard of style they stood for the moment evenly matched, even claimants for a disputed role.

But their exchange was interrupted at this point by the audience, who, coming to hear the first and arguably the greatest play in English history were not interested in hearing the rude argument of a pair of jackanapes.

"Shut up!"

"Stick a boot in it!"

"Stuff it!"

And similar exclamations of exhortation. Faust and Mack were forced perforce to desist, for neither of them wanted the truth of the matter to be known. So they glared at each other out of the corners of their eyes while Marguerite and Helen, on either side of them, patted their hands and whispered to them to remain calm. On stage, the actors had gotten beyond Faust's dialogue with the Seven Deadly Sins, who remained onstage with colored cardboard costumes and lugubrious faces, and proceeded to the entrance of several devils.

Mack's mind was working with lightning speed, both defining the game he was involved in and planning out his next move. It was obvious to him that he had more to gain here, and therefore more to lose, than he had thought at first, back in Cracow when he had broken into Faust's studio and accepted Mephistopheles' offer. It was true that the real Faust was here trying to claim his own; but what did that matter to Mack? Mack's reality was more important to him than Faust's, and his reality seemed to have led him to *become* Faust. Therefore this other Faust, whom he had taken over from, had no real claim to the Faust persona.

Still, it was going to be quite a problem. He needed a way to handle this, get Faust off his back, give him a chance to do his thing. If he let Faust oust him now, what would he be?

An advantage! He needed an advantage. Surely that was the point of all military strategy—to realize when you are in a spot and to seek—the Equalizer.

It was at that moment that he bethought himself of Dr. Dee's Magic Mirror, pressing against his side in its chamois case.

He realized that by peeking into Dee's Magic Mirror he might get a glimpse of the future, and thus he could know what to do in this encounter between him and Faust.

He slipped the mirror out of its chamois case, disguising the noise by grinding his feet in the peanut shells on the floor and remarking to Marguerite, "It's disgusting, how they keep these places." Now the mirror was in his lap.

Just as he was about to look into it there was an explosion on stage, and a bright flash as of hellish lighting. Mack had seen that light before. It was Mephistopheles, conjuring himself.

The tall and handsome demon stepped out of the smoke, adjusted his evening clothes, advanced to stage center, and, peering around at the audience, spotted Mack. "The mirror!" he shouted.

"Yes, I've got it!" Mack shouted back. "Don't worry, it's here!"

"You must destroy it!" Mephistopheles shouted.

"Beg pardon?"

"Get rid of it at once! They've just passed a ruling! By looking into it you'll invalidate the whole contest, since contestants must not be granted foreknowledge of events. It would skew the result, you see."

The audience was mumbling to itself uncertainly at this point, and sniffing often at the perfume-sprayed nosegays that they held in their dirty, lace-gloved hands. Feet clad in various materials shuffled noisily in the peanut shells, and there was something ominous about the sound, some strange over or under cadence, or both, some unbelievable bass note of madness which had an effect on the ear as a tremendous and perhaps bloody happening waiting in the figurative wings that is Everyman's heart from which it would soon be born.

Time to get out of this crowd. Mack got to his feet and edged his way out into the aisle, the better to get the hell out of the place if something happened — because the feeling that theaters are places where sinister things may happen is a notion that sprang into existence contemporaneous with the first theater itself, and it may be this selfsame first performance of this play of Faust that gave rise to the legend. Marguerite followed along behind him, hanging on to his coattails so as not to get lost in the crowd that had begun to roil and tumble around them.

There was a reason for their panic. One member of the audience, not as simpleminded as he looked, had counted the number of actors on stage and seen that this was not the number given in the playbill. When he relayed this information to others — "There are supposed to be seven devils onstage, but I count eight —" A wave of uncertainty came over those watching. Wooden-framed spectacles were hastily clapped on the long noses that were prevalent in that day as all the spectators consulted their playbills. If there were too many devils on the stage, one at least of them had to be real. It didn't take any Thomas Aquinas to figure that out. Any rightminded person who viewed the matter without prejudice could see beyond a doubt that the tall thin guy who had suddenly appeared bore more resemblance to the devil of our dreams than the other guy, the actor in the shabby red cotton suit and ill-fitting slippers. And seeing that, a sudden *let's get the hell out of here* mood swept over the audience, and they began to rise and scrape their feet in the peanutshells, prefatory to stampeding into the exits.

Eight devils. And then a ninth appeared. For it was then that a dapper-looking fox-faced demon made his own appearance on stage, in a bone white lounge suit with white penny loafers and a turquoise scarf with a Tibetan mandala painted on it draped around his shoulders. Seeing this, the crowd went a little wild.

"Hang on to that mirror!" Azzie shouted to Mack. "You can never tell when an item like that will prove useful. Anyhow, you need it for the contest!"

"No he doesn't!" Mephistopheles cried. "It's only one of his possible choices."

"Then who are you to tell him he can't make that choice?"

"I'm not saying anything of the kind," Mephistopheles said. "I'm merely advising him not to look into it himself, since foreknowledge would compromise the contestant, to the mutual embarrassment of Dark and Light."

The audience, driven into a superstitious mania by the trip-hammer succession of downright weird events with sinister overtones, began to panic. Grown men flung ladies' hampers filled with the most delicate hams, roast beefs, sides of pork, and the like, out of their way to get to the nearest exit. In vain the orchestra struck up a toccata of Gallupi's.

Bantam Spectra publishes more Hugo and Nebula Award-winning novels than any other science fiction and fantasy imprint. Celebrate the Tenth Anniversary of Spectra—read them all!

## HUGO WINNERS

| | |
|---|---|
| A CANTICLE FOR LEIBOWITZ, Walter M. Miller, Jr. | \_\_\_\_27381-7 $5.99/$6.99 |
| THE GODS THEMSELVES, Isaac Asimov | \_\_\_\_28810-5 $5.99/$6.99 |
| RENDEZVOUS WITH RAMA, Arthur C. Clarke | \_\_\_\_28789-3 $5.99/$6.99 |
| DREAMSNAKE, Vonda N. McIntyre | \_\_\_\_29659-0 $5.99/$7.50 |
| THE FOUNTAINS OF PARADISE, Arthur C. Clarke | \_\_\_\_28819-9 $5.99/$6.99 |
| FOUNDATION'S EDGE, Isaac Asimov | \_\_\_\_29338-9 $5.99/$6.99 |
| STARTIDE RISING, David Brin | \_\_\_\_27418-X $5.99/$6.99 |
| THE UPLIFT WAR, David Brin | \_\_\_\_27971-8 $5.99/$6.99 |
| HYPERION, Dan Simmons | \_\_\_\_28368-5 $5.99/$6.99 |
| DOOMSDAY BOOK, Connie Willis | \_\_\_\_56273-8 $5.99/$6.99 |
| GREEN MARS, Kim Stanley Robinson | \_\_\_\_37335-8 $12.95/$16.95 |

## NEBULA WINNERS

| | |
|---|---|
| THE GODS THEMSELVES, Isaac Asimov | \_\_\_\_28810-5 $5.99/$6.99 |
| RENDEZVOUS WITH RAMA, Arthur C. Clarke | \_\_\_\_28789-3 $5.99/$6.99 |
| DREAMSNAKE, Vonda N. McIntyre | \_\_\_\_29659-0 $5.99/$7.50 |
| THE FOUNTAINS OF PARADISE, Arthur C. Clarke | \_\_\_\_28819-9 $5.99/$6.99 |
| TIMESCAPE, Gregory Benford | \_\_\_\_27709-0 $5.99/$6.99 |
| STARTIDE RISING, David Brin | \_\_\_\_27418-X $5.99/$6.99 |
| TEHANU, Ursula K. Le Guin | \_\_\_\_28873-3 $5.50/$6.99 |
| DOOMSDAY BOOK, Connie Willis | \_\_\_\_56273-8 $5.99/$6.99 |
| RED MARS, Kim Stanley Robinson | \_\_\_\_56073-5 $5.99/$7.50 |

**Ask for these books at your local bookstore or use this page to order.**

Please send me the books I have checked above. I am enclosing $\_\_\_\_ (add $2.50 to cover postage and handling). Send check or money order, no cash or C.O.D.'s, please.

Name _____

Address _____

City/State/Zip _____

Send order to: Bantam Books, Dept. AA 2, 2451 S. Wolf Rd., Des Plaines, IL 60018
Allow four to six weeks for delivery.
Prices and availability subject to change without notice.                    AA 2 2/95